FIGHTING SPIRIT

DARK URBAN RISING BOOK 1

S M HENLEY

FIGHTING SPIRIT

Copyright © 2026 by S M Henley and Darkish Fiction.

All rights reserved.

No part of this book may be used or reproduced in any manner whatsoever without written permission except in the case of brief quotations embodied in critical articles and reviews.

This book is a work of fiction. The characters, incidents, places, and dialogue are drawn from the author's imagination or are used fictitiously, and are not to be construed as real. Any resemblance to actual events, locales, or persons, living or dead is entirely coincidental.

3rd Edition February 2026

2nd Edition January 2019.

First published March 2017 as *Scratching in the Dirt*.

A QUICK HEADS-UP
FROM THE AUTHOR

Before you dive in, I want to make sure the Dark Urban Rising world is the right kind of dark for you. While there is plenty of gritty humour and fun to be had, these stories are unapologetically adult and don't pull their punches.

In this universe, innocence won't save you. The series explores the harsh realities of its characters' lives, featuring graphic supernatural violence, emotional distress, and the echoes of past trauma.

If you like your fantasy sharp, your darkness balanced with humour, and a plot where survival takes precedence over romance—welcome. You're in the right place.

Want to a free journey into the dark?
Before you start, sign up to **The Spoil Heap** for a free prequel novella.

https://darkishfiction.com/sign-up

A father in Hell, a dead lover, and a demon gangster on her tail. Today is the best day of Tazia's life.

Anastasia Savoy's had a hell of a time. Literally. She's been stuck underground since the end of the last Demon War. One hundred years holed up in her father's miserable company, only permitted to run a few guns, take a few contracts, and collect the blood money. She's been a model daughter. But now she's free. Well almost.

With the world brought to the brink of perdition, all Tazia wants to do is pick up her cash and get outta Dodge. Then a psycho angel interrupts her plans and instead of a life of tequila on the beach, she's forced into an alliance to save the demon who was her jailer. It sickens her. But if Tazia refuses, not only will she die, she'll put those she loves at risk too…

Tazia is a smart-mouthed anti-heroine who attracts trouble like a magnet, and gives it back—in spades. *Fighting Spirit* is her first adventure in the *Dark Urban Rising* trilogy. It is a supernatural thriller set on the streets of modern-day Turin, London, and Detroit. It treads lightly in the darkness, with not a small amount of blood and gritty humour.

I would dedicate this book to my mother, but there are too many curse words. So, instead, because of the blood, sweat, and tears, it is for me. Sometimes you have to be selfish.

Next time, mum.

1

───────────

SHOT IN THE DARK

A SECOND BEFORE Tazia punched each rock from her path, the faces of her enemies swam in front of her. Her father's image figured prominently. As did that bog demon who'd made her sing "Like a Virgin" on a tabletop in Rome back in eighty-eight. The reward, tequila, had tasted like nectar, but she hoped the arsehole was now being rickrolled into oblivion.

The rock exploded under her fist, taking that rat-faced scumbag's beady eyes and stupid mullet with it. She paused and extended her fingers, knuckles crunching as she flexed. Her bones were strong, but even they weren't holding up well. For a moment she felt pathetic, weak. Even human.

She'd been climbing up this damn rock face for ages, squashed between razor-sharp walls of granite, sweat streaming down her face and back, hands cut to ribbons. Way below, wet bloody handprints caught the light of fading embers, every excruciating grip she'd made on the way up.

As she ran her hands over the blade-like rock surface, exploring for handholds, she smeared more blood behind.

She'd have to replace what she was losing soon. Breakfast had been so long ago.

After finding a hold, she levered herself up a few inches until her head hit solid boulders again. With her feet wedged on either side of the almost vertical tunnel, she rabbit punched at the next rock: that was her CO from North Africa who'd got handsy with her in a bunker in seventy-three. *Pervert!*

As she twisted to let debris fall past, she held tight with her left arm and shook out her right. Every muscle seized. Unable to form a coherent curse word (probably for the first time in her life), she hissed until the burn faded to a rhythmic, painful thump.

Tazia flexed her hand again, smeared the sweat still trickling into her eyes with the filthy palm, and sniffed loudly. Before she found the next handhold, the rock directly above her creaked, shifted, and let loose a cascade of chippings. They bounced off her head and shoulders before skittering down into the darkness below.

A sliver of light now cut into the darkness a few inches above her head.

Yes!

She pounded harder. Finding her rhythm. A song played in her head, driving her forward—"Shot in the Dark." She sent rocks flying, getting closer to freedom.

When she scented the fresh air seeping through the gaps between the boulders above, it tugged her on. Using her knees for leverage, she pushed up further, grinning.

Moments later, she got her first clear view of the world outside: a sky painted the pale blue of early spring. She pushed aside the last boulder and, with her eyes forced shut against the burst of light, she dragged herself up onto solid ground and into a delicious mountain breeze. *Thank you, Ozzy!*

Icy cold soothed her ripped skin, but the relief was brief.

The afternoon sun sizzled blisters over the gooseflesh, forcing her to stumble to the shade of a rock overhang close by.

She collapsed, breathing hard. Acrid smoke rose from her skin and caught in her throat. *Burning, like him.* After the shot caught him between the eyes, the rock floor split open and flames claimed him. Her father's body ignited as it descended. Soot and embers had risen around her on the heated air, clinging to her clothes, gritty in her mouth still—

Her stomach lurched. She rolled over, just in time to vomit blood, dust, and her Dutch-courage breakfast.

As the spasms receded, she groaned, wiped the mess from her mouth and smeared it on the side of her jeans before returning to lay on her back. Her thoughts shifted to her father's killer. He'd died in the rockfall too. Her eyes flicked to the hole behind her. *I fucking hope.*

Drifting between sleep and memories, the sun dipped to reveal shadowed gullies across the Italian landscape. Behind her, the Alps cut sharp against the sky, snow-capped and beautiful. Trees covered the slopes below with pines and deciduous trees all mixed, thick and green. This view always made everything better.

Time to go, Taz.

Rising, she groped for the silk bag hanging around her neck on a thin leather cord. It contained her father's fangs. At his urging, she'd removed them a few hours earlier using metal pincers and brute force. Teeth popped from his jaw, blood spraying her face and neck. His smile as he licked it from her. His final act of control.

After tucking the bag back under her shirt, she assessed the path down from the rocky outcrop.

Turin spread out below her, just a few miles south. Old church spires stuck up between the modern office and apartment blocks. Red roofs mixed with the cream stone of the old buildings and the shiny glass of the new. Industrial areas stretched out into the distance.

It would all begin down there. Her life would start over, on her terms—ideally with a bottle of Don Julio in front of her and a nice pile of cash. She heard Billy's voice in her mind: *La dolce vita, baby!*

With a final glance at the sun's position, Tazia began the descent down the hill, keeping to the deeper shadows as much as possible. From the treetops, a few songbirds serenaded her first steps. As she entered the city, they would leave her to continue on alone, but for now she whistled alongside them.

She didn't look back at her father's resting place. After one hundred and fifty years of servitude, it was time her life began for real. Time to make a deal with a demon.

2

———————————————

DEMONS EVERYWHERE

IN A WELL-REPEATED MANTRA, Tazia recalled the kill spots of the demon breeds she singled out: brain, heart, stomach, or eyes. Always the eyes with the sneaky ones.

The patio was crowded. Patrons shunted up against each other. Table tops touching. Scents of coffee, wine, and garlicky suppers. Her mouth watered.

Tazia sucked on her straw. She'd forgone the full bottle, but a nice hit of tequila nestled at the bottom of the glass underneath the Coke. She'd yearned for a buzz ever since her climb from the cave, but it was proving elusive. Did they water the shit down in here? She sucked harder, rewarded with a swimming sensation in her head that reminded her she'd left her breakfast on the mountain. The *agnolotti* looked tasty…

A fresh wave of specimens moved through her field of vision. A mixture of tourists and locals, both demon and human, milled around the *piazza* oblivious of each other, and of her attention. She examined each through squinted eyes and made an identification before turning back and crossing her arms over her chest.

Tick-tock, mister, tick-fucking-tock.

Her movement made the metal tabletop clink against the one squashed alongside, and the man sitting there paused his loud phone conversation to shoot her a pained glance over his Ray-Bans. He smelled human. Business suit, briefcase, but biceps and tribal tattoo that said *Fight Club* not JP Morgan.

She returned his look with sparking amber eyes just to see if he'd react. He didn't even blink. He seemed aware of the demon element in this melting pot of a city.

Turin. She'd been back two decades, ever since her father dragged her home from that English prison. Jail time had been... interesting, but keeping Daddy happy was survival. Until that morning, anyway.

Tazia smirked as she recalled the fire licking her father's body, but the glass she pushed around the table stuttered rather than slid over the little pool of condensation underneath it. No, she wouldn't think about her father anymore.

Where the hell is this guy?

Across from her, sat a woman in a dark Chanel suit. Mixed breed. Flesh Gobbler. More evil than average. She eyed the waitress rushing from table to table while grinding her teeth along the edges of her espresso cup, sharpening each one against the place where the glaze had worn off.

Testing a theory, Tazia peeled off a flap of skin the rock face had almost sliced from her palm and flicked it to the pavement below her table. Instantly, the demon snuffled the air and turned her head toward her, teeth chattering. Her eyes flashed a brief, hungry red.

Grinning, Tazia pushed the skin, now curled and speckled with dirt, further under the table with the toe of her boot, the metal toe cap tapping off the mosaic tiles.

You want it? Get on your knees!

The demon looked away, her pinched cheeks turning as beet red as the umbrella that sheltered her.

Giggling, and pleased she'd been correct, even if she'd used her own rather more colourful classification system than those in her father's dusty books, Tazia turned back to the cafe building. The only things visible inside were small pools of light cast on the wooden bar and stainless fixtures from the spotlight-studded ceiling.

By rights, it should have been the assassin waiting to collect the money, of course. The image of Soren Huxford's face (that flash of betrayal when she'd left him to die) had been unexpected. It bothered her. Should she have gone back? The skin shifted over her spine. She scanned the square again. If he'd shaken off the cave collapse like so many other injuries in the past, he'd be gunning for her next.

Once she had the money, you wouldn't see her for dust.

One of the service staff approached her table, stepping cautiously into her line of vision, and coughed to attract her attention. It was the same lanky teenage boy who'd served her the drink. He kept several steps away from her, shifting from foot to foot.

She caught his eye, and for a moment, blinked amber eyes over her deep chestnut ones again, keeping her lids soft and heavy, just for the hell of it. The veins in his arms were thick and ran close to the skin, marbling his flesh, blood running through them like her favourite Morellino. She stood, licked her lips, and took a step towards him as the stink of his sweat rose. "*Beh?*"

The boy snapped the metal tray he was clutching up to his chest and held it like a shield, shoulders tense, and head and neck pulled back as far as they would go. "Signorina. *Il direttore…*" He nodded towards the cafe, where Tazia now made out the shape of a man in a dinner suit standing with arms crossed gazing out at her.

He looked pissed.

Even from the depths of the building, she made out waves of scarlet and black coursing from his body. The supernatural shine in his eyes flashed from red to a pure cornflower blue as she looked. It was the only attractive thing about him.

Tazia parked the idea of supper, inclined her head at the boy in thanks, then walked into the bar. All she needed was her cash to buy herself time to figure out what freedom actually meant. What could go wrong?

3

———————

SAHARA DUNE

THE SOUL SUCKER'S aura hit Tazia before she'd fully stepped into the cafe. Scarlet energy probed her skin looking for an opening and the tats burned a warning under her shoulder blades.

Her hand fell to the sheath on her right thigh and came up empty. The Bowie knife was still lying on the cave floor where she'd discarded it for the climb. Great. Nothing like negotiating with a demon unarmed.

The fangs in the pouch around her neck felt heavier than they should as she stepped into the cafe. Hopefully, her ticket out.

"Signorina!" Signor Bello, the bar manager, hailed her with a smile. *Fake bastard!* "Come sit here, please." He pulled out a chair at a small table crammed between the restrooms and kitchen, the perfect spot for a private conversation—or a quiet murder.

Tazia smiled her thanks and sat down, counting exits. Four steps to the kitchen door, ten tables between her and the front entrance, one visible staff member, and guaranteed hidden muscle somewhere in the shadows. Soul Suckers always had their bully-boys.

The manager took the seat opposite hers. It creaked under his girth. She scraped her own seat back, away from the table. He had recently fed, bloated with the victims' souls, which now surged under his skin rhythmically bulging against the dinner suit he wore.

Tazia mostly contained the shudder, but her skin prickled as his energy swarmed the injuries on her hands, arms, and knees. Not for the first time, she cursed her human side. Healing took too long.

"Comfortable?" he asked, lips tightening.

Ignoring the smirk, she matched his charm. Also fake. Batting her eyelashes, she said, "Perfectly, thank you. I appreciate you seeing me at such short notice, Signor." At least the stink of his rotting flesh and whiff of lavender perfume made her less self-conscious about her own rather ripe aroma.

Bello's eyes barely flicked an acknowledgement over her face.

Okay, the eyelashes were overkill.

"My name is Sahara Dune."

If he lifted his eyebrows in response to the unlikely pseudonym, she could not see it under the drooping flesh of his forehead, reminding her of a not-so-cute Shar Pei puppy.

"I understand, Signor Bello, you recently engaged the services of myself and my partner, Soren Huxford, to eliminate the Abbot of Savoy?"

"Ahh, bella, call me Sergio." His words were affectionate, although his tone was not. In fact, the electrical charge that surged from him at the mention of the Abbot crackled and fizzed in the air between them like scarlet lightning. She hoped the anger was directed at her late father rather than herself.

"And where is Signor Huxford?"

Not wanting to meet his eyes, Tazia studied the sign to the

bathroom; a little blue painted rabbit pointed the way. She looked back. "He's… indisposed." Bello didn't need to know the truth. Under the table, she scratched at her wrists and knees. They prickled as his fetid aura chipped at the grazes.

"How unfortunate for him." Bello gazed steadily at her.

Tazia blinked and changed the subject. "I have good news, sir. The Abbot is dead."

"Bella, may I get you a glass of wine or… blood?" Before waiting for her answer, he raised a finger toward the server, who'd hovered at the bar this whole time.

"No thank you, Signor. I expect you wish to see the evidence?" She pulled the pouch out from under her shirt.

"And I expect you want to see the payment, *carina*." He gestured toward the inside top pocket of his jacket just as a soul circled his body again, pushing a lumpy package into relief under the material. "But for now, we will drink. You would not insult me by refusing again?"

Bottles and glasses clinked behind her, and she fought to still her fingers drumming against the leg of the table.

After the wine was brought to them, and Sergio had affectionately fondled the waitress's behind in such a way that made Tazia's stomach heave a little, he raised a glass. "To the destruction of blood-sucking mutant vampire scum. May their offspring suffer prolonged abuse and slavery at the hands of superior demons everywhere. *Saluti!*" He paused as he held his glass high, awaiting her agreement.

She gave it. "Sure, yeah."

Before the Demon War her father had extorted money from local businesses and families. Bello apparently had a long memory.

He downed the full wine glass as though it was a vodka shot, a swift movement that left deep red trickles flowing down his chin and onto his white shirt, creating purple stains. They spread rapidly, saturating the surrounding cloth.

An idea sparked.

Acting quickly, she lifted the bag over her head, poured the two fangs into her hand and offered them to him. "The evidence, Sergio."

Get ready, Taz!

Bello widened his eyes slightly. He fumbled inside his jacket's side pocket to extract a small tin box and put it on the table in front of him. As he did so, she got a clear glimpse of a brown envelope in his inside pocket. He plucked the fangs from her palm and inspected them closely.

Casually picking up her wine glass, Tazia finished the contents, making the most of each drop, even licking the rim while she watched him. *This had to work.*

Three—

He placed the teeth on the table and, while muttering a short Latin incantation, sprinkled the teeth with powder taken from the box.

Two—

As the powder came into contact with the teeth, they slowly took on an eerie pink glow, gradually intensifying to luminous orange reminiscent of a burning candle wick.

One—

Bello gave a small tight smile, and his shoulders appeared to relax. The magick proved the ownership she had claimed. The Abbot of Savoy was dead.

Go!

She leapt up, stretched across the table and smashed her glass into his neck, aiming for his carotid. As her right hand struck, she reached inside his jacket with her left and snatched the contents of his inner top pocket.

The glass shattered. A long shard slashed across his neck deep enough to spurt blue blood across the table and Tazia's arm, but he wouldn't bleed out. The distraction worked. The shrieking souls of half a dozen entrees bulged against the opening looking for escape.

As the pain hit, Sergio let out a piercing animal screech.

Sensing a presence behind her, Tazia kicked back her chair, heard it skid across the floor and collide with something that shouted a colourful Italian expletive before the chair clattered to the ground.

She turned in time to see a lumbering goon finish his fall over the chair, hitting the floor with a massive thud, his breath forced from him.

Without hanging around any longer, she leaped over tables blocking her exit and ran out into the evening sunshine towards the piazza. A couple of gunshots echoed after her, but she was moving too fast and they whizzed uselessly past. People dropped to the ground. It aided her escape, and she swerved her way through them, across the square, and down into a nearby alleyway.

After a few blocks, she checked behind her. No one was chasing. She was safe, for now. But Sergio Bello would never allow the insult to be unpunished. *Oh well, get in the queue.*

In the relative safety of the shopping district, Tazia wove her way through the evening crowds to another little passageway. This one empty. She squatted against a wall to catch her breath. The envelope she'd taken from the demon's pocket felt light. She counted out the contents just the same. *For fucksakes—less than half.*

Still breathing heavily, she slid down the wall, legs sprawling in front of her. "Well, what do you think? Will it be enough to start over?" She addressed the aged yellow brick wall opposite, an old habit she couldn't shake.

When the wall remained silent, Tazia sighed, and shoved the money into her DM boots for safekeeping. She stood. It has to work. *I'll make it work.*

4

NO MADDER THAN USUAL

BOTTLE IN HAND, Tazia sat on the wide stone ledge surrounding Turin's most notorious fountain: a kitsch monstrosity of naked cherubs and dancing lions. In the centre, on a marble plinth, a horned demon groped a tarty-looking Venus.

Tazia stuck her tongue out at the demon statue. She had no use for Satan. After watching her father's lifelong allegiance to the Old Goat, she was relieved he was now safely ensconced in Hell alongside him. Her own ambitions were simpler.

Taking a swig of tequila, Tazia shook off thoughts of her father, seeking instead to sink into the soft cushion the drink provided—

But the hair on the back of her neck shot to attention. Someone was watching.

The goons from the cafe? She scanned the square in the direction she had come. Nothing. No one barrelling towards her.

Soren Huxford, then? If he'd lived, gone to the bar for payment and found the chaos she'd left behind, he'd be fuming. He was not the type to let anyone mess with either his money or his killer reputation. If he were alive, he'd be after her. But the doorways, rooftops, and windows of the buildings that overlooked the fountain were empty. No telltale flash of light reflected off the end of a rifle, either. Just the final rays of the dying sun winking back at her.

With the hairs still pricking on her neck, the sensation intensified, as if someone was creeping up behind. Turning, she looked up at the statue of Venus and drew a breath in alarm as the goddess slowly blinked at her, then curved her full lips into a stiff and awkward smile.

Without taking her eyes off the statue, Tazia reached into her pocket for the small bottle that was her constant companion. Opening it, she pulled out two pills and put them in her mouth. She crunched and swallowed slowly with the aid of another mouthful from the bottle.

The "hallucination" continued.

In fascinated horror, she watched Venus straighten up, pull free from the grasp of the lustful Satan, step off the marble dais, and wade clumsily through the water. The statue settled beside her with a grinding scrape as its stone bottom settled on the ledge.

Even for Tazia, this was new. She froze. If not hallucination, then possession, or some kind of projection?

The statue gently put a marble hand onto her arm, the smooth stone icy against her skin. "It's okay, Anastasia, you're not going mad. Well, no madder than you usually are, anyway." She tittered at her own joke.

The tiny bell-like sound echoed around the plaza, strangely twisting into a distorted groan as it hit the stately basilica standing at its northern end. Alarmed, a small flock of pigeons took off from the ledges of the baroque facade. Tazia tracked them flying high into the sky before circling and landing again in a part of the square that didn't contain odd-sounding statues.

"Not talking, Anastasia?"

—Tazia jerked her head and made a strangled grunt. *Words. Form words.*

"I didn't really hear that, pet?"

—She sucked her teeth, loosening pieces of reluctant medication, and swallowed quickly.

Venus adjusted her position so that the wet marble folds of her robe loosened their attachment to her legs with a squelch. Water rolled off her clothing and splashed onto Tazia's boots. "How about I talk and you just listen, eh?" She adopted the tone of a kindly schoolteacher greeting a brand new class. "I'm not really Venus, of course, but you probably guessed that?"

Tazia blinked, still expecting the vision to disappear any minute into a puff of smoke, or glitch out like a hologram in a sci-fi movie.

The statue sat back, apparently collecting herself before straightening with a stiff flourish of her arms, and declared, "I am the High Advocate! That's fancy talk for an angel." When she still got no response, her tone abruptly changed. "An important one, actually!"

Silence ticked by.

Tazia bit down on her cheek. Even her blood tasted weird. *Why is it still here?*

Venus sighed and wriggled, grinding her bottom like a pestle into its mortar. "Do you know what an Advocate does?"

Tazia shook her head.

"We decide the fate of a human soul. Whether it deserves to go to Heaven or Hell. You know, have you been a good boy or a bad? A bit like Santa." She shrieked at her own joke before drawing the laugh to a sudden halt. She lowered her mouth close to Tazia's ear before hissing, "I am the *High* Advocate, however, Anastasia. I look after those difficult cases where the balance of good and evil is often unclear. Royalty, presidents, and ecclesiastical types like, oh, I don't know… abbots."

"Oh!" Tazia backed away, her mind spinning. "You're here about my f-f-father?"

"Bingo!" Venus clapped her hands together. It sounded like a gunshot ricocheting around the square. Every pigeon in the neighbourhood took off once more, blocking the low sun and plunging them into darkness.

Palms slapped tight over her ears, the high-pitched ringing persisted in Tazia's head.

Venus didn't look in the slightest perturbed at the flight of the pigeons or her obvious distress. Instead, she gazed across the square, a little wetness forming in her eyes. "When your father was still human, he was rather important to me. I saw his… potential, let's say. And then he was dying."

Tazia shuffled slightly closer. "Are you crying?"

Venus turned back to her. "Of course not." She sniffed dramatically. "I tried my best to persuade Heaven that he should be forgiven. But they denied him and ridiculed me. Too many sins, they said. He was true evil, they said. Said my head was turned. They didn't know him like I did. He was a great man. Strong and powerful. Vigorous."

Eyes now bone dry, her lips curled into a wide and lustful smile that brought gooseflesh to Tazia's skin.

"So, in those moments before his death, I offered him the chance to be reborn as a demon. He would be the greatest vampire ever known, eventually sit by Satan's side, his ultimate reward for devotion to the dark. To get there, he needed to do one simple thing." She got close to Tazia's ear again and whispered, "To create you!"

This part of the tale was all too familiar. Tazia's father had spoken often of the voice whispering in his ear, telling him to create a child through murder and magick. The perfect creation to help him achieve his dark desires.

Venus brought her unblinking eyes level with Tazia's. She gazed back into the cold grey stonework and the shallow holes that the sculptor had shaped to resemble pupils.

The statue's voice was steely. "Only he messed it up!"

Flinching, Tazia tried to edge away. It would take around five seconds for her to clear the plaza at an all-out sprint. But for some reason, her legs wouldn't respond to her urgent demands for them to move. Even her ink gave her nothing.

"He didn't keep you the way I told him to. He cut you off from that human soul I worked so hard to ensure you were born with."

Legs, move.

"So, you're here for my fucking soul?"

"Oh no. I don't want that."

"Then, what?"

"*You* do. *You* want it back, Anastasia. You *need* it back. You are more important than he ever knew."

"Lady, I don't understand."

Venus gained a wistful look. "Let's say it's a Fate thing."

What the fuck? It was the sort of bullshit answer her father had always given her when she asked about her impossible existence.

Tazia finally managed to shift her legs, jumped up, and pulled in a deep lungful of air.

Clouds had gathered since the sun lowered, and rain fell on them both. It soaked her hair to the roots and dripped down her neck, reviving her. She took a few steps away from the ridiculous statue with her stupid laugh and cold hands.

"Don't run away, pet. I haven't told you the best part yet."

"God, there's more?"

"Now, Anastasia. No attitude, please. It seems daddy took a bit of a wrong turn when he got to Hell. Instead of finding that seat next to Satan like we planned, he dropped into the Red River. The river of fire, of blood, and bone. Liquid destruction." Venus came up behind her and whispered, "But you can get him out."

Tazia turned and glared. "Why would I do that? I'm free. Finally. Why would I help him?" She'd suffered years of imprisonment and cruelty at his hands. She'd earned this!

"Because despite everything, you can't escape him. His control is buried too deep, pet. We both know it's still there."

"You're fucking kidding me!" The comment was ridiculous. Still controlled? Even after his death? The suggestion made her skin crawl. Yet, when she tried to argue more, her tattoos pinched a warning.

She turned her back and set out across the square.

"Don't leave, pet. I'll just bring you back…" The Advocate called after her.

With that, the atmosphere thickened. Drops of rain stopped falling, suspended in mid-air. She turned back. Her body felt disconnected, a hundred times heavier, like she was twisting in thick molasses. Sound dampened. The talking statue was now the only thing that seemed normal. She continued moving as she had been, while all else was held in a sweet static fog.

"We won't debate the point, Anastasia. But if you are unconvinced perhaps you'd prefer to take a trip back to Hell yourself. That cell by the Red River is empty right now, I believe. Perfect for a little sojourn."

The threat froze Tazia's blood. Could this bitch send her back?

Now pinned to the spot, the final vestiges of excitement she'd felt that day faded. Her shoulders sagged.

Venus smiled. "It doesn't have to be this way. No Cells of Permanent Incarceration. No Hell." Her childish giggle bounced through the air. "Do what you're told, and Daddy gets the eternity he deserves. A place by Satan's side just as I promised him. He'll be out of your hair forever."

"And if I don't?"

"I will make every step you take extremely unpleasant," Venus hissed. She glanced at the fountain, and the serpent wound around Satan's spear hissed back. It unfurled itself, flashed through the water, and slithered over the stone ledge heading straight for Tazia.

Trapped in the thick air, she couldn't move back.

The snake rose up—

No! Tazia jerked her head away. The tattoos on her back pulled taut.

Mouth opening—

"No. Please. Don't!"

Fire shot from the serpent's mouth. It burned up the water in the air, and boiling steam blasted into her face. Pain shot across her cheek and up to her forehead. Instant blisters formed, burst, and splashed blood back over her face. She tasted iron.

Tazia screamed—

Then the snake was gone.

The atmosphere returned to normal. A few pigeons caught on the fringe of the stasis were released and flew rapidly into the sky. The serpent was again curved around Satan's spear.

Tazia whimpered and dropped to her knees, but the blood and pain of her scorched skin were already gone.

"Just a warning. I'll leave you to think about it." Venus twisted her body so that her feet were once again in the water, and she heaved herself up. "*Buona sera*, Anastasia. I'm always watching. Call for me when you are ready to make a decision. Don't leave it too long, pet."

As her words faded, Tazia found herself staring at a stone-still statue standing on its pedestal, water splashing over its feet, and glaring at the amorous devil.

5

CHURCH GOING

CLOSING the door of her apartment behind her, Tazia leaned back and exhaled. The shaking in her hands all but stopped, though her breath was still shallow.

The apartment was on the first floor of a slim, tall sixteenth-century townhouse on a narrow street in the older area of Turin. She'd lived here for thirty years, off and on, sharing it with Hux for the last two of those.

After seeing the angel by the fountain, she couldn't face going straight home.

Instead, she had gone to the little church a couple of streets away. It was her refuge. No one ever thought to search for a demon in a church. It was a place to sort good from bad. Not as clear cut as religion or fantasy would have humans believe. Angels could be bastards; demons could surprise you. She'd seen both.

The calm, cold air in the church had worked for a while. Then it changed into freezing fingers clawing at her.

She dropped into the overstuffed purple easy chair by the fire and pressed the remote control. Usually comforting, today the warmth was not enough. She scanned the room, looking for familiarity in the clashing colours, the book-covered shelf, the painted landscapes on the wall, and the battalion of video game collectibles that stood guard on the mantelpiece. *Yes, this is home.*

The church was the exact opposite. Plain, simple. Unadorned white plastered walls.

But for the painting.

The canvas hung on the side wall at the end of the pews, a new addition to the décor. She'd never seen it before.

In style, it reminded her of a Bruegel. In subject matter, it depicted the division of Heaven and Hell. Angels with halos and wings, and demons with red horns and pitchforks slicing up their territories, hauling people this way and that. The painter had not been concerned with challenging stereotypes.

Above were the luminous white clouds and flat expanse of sky, while below, the Red River carried its cargo of condemned men and demons to Hell. The water ribboned over the ground, ending in the dark Cells of Permanent Incarceration. The hole she'd been trapped in until she was thirteen years old.

The painting intrigued her. She'd been drawn to the image of an elderly man shunted under the red burning water with a long thin pole yielded by a skeletally thin angel. The man's stalk-like arms were raised in supplication to the sky, the flesh already peeling from the bone in wilted leaves by the action of the acid water.

Tazia shivered. Even the memory made her cold.

She grabbed the fringed blue blanket from the back of her chair and draped it over her shoulders, then pulled herself closer to the fire. She didn't mind the fake flames. Illusion was the story of her life. The pills helped her figure out what was real and what was imagined, but not today, there in the church.

As Tazia examined the figure of the man, faint screams emanated through the air. Alarmed, she'd looked around to pinpoint the source of the sounds. There'd been no one else there.

The screams changed. A male voice pleaded for help, now one moment calling to God and the next to Satan. When it uttered her own name, it clicked: her father.

She'd stepped back, crashing into the bench as the painting came alive before her eyes. The river surged with pink-foamed waves washing over screaming victims, and among them— unmistakably—her father's face, his hand reaching toward her.

Tazia tried to shake the memory of the picture. She stood and crossed to the sofa where she ran her hands over the soft cushions and throws, grounding herself. *This is real. This is home.*

In the church, she'd raised a hand there, too.

Stupidly, she touched it to the painting, looking for the comfort of its rough oil and canvas, but under her touch the vision escalated. She found her fingers wrapped around the cold iron bars of an old wooden door, the scent of rust and decay rose around her as she looked through the bars and out into the church.

She was inside the painting now. She could see the rows of empty pews and the crucified Christ statue that stood on the far side of the central aisle. To her right, the flickering votives on the altar cast moving shadows across the walls.

Looking behind her, she realized she knew this place. She was back in the cell that had held her for so long. The walls were rough-hewn slabs of stone cemented with damp dirt, and the floor a mess of mud and blood. Metal and rancid fat tainted the earth as water from the Red River got sucked up by the heat, condensed on the walls, and dripped to the floor.

And there, on her left, was her old friend. Over thousands of years, the rivulets of water had carved a crude face into the wall. Hollows for eyes, a ridge for a nose, and a deep gully that almost resembled a smile.

She'd spent the first years of her life in this cell, whispering her secrets, fears, and hopes to that face. It's the one habit she'd taken from this place to her life above ground. The one good thing that got her through.

When she was old enough to be useful to him, her father replaced the walls and bars with the tattoos etched on her back, binding her soul. He'd told her it would make things easier, make the human side less intrusive. Promote loyalty to the dark. To him.

But the magick made her lose herself and hallucinations distorted reality now her soul was out of reach.

"I can't go back!" she'd whispered, and dragged breath into her lungs. Panic rising. The scream came from her throat. She felt it, but all she heard was the deafening roar of blood in her ears and her heart pounding. She'd snapped back to reality, standing beside the painting. The priest was running from the back of the church up the aisle towards her. "Signorina?"

He hadn't stayed to comfort her. He'd caught sight of her wild amber eyes and double-backed to his office at speed. "*Mi scusi*, Signorina, *mi scusi*."

Here at the apartment, she moaned again. The pain of that place deep in her belly. Would she ever forget? Could she?

Tazia crossed to the window, looking out at the street below. She'd left it open to air out the room after Hux had been too liberal with his cologne that morning.

A crow settled on the roof of the house opposite, flapping its wings and cawing discontent. The iridescent shine of its feathers caught occasionally in the moonlight.

With a deep inhale, her thoughts returned to the church.

She'd addressed the angel in the painting. "All right, you win, I'll get my soul back. I'll save my father. Don't put me back there."

As she spoke, the atmosphere in the church changed. Around her, the air crackled, chilling her skin further and raising the hairs on her arms.

The painting came to life once more. The angel looked up from the Red River, her voice seeping into Tazia's mind. Venus from the fountain. "Do I have your promise, Anastasia? A promise is binding."

"Yes, I promise." She had no choice but to serve him still.

The angel nodded and removed the pole from the man in the river. He bobbed up and floated away on the current, the flesh reforming on his bones. "I'll pop in now and then, pet, to help you if I can. I'm not the tyrant you take me for." Her fake tinkling laugh followed.

Tazia returned to her place by the fire and slumped forward, holding her head in her hands. With that promise, her freedom slipped away.

Now a different question rose: what would removing the walls to her soul mean? Not only for the Advocate—fuck knows why she needed it—but for herself? Would she finally be able to love, or just drown in more shit she didn't want to feel?

For almost an hour she sat stock still, raising her head only when the apartment was pitch black and luminous red flames danced crazy shapes on the walls. Outside, the crow swooped at the window so close its wings beat against the glass. There every night, it would fly off soon to report God knows what, to God knows who. *Little fucker.*

Beneath her outward surrender to the Advocate, defiance hardened in her chest. She would not let all hope of freedom die. She'd struggled far too long, fought too hard. She returned to the window and struck the frame with the flat of her hand. "I've got friends to help you know! People that love me."

The bird squawked and flew off.

Well, one friend anyway.

6

THE BACK END OF A HORSE

TAZIA PRESSED the keyboard on her desktop computer to make the Dark Souls screensaver disappear. She selected the video call app and clicked on the only name listed: William Nadig.

While the call connected to London, she disappeared into her bedroom, threw off her ripped and demon-blooded clothes and boots, and returned to sit in front of the screen dressed only in a pair of boy-cut underwear and a black sports bra. As she shrugged a clean top over her head, Billy picked up.

"Hey, love, slow down. This is too good to miss."

Tazia finished pulling down the top and found herself staring at a young man's grinning face. They looked the same age. His twenty-six was her one hundred and fifty-some. That's where the comparisons stopped. His parents, Pakistani, hers were Italian. His short black hair, impeccably cut and styled, hers blonde, overlong and hacked with a knife for practicality.

Tonight he was sporting the rectangular, heavy-rimmed glasses he only tended to wear if he was tired or deliberately geeking out.

Despite the trauma of the last few hours, she couldn't help but return the grin. "Hi, Billy. What's up?"

"Nothing much, but go back and do the undressing thing again, and I'll have something to report." He winked at her.

Tazia had no retort, unusual for her. Trading sexual innuendo with Billy was standard.

"You called me, idiot!" he said lightheartedly, but frowned. "What's up with you, Taz?" The picture flickered slightly as the connection bombed for a moment, and it looked like he'd made a small staccato jump in his seat.

"Trouble." Debating which shitstorm to dump on him first, she tapped a little Princess Elsa figurine (a gift from Billy) against the tabletop in front of her. Billy had sworn Hux and Elsa shared the same wig. The joke remained between them, much to Hux's frustration.

"I had a run-in with a guy who owed me some money. Ended up a bit… messy." She remembered the blue blood spewing from Bello's neck and shuddered. A shower would have been a good idea.

"You all right?" Deep concern.

"Fine. Got the cash. Well, some of it, at least. That's not why I called, though. I need help with something—a couple of things?"

As Billy was about to reply, a well-manicured hand snaked over his shoulder and settled on the back of his neck. It appeared to giggle for no apparent reason, and a voice whispered, "You coming back to bed, Billy?"

Looking annoyed, he said in a pleasant enough tone, "I'm working, love, piss off."

There was a deep sigh, as if the hand had heard it a thousand times, before it was abruptly removed.

Tazia waited a respectable enough three seconds to allow the owner of the hand to get out of range before asking, "Is she called Chastity or Candy?"

Billy snorted slightly. "Actually, it's Tiffany, love—classy, innit?"

"Figures," said Tazia. "When you gonna get a girlfriend who looks more like the back-end of a horse? At least they might be able to hold a conversation." She didn't pull off the flippant tone she was attempting. She was being mean, sexist, but hell, she'd had a very bad day. She fiddled with the figurine under the table, turning it over and over.

"Love, if I wanna talk, I've got you, innit?" Billy's accent and dialect veered regularly from highly respectable West London to the more street-smart East End when it suited him, often throwing those who didn't know him well into confusion. Few people knew him like she did.

"That wasn't a compliment, was it?"

"You're the one who brought up horses' arses…"

Tazia rolled her eyes. "Can we get back to my problem?"

"Fire away." Billy settled back. He picked up a bottle of expensive imported beer from the desk beside him to swig as he listened, his seat twisting slightly from side to side. The signal she had his undivided attention.

"Can you pick up anything about Hux? I think he might be dead. I want to make sure."

"Make sure? Did you finally stab the tosser with that splendid knife of yours?"

Tazia thought wistfully about her Bowie lying under the rubble at the bottom of the cave. "No."

"Then how?"

"He got squished."

Billy frowned.

Tazia acted out Hux's demise with her hands. Using Elsa as the muscular gunman looked a bit odd, but it did the job. She held it in the palm of one hand. "Hux here. Rocks here. Squish." She slapped her other hand down on top of the figure with a smack that, for a moment, wobbled the webcam.

"But how?"

Talking about her father would worry Billy, so she'd been avoiding it. He'd get stressed out and angsty, and she wasn't sure she could cope with that right now, but what was the alternative? She would stick to the facts. "He shot my father dead—who got sucked down into Hell—and the cave collapsed on top of him." *Pithy*.

As predicted, Billy's response was intense. He leaned forward in his seat, filling the whole screen with his face, eyes wide. "Your dad's dead? Love, I don't know what to say. You okay? What can I do? Let me help."

Tazia sensed the buzz of his energy reaching out to her from the screen. She gave a little smile of resignation. "I'm fine, honest." Coping, anyway. "But it's Hux I'm worried about. If he's alive, he'll come after me."

"Why would he come after you?"

"I sorta… well, I… um… left him there to die." A little heat rose into her cheeks.

Billy nodded approvingly. "Good job! He was a dick."

"I know you thought, well… I know he was… probably. Oh Jesus, just tell me if he's alive or not, Billy. Please."

He moved back from the screen, took another swig of beer, then focused deep into her eyes, creating an even deeper connection between them. A magickal connection. "Okay, give me a minute. Is he still wearing the pendant?"

"He told me he'd—" Tazia dropped her eyes from the camera "—never take it off."

Billy had crafted a pendant for Hux at Tazia's request nearly a year ago so she could keep track of him. A simple silver square inscribed on the front with a sigil created from an entwined "S" and "A" standing for Stalk and Acquire. The idea of a tether wasn't unfamiliar; she'd been wearing one on her own back most of her life.

When she gave it to him, he'd told her he'd wear it forever. He took it as a gesture, a gift of love, even. He interpreted the letters as the "S" of Soren wrapped around the "A" of Anastasia. She didn't contradict him. Fake relationships were good cover.

But now her intentions felt cruel.

"It's okay, love. We do things sometimes. All of us. Not good things. Let it go."

Is he a damn mind reader too?

Her eyes returned to the screen. "The spell will connect to the sigil?"

"Yes, the charge should have lasted. Where is the cave? In Turin?"

"Close by. I showed you once on the map. Remember? It was on top of the place my father had me locked up as a kid."

"I remember. The one on the Sword of Saint Michael ley line. Not unusual to find the old archangel close to an entrance to Hell. We can use that for some extra oomph. Follow the signal, ride the line, and—*et voila*—we see if the wanker's still breathing."

Tazia had seen Billy work magick many times before; the blank eyes, focused intention as he typed, code flowing from his fingers like water. As she watched him, a code-string appeared on her screen, in a little text box in the corner. The Latin words interspersed with punctuation marks, numbers, and random letters made no sense to her, but the air in the room felt the power and emitted a low buzz. The hair on her skin rose.

The code lifted from the screen as wisps of silver smoke and reached into the room before passing into the electrical sockets, searching for the nearest communication hub or pathway, then on to the next, and the next until it found its target.

As a technomancer, Billy had charmed everything from an electric razor to a NASA telescope in the past and earned bags of cash doing so. The resulting magick was fast, laser-precise, and powerful.

This spell, drawn by the sigil on Hux's pendant, took a while, though. Seconds turned to minutes; five minutes turned to ten. Tazia stood, sat again, stood again, circled her apartment, and now sat once more tapping Princess Elsa against the desk top.

"It doesn't usually take this long," she said.

"He's deeper than a Soho alley at 3 AM, love."

"What?"

"He's a long way down, babe." His fingers had been tapping away all this time, while hers casually stroked Princess Elsa's hair. Any distraction.

"Oh. Right."

After a pause, Billy asked. "Do you remember me telling you about my old mentor, Charlie?"

Tazia nodded, still stroking.

"He pulled me off the streets to teach me technomancy when I was fifteen, gave me a roof over my head. It wasn't charity, he certainly liked the benefits. Twisted, bastard. But he knew his stuff. Told me casting a spell this way was like navigating a digital sea in a sailboat. The electricity, or in this case the energy of our ley line, fills the sails and pushes the boat along. With Hux so deep, there's no wind just a weak current, the boat's… drifting. The magick will get there, we just have to be patient."

"The sigil is like a lighthouse, then, guiding the boat in?"

"Exactly!"

"I'm sorry about Charlie, Billy. You miss him, you—"

With an audible bang, silver light surged into Tazia's apartment and flew back into her PC and through the network to Billy's machine in London. "Current's shifted. Almost got it, Taz." He tapped away frantically.

"What does it say?"

"Hold on." Billy deciphered the code as it appeared on his screen. His face dropped. "You're not gonna like this, love. He's still alive. Vitals are strengthening." He looked at her, forehead creasing. "You'd better get out of there, Taz. The cave's only an hour or so away, right?"

Any thoughts of regret about what she had done to Hux vanished instantly. Now it was about survival.

She threw Princess Elsa across the full length of the apartment into the kitchen, where she ricocheted off one wall to come to rest in the greasy washing-up water still sitting in the sink.

"Taz? Did you hear me?"

In her mind, Billy's voice faded. In the street below, every pedestrian, every parked car now held a potential threat. Soren Huxford wasn't just persistent, he was a goddamn animal when it came to revenge. He didn't gnaw at a bone; he crunched it into a million pieces with a big smile on his face. And now he'd be coming for her. She was the fucking bone.

Billy's voice cut through her spiralling thoughts. "Tazia? Talk to me." The determination in his tone pulled her back to the present.

She turned from the window, decision crystallizing. "I need to disappear, Billy."

He was ready even before she got back to the desk and gazed into the camera. "Come here, love. To me. We'll sort the rest out later." His eyes looked hopefully at the screen.

This wasn't the first time she'd run into Billy's willing arms to lie low for a while. Plus, there was the Advocate. She hadn't even told him about her yet. Billy was the only one who could help with that. He loved her. The only one who did. If her bricked-up soul could feel gratitude, it would be endless. She nodded, "I'll need a flight—"

"Already done." He lifted his fingers from the keyboard, leaned back, stretched hands behind his head, and grinned. "You're on the midnight out of Turin flying into Heathrow under that famous pseudonym of yours. See you later, 'Sahara.' Stay safe. Over and out." He leaned forward and ended the call.

Tazia went to the bedroom and pulled on some jeans, emptied a drawerful of clothes into a bag, grabbed a toothbrush and paste, her fake passport and driver's license, and the money she'd just collected from Sergio Bello. She locked up the apartment and left.

She deliberately didn't even glance at the racks of Hux's expensive clothes still hanging in the wardrobe. She was trying hard to forget the two years she'd spent living here with him as his lover, while all the time scheming and deceiving. The plan her father had hatched was supposed to have given her the freedom to start over. Hux's death had been integral to that plan. It had failed. She had failed. Her father would have found that totally unacceptable.

———

At the airport, Tazia breathed more freely. She'd navigated check-in and made her way to Security behind the clear plexiglass partition. A few more steps—

"Anastasia! Stop!"

Her muscles locked mid-stride. He hadn't even had to shout to make her freeze. Only raise his voice enough to carry over the noise of the busy concourse, bee-lining to her.

Icy cold, she turned slowly to see Soren Huxford watching her from twenty feet away on the other side of the screen, a giant among the smaller, darker Italians rushing around him.

He stood perfectly still, framed by the clean grid of the plexiglass with the crowd blurring between them.

Their eyes locked together.

Dressed in fresh clothes, his chin-length blond hair was disheveled, but clean. No evidence to suggest he had been lying under a pile of rocks for hours.

He was protected by some magick charm, she was sure. An amulet maybe, or invisible tattoos. But despite doing her best to coax his secret from him, he'd remained stubbornly silent in the two years they'd spent together. Human, yet she'd seen him recover from bullet wounds that would kill a normal man dead, and watched as cuts in his skin had healed in front of her eyes.

She moved her balance to the front of her right foot, ready to run. The intensity in Hux's eyes dialled up a level, daring her to continue. His body too was poised ready to pounce, chest moving up and down, deep and steady. His clear blue eyes bore into hers, still holding her immobile.

She knew she was safe, and he knew it, too. He couldn't get to her without causing a scene; the partition stood solid between them. He couldn't shoot her despite the ever-present handgun holstered under his jacket; he'd likely hit someone else in the moving crowd. He had to let her go. It would be maddening to him.

As she watched, he seemed to accept that it was hopeless. He gave her a rare, tight smile. Grabbed at the pendant hanging around his neck, pulling it free to break the chain. Then, still with it in his hand, drew his thumb slowly across his throat. The threat was clear.

Something twisted in her chest. Fear, yes. But more. Guilt? Regret, even? *Hell no!*

He took two steps back, eyes still boring into hers, turned, and walked away. She watched as he left the concourse, saw him slam the broken chain and pendant into a waiting garbage bin and go through the exit.

Still she stood, not moving.

Breathe, Tazia, breathe.

A formal Italian voice announced last call on the tannoy; her plane was boarding. She had to hurry. Her legs unstuck, and she sprinted to Security.

7

THE LOVE OF A GOOD WOMAN

TAZIA GOT to Billy's Docklands penthouse at around five am London time. She'd exchanged insistent banging to rhythmic kicking by the time he finally pulled open the door, narrowly avoiding a kick to his crotch.

He froze, raising his eyebrows. Then grinned a greeting.

She glared.

Her hunger peaked on the late shuttle train, so she'd grabbed a quick bite. A businessman. He didn't go quietly and during the struggle her feeding knife slipped. Too deep, too jagged. The punch to the head made him easier to deal with, but too late with the botched cut. He bled out. An ambulance would've been pointless.

A messy kill. The Abbot would have sneered. Another failure to add to the growing list. Her control was slipping, and some random corporate fucker had paid the price for it.

Billy opened his arms in greeting. Still grinning, of course.

She ducked under his arm and walked in.

The designer underwear and a shirt was a nice touch. Sometimes he didn't bother. She waved a hand at his clothes. "Thanks for the effort!" Tall, gym-toned, the whole package.

He chain-smoked, drank too much beer, and still looked good. *Bastard.*

"Anything for you, love!"

From her angle in the hallway, she saw the end of Billy's bed. A pair of long naked legs stretched out. They looked asleep, red-painted toes occasionally twitching as she watched. "Tiffany?"

"Tracey." Billy shrugged like a man reporting the weather.

"Ah, of course. One a day wouldn't be enough," Tazia said.

She dropped her duffel bag on the floor where she stood and walked further into the flat. Billy picked it up and repositioned it against the wall. *Of course he did.*

"When you've got a body like mine, love, it seems unfair not to share." His bragging was good humoured. The tiredness in his tone, new.

As she walked away, she felt his eyes on her. His energy curling around her middle and holding on tight. Trails of pink and gold glittered one moment, tickling, the next, caressing her. The ink gave a faint shiver. He'd already forgotten the sleeping blonde in his bed.

She milked it.

Stretched up her arms slowly, dropping one hand to pull up her hair to reveal the smooth skin on the back of her neck for maximum effect. *Did it land?* She turned. Billy's wide smile and shining eyes said it all. They both cracked up laughing.

Friends. Always only friends. He'd wanted more, she'd shut it down flat. Half-demon wasn't a fair match for him. He disagreed, but let it slide. He'd never give up.

She looked around. Eighteen months away, yet little had changed here. Same urban bachelor style: red brick and black leather. Not a squashy cushion or shade over grey anywhere. Comfort didn't meet the aesthetic. A few more modern paintings hung between Billy's footwear photography: mostly women's shoes throwing animal-like shadows through lighting and angles.

A single full-length mirror reflected the entire flat. Handy for his hair checks before leaving for the day—she caught her image—and for cleaning blood spatter off your face, too.

A new leather sofa, nearly identical to the old one, faced the massive flat-screen bolted to the brick. Despite the cash, Billy was a lad at heart. Give him beer, footy, and someone to hang on to at night, and he was happy enough.

Billy handed her a damp towel, hugged her tight from behind, tucking his face against her neck. His scent washed over her. She allowed herself to relax back against him for a beat, then wriggled free.

"The hug was for your loss, love. So sorry." He meant it, but it had made her itchy.

She collapsed onto one of the armchairs, bookending the sofa, putting space between them. "I'm okay. Honest."

"If you say so." His eyebrows said *liar*. "You look knackered, by the way. And what the bloody hell happened to your skin?"

"Sun got a bit hot. It's healing. The blood will help. By tomorrow, I'll be fine. Are you tired? There's something. It's urgent, there's—"

"Any sign of Hux?—"

Shit! He was going to dig.

"—Murder seems an extreme way for a bloke to get permission from a dad to date his daughter."

She winced. *Joking? Really?* She'd kept life with Hux to herself. But if she lied, he'd know.

"He found me at the airport just before takeoff. He was pissed, but not a lot he could do. He doesn't have the pendant anymore." She shrugged. "I don't care."

Billy raised his eyebrows.

"Don't!" she said. The ink bit down along her spine.

"What?"

"The eyebrow thing."

"This?" He raised his brows again.

"Yes! I'm telling you the truth." *Yeah, right.*

"Coffee?" he asked, pointedly changing the subject.

"Look. It's not even him we should talk about. There's… other stuff." Perhaps telling him about the Venus in the *piazza* would stop him reading her so fucking well.

He ran both hands vigorously over his hair so that it, once again, stood to attention. "Again. Coffee?"

She shook her head. The new blood in her stomach had revived her enough.

He did it anyway.

In the sleek kitchen he assembled an Italian coffeepot, screwing the pieces together after filling it with espresso and filtered water. She got talking. It was easier to tell him her broken story while he kept busy shining up the stainless steel and the pristine cupboards.

She didn't tell him everything, not that the angel had threatened her freedom, just that she had to bring down the magickal walls around her soul to save her father. That got him right where it hurts.

"You want him back?"

"No!" *Too sharp.* Her eyes widened. "I need to free him. That's what he died for, wasn't it? That's always been my purpose."

Her father's words.

"Your bloody 'purpose'? What the fuck, love? He was a bastard to you. You're finally free—let him rot!" He spat out the final words and spun away. She'd told Billy her past in weak moments. The cell he kept her in. The violence. She regretted it often. It was life to her, for him it broke every code between parent and child. Between monster and innocent.

The coffee bubbled.

Billy broke first. He always did. Crossed the room, and offered a hug. "Sorry, love, I just don't get it. All I want is you safe. Your dad never wanted that for you and yet you love him."

"Not love—I can't—" The words rushed out. "Thirty years ago, I would have left him to the River. But then, things changed… He kept his word. Oh, it doesn't matter. There's nothing he can do to save himself now. It's down to me. As always." *Whiny bitch.*

Pushing him away, she dumped herself onto the sofa and crossed her arms over her chest, her back to him, shoulders hunched. The room seemed to shrink around her. "Do you think I really wanted this? I was ready to start over. But I can't until this is done!"

She tried to suck in a breath. Her lungs seized. A cold sweat prickled her skin, starting at her hairline and racing down her spine. *Not now!*

The edges of her vision narrowed. Tattoos digging deep, bastards loving every minute of the coming attack.

With his usual sixth sense, Billy vaulted the back of the sofa and squeezed himself into the gap between her and the hard, square armrest. A steadying hand on her back. "I got you, Taz," he murmured, his voice dropping into a familiar cadence she'd heard dozens of times before. "Breathe. In. Hold. Out slow."

No big deal, he just handled it.

Inch by inch she relaxed against the steady pressure of his hand.

"That's it, love. You're alright." Matter-of-fact. No fuss. Just Billy.

Breathing in and out for five minutes more and then she unclenched her fists, not remembering when she'd balled them up.

"Dammit," she muttered, the word barely audible as her breathing normalized.

Billy gave her shoulder a final squeeze. "Right then. Let's figure this out properly, shall we?"

————

Fully recovered, Tazia drummed a teaspoon against the kitchen countertop like she was auditioning for a rock band. Hands full, Billy poured the coffee. The moment the last drop hit the cup, he slammed it down with a *"shush!"* and snatched the spoon from her hand. To add to the drama he pantomimed carefully feeling for pits in the surface of the granite.

She hugged him, smoothly stole his coffee cup, and headed over to the monster PC he called his "workhorse." It had a chunky keyboard that clicked and clacked like it was nineteen-ninety-five. She remembered them the first time around. "Where shall we start?"

He poured another cup and joined her, pulling up a wheeled office chair, and pushing hers along the desk to give himself space. He cracked his knuckles. "Right, saints, angels, demons—always start with the Catholic records."

As he started to type, the hum from the CPUs was more than electrical. A faint fizz stroked Tazia's skin, a static prickle of magickal energy; a boost to overcome a few of the trickier issues. Billy pulled up all the results concerning 'Angelic Advocates.' A few hits stood out. Venus had been right when she'd said the Advocates were not well known.

"This is a good one." Billy scanned with blank eyes and a hand on the screen, little white sparks flying from his fingertips, picking up details far faster than Tazia could read. She sat back while he paraphrased, her head resting on his shoulder in between sips from her cup.

"It seems the Advocates rarely show up in their true

form. Usually just flashes—like light in your dreams, voices in your head, creepy shit with mirrors. And, apparently, they speak through artwork. Paintings, statues—"

"A tarty looking marble goddess? That's her!"

He scanned on. "There's more about their job here. Like she told you, they speak for the souls of dead people, picking Heaven or Hell for them." He looked at her, "Like she did for your dad."

Tazia's body tensed against his. Maybe caffeine had been a bad idea.

He put a hand to hers. She jerked hers away, got up, and paced to the large picture window to stare out at the river. The water reflected back the deep grey sky like dirty steel. Cold. Dead. "Have all the songbirds gone?" she asked, her breath fogging the glass.

Billy left the computer and joined her, his shoulder barely brushing hers. "Mostly. The portents started for real in January. That was the last time I saw a robin."

"Sad." Her left hand reached for his. "They will be here soon."

To lighten the moment, Billy nudged her gently and pointed toward the riverbank. "See that bench over there? Had a rather spectacular night with twins from Manchester. Nearly fell in when the police boat went by. Then there was the guy with the massive barge…"

She smiled. "You're a disgrace."

"And yet, they love me for it!"

"Not Tiffany, she's gonna be pissed tomorrow when she finds out Tracey was here."

"Who'll tell her?"

"Well, I could…"

He chased her back to their seats.

After scrolling further, Billy said, "It sounds like this angel whatsit must have some pretty big mojo going on. I guess Joshua would know more about her."

They both turned and looked at the massive metal box that stood by the wall a few feet away. The computer was old: four feet tall, two feet wide, and the horrible silver-grey colour she remembered from her time in fall-out bunkers in the fifties. Tazia almost expected to see magnetic tapes turning at the top of it.

"You still have a necromancer in your computer?"

8

A LONG HARD KISS

BILLY NEEDED time to rig the giant processor, so Tazia claimed the leather sofa and a fleece throw he'd removed from the bed (and from Tracey) to grab a nap. At the same time, he woke the sleeping woman to suggest she go home. "Time to bugger-off, love."

Tazia vaguely heard the exchange and watched through one semi-closed eye as a flounce of blonde locks made its way past her and out the door, then she fell asleep.

Raised voices and laughter pulled her from dreams of mangled limbs and cascading rocks. Billy's voice, sharp with frustration: "What the fuck do you mean? You told Dr. Mackenzie I wanted—"

The words cut off as his companion laughed hysterically.

Billy continued. "I knew he was looking at me funny the other night. Bloody hell, Josh!"

Tazia sat up. Billy glared at the computer screen in front of him. "Trouble?" she said.

"This little git!" He jabbed at the screen with his thumb.

"You should have read the message he sent you, dude. It

even mentioned the cops." The voice from the computer cracked up again.

Tazia crossed to the desk and rested a hand on Billy's shoulder. His muscles stretched taught underneath. He absently covered her hand with his own, still looking daggers at the screen, but she felt him release.

The kid's face on screen looked around seventeen. He was still rolling with laughter but the picture showed only little repetitive expressions cycling through. His chin-length dirty blond hair hung limp from the centre in eighties skater style. He looked like Kurt Cobain's little brother, but with piercings.

"Hey, love. Come sit. Meet Joshua. Nearly a thousand years old and going on twelve." He readjusted the camera on top of the screen so that it was facing both of them.

The boy peeked at her from between half-closed lids, giving a good approximation of a shy expression. "Hi, Taz."

"Hey, Josh, how are you today?" Tazia looked in fascination at the kid. Just a picture from a magazine Billy had scanned into the computer with a voice he'd recorded from a Californian student.

Joshua was an old-school necromancer, the kind who body-hopped through corpses and coma patients for centuries. Last year, Billy caught him mid-transfer between the body of a pharmaceutical CEO who'd dropped dead snorting cocaine, and a young kid dying from exposure on the cold London streets.

As the CEO, Joshua had been selling cancer medications dirt-cheap to non-profits worldwide, resulting in a trillion-dollar loss for Billy's client. He admired the Robin Hood act and offered him digital refuge instead of oblivion.

"What was that you were talking about? Doctors?" Tazia wanted more gossip.

"Nothing!" Billy glared at Joshua.

The kid dropped his shyness for a second and smirked. "I'll

keep quiet, Billy, if you let me stay in the Mac, get out of this dinosaur. I could have some fun. Maybe edit all that video you got. You know the stuff. I liked Tiffany, she did that thing with the—"

"I'll mute you!" Billy cut in. "He's been sending emails, Taz, pretending to be me. Little shit."

"Dissing me won't make me help you, bro."

Billy was about to speak again, but Tazia squeezed his shoulder to silence him.

"Hey, Josh, he insults everyone. You tell me all about it later, okay?" She winked, making the young man grin. "What about this angel? Do you know how I get my soul back?"

"Billy's filled me in. Advocates are tricky and if this is the High Advocate—really bloody sneaky! I bet there's more going on than you'll know." Josh's face cycled, with brief movements of the mouth and eyebrows, and slight furrows appearing between his eyes. *Impressive.* Pre-AI and not gaming standard, but Billy had done a pretty good job.

"The ink on your back is just a cage. Soul's not lost or stolen. It's imprisoned. We don't have to summon it back from somewhere, just let it out. I bet you feel it sometimes, right? Leaks through a bit?"

"Perhaps." Tazia remembered being forced awake by sudden flashes of regret for her victims. Lying in the dark, she'd panic, wondering if the ink was cracking. If the spell was broken, would she wake up different? Did she even want to know?

"Have you tried removing the tattoos? Or covering them?" Billy asked, shuffling over to make room for Tazia to share his seat.

"Yep, doesn't work. Laser craps out or needles break. Poured a bit of acid on the top one. Hurt like hell, but didn't touch the tat itself. The magick's clever—"

"Or the shaman that worked it was." Joshua finished for her.

Her spine spasmed at the memory. Fire and ink, drums drowning out her screams. The helplessness had been worse than the pain.

"We need to figure out what type of shaman it was." Joshua continued. "Besides true necromancers like me, they're the magick workers who know the most about souls. They all have different ways of working, different ways of breaking the spells once they've been cast, too."

He glitched into a sneakier look. "Course, the other, quicker option is that I summon Taz's dad so you can talk direct to the bloke. Find out exactly how to break the spell. You'd need to let me out for that though."

"You can do that?" Tazia's eyes widened. "Really?"

"Yeah. Just a quick trip to the nine circles!" His eyes glitched wide.

"Seriously, Josh? If I let you out of there, how likely are you to come back? How stupid do you think I am?"

From the screen, Joshua blinked. Billy hadn't programmed in a glare.

Tazia turned to him. "Billy. If it's the quickest option..."

"No. He won't come back! Remember the hell it was to get him in there? All the havoc he was causing?"

Billy hesitated, and she knew what that meant. *Time to play dirty.*

She caught his hands, held his gaze. "Please."

Still nothing. *Fuck it.* She leaned in and kissed him—long, hard, breaking every rule they'd established. Not fair, but she needed this too badly.

Billy pulled away. "Fuck!" He hesitated, staring deep into her eyes, looking for something. She knew he wouldn't see it, but held his gaze without flinching. *Come on.*

He shoved his hand through his hair and gave her a gentle

push from the seat they shared. She stood while he faced the screen again, his fingers poised over the keyboard. "How do we do this, Josh?"

Joshua explained he'd fetch the essence of the Abbot from Hell itself. Nothing more than a flicker of the man he used to be. They'd have minutes at best before he snapped back, so Billy would have to keep the channel wide open and Tazia would need to talk fast.

Billy didn't argue. He bent to the keyboard, fingers flying, the code spilling faster and faster. Tazia barely followed the blur of commands before Joshua's image began to thin then fade. His face dissolved one pixel at a time, as if someone were erasing him with a slow, steady hand.

A pinprick of light winked in the air above the desk. Then another. The fragments gathered until a single orb formed, bright as a candle flame but swelling, strengthening, until Joshua's picture was gone completely. The ball of light pulsed once, like it was catching its breath, and then streaked past her in a white-blue blur, vanishing into an unused electrical socket with a soft snap.

At the sound, the tattoos under Tazia's shirt thrummed like a struck cross-bow cable as the orb pulsed past. It's like it took a piece of her with him. She rubbed her hands quickly over her arms to shift the feeling.

Billy typed a final line, checked the session read *OPEN*, and shoved back from the desk.

Without a word, he took Tazia's hand, led her out onto the large terrace that ran the length of his penthouse, and pulled her down onto the teak bench to sit beside him. She hung back, he just pulled harder. After lighting two cigarettes, he passed her one and they sat, still and silent, watching London come to life.

She repeatedly glanced sideways at him while she smoked,

her stomach flipping over. The kiss was a step too far. What did he expect? He stalwartly ignored the looks.

Itching to move, she got up and leaned forward on the balcony railing. For a big city in spring, there was still little smog around, just a slight yellow mist that hung above the Thames in the middle distance. The lights in the tower blocks were going out as the sun came up, and ghost-like people trudged to work. *Enjoy your lives while you have them.*

After his last drag, Billy stubbed out the cigarette butt on a heavy silver ashtray sitting on the arm of the bench. It was in the shape of an upturned taloned hand (a gift from Tazia). He leaned forward with his elbows on his knees. "He won't come back, love. And now we've got nothing to help us figure this whole soul stuff out. I shouldn't have let him go."

"Did I screw up?" *Of course I did.* She threw her own stub on the floor and squashed it with her toe, then continued scuffing the ground with one foot like a five-year-old.

Billy picked up the stub and deposited it in the ashtray alongside his own. "You got carried away. With *everything!*"

"I needed to do it. And I found a way to make you." She felt her colour rise. *So, pathetic.*

He blurted out a laugh. "At least you're honest about being a manipulative cow. Most people lie after they've played you."

She threw up her hands. "Guilty! So, what now?" *Can we move on?*

"We wait. See if he comes back, I guess." He lit a couple more cigarettes and handed her one. "You hungry?"

"Nope. Why?"

"I was going to offer you Tracey. She's really getting on my tits. I can call her back?" His joke sliced through the tension that remained.

Tazia grinned. "Tempting, but I prefer my meals without a spray tan."

He smacked a quick kiss onto her lips. "Sometimes, I forget

you fuck up. I know you're more than a hundred and fifty-odd, but I'm the grown-up here. As usual, Miss Dune, I forgive your failures."

She stood and mock-bowed her thanks. "Are you tired?"

"Yep."

"Bed?"

"Yep."

She offered her hand and pulled him up from his seat. They were halfway into the bedroom when Tazia spoke again. "Billy?"

"Yeah?"

"Thanks."

———

Jegudiel leaned back from the mirror and shook away the concentration. She smiled, pleased with the progress; a few more pieces had just clicked into place. When she'd appeared to Anastasia at the fountain, she wasn't sure how that meeting would play out, but progress was good.

She stretched herself, elongating each long limb, feeling the pulse of energy flowing just beneath the translucent skin. A bright yellowish light shone from her, collecting in layers like a second covering, and as she moved, a subtle amber trail remained.

With a blink of her large oval eyes, she summoned a glass jar. It flew to her hand, and she peered inside. There was a little light there. A dim glow, like a weak lantern shining in thick fog. There were sighs, too, vague and pathetic, the sounds of someone long past caring.

"Anastasia thinks she's clever," Jegudiel purred, fingertips stroking the glass jar. The trapped soul inside moaned softly. "A kiss here, a trick there. Such petty human theatre. Let's hope she is just as persuasive with the Soldier."

She leaned closer to the mirror, to take a closer look as they disappeared into the bedroom then she stepped away, jar still in hand. "But I have eternity, pet. I have patience. And when I am finished, there'll be no kisses left to steal."

With her free hand, the angel slowly scraped her long fingernails down the edge of the jar, creating the noise of a blade on glass. The glow inside flared in panic, and darted away from the side where she played. A female voice pierced the air; a single note stretched into a scream and then withered to silence.

Smirking this time, the angel flicked her wrist, the jar disappeared.

9

———————

LOYALTY

SOMETHING BUZZED against Tazia's ear. Half-asleep, she swatted at it, but the sound grew louder, bouncing off the walls like it was in her skull. *That's not a bloody fly.*

One eye cracked open. Billy had buried his face against her back, arms wrapped tight around her waist, dead to the world. The buzzing intensified.

"Fucksakes!" She sat up, shoving Billy's arm away to wake him. "Look!"

A white ball of energy zipped around the room, bouncing from wall to wall; Joshua had returned.

Billy snapped awake and raced past her to the desk, banging code into the keyboard even as he sat down. She dawdled into the lounge. The light outside looked different. Weak afternoon sun struggled through drizzle that had gathered on the windows. Perfect weather for a family reunion.

Three crows landed on the balcony rail outside, wings twitching. The advanced party from Hell.

Avoiding the desk and chewing on her thumbnail, Tazia paced. She was about to see *him* again. Memories surged from her childhood. Footsteps on the threshold, his shadow in the doorway, his roar of disapproval. But she was not a kid anymore.

She shoved down the rising panic and steeled herself; shoulders straight, big breath. *Ready.*

The ball of light hung over the PC for a moment, and then gradually disappeared as Joshua's face reformed on the screen pixel by pixel. "Hope you two weren't getting too cozy in there." His smirk glitched back to a straight face when Billy yawned, too sleepy for banter.

"Did you bring him with you, Josh?" Tazia spoke from her spot by the window, her eyes flicking between the room and the view outside. She kept her voice steady. The jump down into the murky river was looking increasingly tempting. The crows winked red eyes at her. *Whatever.*

Hearing Joshua's voice, her attention snapped back. "Yeah. It wasn't easy. Dude's not that happy, Taz. Give him a moment to catch up—I travel a bit faster than him. You won't have long, so talk quickly."

No pressure then.

As he finished speaking, the air in the hallway buckled, spitting red and amber sparks. Sulphur hit her square in the face. She stepped back, coughing, as black smoke rolled towards them.

Then *he* pushed through.

For a split second, she saw the man she remembered: handsome, severe, absolute. The father who'd raised her as his foot soldier. Every beating a lesson. Every contract a chance to win his favour—

Then Hell claimed him back.

Flesh peeled away to gleaming bone, blood and fat siphoned into the air hanging like an oily fog before reforming into flesh again. It didn't feel like justice. It felt like cruelty. This cycle would be his eternity if she didn't save him.

As she watched, her tattoos cooed happy vibrations. Their maker was close.

The Abbot turned his face in her direction. "Anastasia?" His voice sounded distant like he was trapped inside a thick bell jar.

Her response immediate, Tazia stepped closer. "Yes, Father."

Joshua's voice piped up from the computer screen. "Tick tock, dudes!"

When she tried to speak the stink and heat coated her throat, dragging at her breath. But once she started, the words tumbled out, still stumbling and desperate, but honest: the Advocate, the promise, his release from the Red River. All of it. Then she braced herself for the fury that always followed her failure.

He said nothing. The worst punishment.

"*He* caused this by binding your soul, Taz, not you. Don't forget it." Billy slid a protective arm around her shoulders.

She couldn't allow herself to sink into it, but his certainty grounded her. Her gaze fell to the flames licking up through the boards around her father, fizzing against the flesh.

Her father's attention shifted to Billy. "Who is this?"

Her eyes flicked back.

"I'm William Nadig. Billy."

The Abbot cocked his head to listen. Flesh falling, bone glistening, wet and white. All the while, though, he stared back at Tazia, sometimes with deep brown eyes, sometimes with empty sockets.

"The angel said we need to get rid of the ink on her back," Billy continued. "Until we do that, you can't be with your... Lord."

"And you, child? Do you want to feel your soul again?" The Abbot's voice whipped around the room, one minute beside her ear, and the next sounding like it was back behind glass.

The flames crackled louder around his ankles. A rumble in the distance grew closer, deeper. She had to raise her voice. "I want your freedom, Father. But, you always told me angels could not be trusted."

"She will have an ulterior motive, no doubt," the Abbot replied. "But I am resigned to whatever Fate brings me now. I've had time to reflect. Time in Hell goes very slowly, child. I have lived a long life and enjoyed great power. Now, I am just like everyone else. Just Brother Stephen lost in a sea of demons."

"Chop chop, guys! It's coming!" Joshua's voice rose from the PC, sounding weirdly casual in the horror in front of her.

Heat hammered against Tazia's skin. The black smoke had thickened around the Abbot's legs, and the flames climbed higher, reaching his knees. She recognized the stench of rotting, burning meat from her long childhood years.

The rumble of fire had become a roar, still distant but getting closer as shadows surged toward them—reaching. *Hell's coming for him!*

But they did not stop at her father.

The shadows brushed against her, hot and clammy. Then pulled back from Billy, splitting and circling him, not touching like he was off-limits. *What the hell?*

She felt his arm slide away from her back as he stood rigid beside her—against the shadows. He seemed taller for a second, or maybe her eyes were fucking with her. When he spoke, his body seemed to glow. Dim, for sure, but it was there, like old, worn luminous paint.

"You don't fool me!" Billy's tone was sharp, more mature. Several voices speaking at once. He wagged a finger at the Abbot like scolding a child. "This act. This pitiful martyrdom. Just desperation. Deceit!"

He turned to her. Something flickered in his eyes. He was

back. All Billy. "He's gaslighting you, love. Can't you see it? He needs you babe."

"It seems as if you ran into the arms of the first man to offer assistance, Anastasia. A shame you did not choose more wisely. This one can only offer side-show magic with his imprisoned necromancing monkey."

"Hey! Name caller!" Joshua yelled from the desk.

Tazia smiled. There was her father. Whatever had happened to Billy, it had drawn the real man out. *The bastard's back!*

"Get on with it, will ya. He's not going to last much longer!" Joshua added.

The flames had reached the Abbot's waist now, the black smoke circling higher, picking up speed. The roar was closer, making her eardrums pulse.

"Only an act of great sacrifice from another will free your soul from its bounds," the Abbot's voice cut through the growing noise. "A failsafe the shamans insisted upon. Understand, my child—souls crush spirit. It was holding you back, keeping you a mewling infant far too long. I gave you freedom from it, connected you to your demon!"

The fire reached his chest. The roar carried waves of heat toward them, forcing them back a step. Joshua's voice crackled with static. "Thirty seconds max!"

Billy had to shout. "Who can perform this act of sacrifice? Can it be me, you fucker? Can I die for her?"

The Abbot smiled, grinning teeth set in bone jaws. "Oh, the hero! Anastasia, you have a prince to serve you!"

Billy's icy hot aura circled Tazia's body beside him. She felt his chest heave against her shoulder, and squeezed his hand.

"Killing yourself for my girl will achieve nothing, William!" the Abbot called over the roar. "You do not yet know what life means. My god, you are not even awake!"

The flames licked at his shoulders. The roar deafening, forcing them all to yell.

"Daughter, will you do as the Advocate asks?" Fire danced in his empty sockets. "Will you give me my rightful place in Hell?"

"YES!" she screamed back. "BUT WHO MAKES THE SACRIFICE? WHO IS THE MARK?"

The fire surged toward his head. His words barely cut through the thunderous crackling.

"The sacrifice has to be of something treasured beyond measure! Something it will destroy the giver to lose—"

The flames consumed his head, drowning him out completely.

"WHO?" Tazia screamed over the inferno.

"One who carries such devotion is—"

The roar was deafening now, a wall of sound.

Billy bellowed beside her: "WHO?"

Through the firestorm that had completely engulfed him, the Abbot's voice sliced the air. "—CONN O'CUINN!"

His final words drifted to them weakly: "Do... not... fail... me..."

The inferno vanished, sucked back into nothing, leaving not a trace. A vacuum of silence broken only by their ragged breaths grasping at the thin air.

———

Tazia ran to the terrace doors and threw them open, taking deep breaths. The stink of him lingered—not the sulphur, familiarity. That twist in her chest when he got near her. *Foul.* She hated that it had rattled her, even for a second.

The crows still watched her. Enjoyed the show, did you? She shooed them away before returning, leaving the doors wide to allow the damp afternoon air to flow inside.

She shoved aside the thought that this was just another Abbot head-fuck. There was no choice now with the High Advocate's threats hanging over her. "How do we find out about this 'Conn O'Cuinn'?"

Billy moved like his joints had seized up. She watched him ease himself into the computer chair, still shaky from whatever had happened to him. She sank into the seat beside him. "What was that back there? I thought you were going to attack him."

"I wanted to—nearly did. I'm a lover, not a fighter, you know that, babe. But that crack about me being asleep! I'd die for you!" He squeezed her hand hard, knuckles white.

He would too. She pecked a kiss on his forehead. "But that weird shiny shit, Billy? I swear you were glowing."

He turned back to the screen, fingers poised over the keyboard. "Taken your pills lately, babe?"

"Patronizing arse."

Billy still hadn't started to type. "Hey, though, Taz. Seriously, the evil coming from that fucker! Intense. My God, I'm not a religious man but I felt it in my soul!"

"Yeah." She nudged him, "At least you have one, eh?"

They shared a smile and kissed foreheads together.

"You reckon this guy is flying the green flag, too, yeah?" She asked.

"With a name like that? Has to be Irish." Billy switched to a Tor client and they scanned the dark web for the name Conn O'Cuinn. Thousands of results came up. None lined up. "Josh, can you help? There's got to be something."

"Sure," Joshua was surprisingly agreeable. "By the way, I never once took you to be a prince, in case you were wondering." He winked, then pixel-faded back into the big processor.

Within moments, classified British Army records (demon division) flicked onto the screen. *Conn O'Cuinn: Noted demon,*

Celtic Soldier. The rest was a patchwork of heavy black redactions, whole paragraphs dissolving before their eyes.

"Magick," Billy muttered. "Someone's protecting the records." He attacked the keyboard, banging at the keys. More sections were revealed as he broke the spell, showing a lot of what she already knew: Soldiers were uber tough, loyal, steel-like bones and with regenerative powers.

"They also have a 'Core' demon inside them—pure primitive, animal-type dude. Lethal!" Joshua said, sounding gleeful. "This guy's a beast!"

"Last known—Detroit address." She read over Billy's shoulder. "He's running a place called the Irish Club. Yeah right. Slap bang in demon central."

She'd seen Soldiers in action during jobs; walking tanks with loyalty that bordered on fanatical. And this one will sacrifice something precious for me? *Right.*

Billy shoved the keyboard away. "I give up. I'm wiped. Still a lot I can't break."

"What if I go pay him a visit? Record what I see? Might help us get a feel for the guy. I can travel on the beams, man."

"Network." Billy corrected. "And in return?"

Joshua shrugged. "The Mac."

"Whatever." He rubbed his eyes and heavily typed the run code.

While Joshua disappeared into the network, Tazia needed something to do with her hands. She grabbed two beers, the cold bottles slick with condensation in the heat of the room, and cracked them open with a vampire-shaped bottle opener she'd bought Billy a while back. The teeth of the little Dracula dug so deep into the bottle caps they wouldn't let go, and she had to pry each one free. She knew just how they felt.

"What do you think it would be like?" She kept her eyes on her beer while handing Billy his. "You know... to actually feel stuff properly?"

The question slipped out before she could stop it. *Stupid.* She wasn't supposed to want things like that. But the talk of souls had her wondering. What would it feel like to be whole?

He looked at her, surprised. "Your soul, you mean?"

She nodded, suddenly self-conscious. "Never mind. Dumb question."

"Not dumb," Billy said softly. "Just... heavy, babe."

10

GREEN EYES

BY THE TIME Joshua returned with a video file just half an hour later, Tazia and Billy had gulped down their second beer each. The tension in the room had eased, their breath flowing steadily.

"This guy's, like, major tough!" Joshua said. "I followed him from the security cameras. He spotted me at the end. Instinct I think, not magick, but I got out of there no problem. Found it?"

Billy nodded and hit play. Joshua's face disappeared from the screen, and they found themselves looking at a prison cell.

The video was in colour. No sound. A man with broad shoulders had his back to them, almost fully blocking the camera. He looked at someone secured by chains to the wall opposite. The object of his attention, also male, curled over, haunches tucked under himself and shaking his head as though responding to something. He eyed the shotgun his captor carried with an expression close to panic.

"That's a vampire," Tazia noted. "The way he crouches. A young one. Terrified."

The vampire said something. The man nodded, but instead

of freeing him, he brought the shotgun around and, without hesitation, fired directly into his chest. The video stuttered as Joshua jumped to another camera, this one situated with a clearer view of the victim.

Billy gasped, and as the video ticked on, his mouth fell open.

The gun had blown a fist-sized hole in the vampire's chest. Blood spattered and gushed from the wound. Another liquid, this one clear, combined with the blood, leaving translucent trails amongst the red.

Tazia gripped his shoulder. "It's eating the chest," she said. "Then the heart. No heart equals dead vamp."

The blackened and broken rib bones turned white as the rivulets of liquid washed over them. Alive still, his body jerked until the final part of his heart was consumed. Then he slumped, head resting on his shoulder, eyes staring.

"Acid?" asked Billy, shuddering.

"As good as," Tazia replied. "Holy water. Poor bastard."

The weapon was adapted to kill vampires. It propelled the water with the shot. She'd seen it before. This one looked powerful.

The man in the video turned. Face and neck patterned with the vampire's blood. Dark hair cut into an army-style crew cut, a square jaw in a tanned face, and striking sea-green eyes.

His eyes roved for a moment and looked up into the camera directly at them. The stunning green eyes instantly turned to ice blue, and his mouth set in a stern line. He reached a hand up toward them, then the screen went blank.

Joshua's grinning face popped back onto the screen. "He's a good-looking dude, huh?" He winked at Tazia.

"Taz, you're not going near him."

Was Billy worried about the demon's looks or because

they'd just seen him kill a vampire so gruesomely? "Relax. This is my world remember. This definitely him, Josh?"

"Yeah. The place is full of security cameras. I did a good reccy first. In one room there's like a stack of guns, rifles as well as those huge grenade launchers, and handguns—pistols, Glocks, old fashioned revolvers. He's got a major set-up there."

"It's our way in, Billy." Her mind was whirring now. Gun deals: Europe, Middle East, UK. In recent years, she'd done them all. Billy doing his digital thing, helping to ease doors open, turn off alarms, follow targets. The States couldn't be much different?

"Yeah, best bet if we have to. Still don't like the look of that bloke. Bet we could find another way to get your soul before I end up scraping you off the floor."

"No, this is it. You heard my father, it has to be him." Her energy surged, "Looks like I'm going to Detroit."

11

CRACKING TEETH

SOREN HUXFORD HAD DRUNK a truckload of whiskey the previous night and taken the opportunity to sleep it off in the Turin apartment, rather than get up and face a hangover.

He rolled over in the empty bed, stretching out into the space that Anastasia usually occupied, and ran his hand over the hollows she'd left. Two days ago, she'd been here. The pillow still carried the warm, earthy scent of the oil she used on her hair, and as he breathed it in, the events of the previous day slowly returned to him. Stroking gave way to thumping before he grabbed the pillow and hurled it at the wall. It split on impact, white feathers swirling to the ground like snow.

Head hammering, Soren hauled himself upright and sat on the side of the bed, gathering himself before taking a shower and breakfast. He had to figure out his next move. At the airport, he'd noted the flight Anastasia had taken to London, and figured she'd run to Billy. His temper simmered, soon to hit boiling point. *Smarmy dickhead!* He was always on the end of the computer ready to pull her out of trouble. He threw the other pillow. It joined its mate on the floor, creating another storm of feathers.

"Enough, Huxford," he whispered to himself. Licking his wounds would have to wait. It was time to take action.

In the shower, the water stung his injuries from yesterday. The cut over his eye where that rock struck still smarted, the exposed quartz drilling deep into his flesh. The memory of the cascade of rocks falling down on him still burned. He soaped the offending scar vigorously and gloried in the pain shooting through his still-mending left hand. Bones knitting back together always took longer. The rest: a deep gash, one cracked rib, three bruises, only irritations.

That initial panic, when he'd woken in the cave and thought she'd been under the rocks too, and frantically searched around him. *Stupid!* The moonlight spilling through the tunnel entrance meant she must have climbed out, cleared her path to the outside. Left him there.

Hearing from Sergio Bello that Anastasia grabbed the cash and ran cemented it: he'd been played. The money was his. Earned. Soren rubbed his knuckles on his right hand, remembering taking his anger out on one of Bello's henchmen: a highlight in an otherwise rough day.

The healing magickal wards that flowed over his skin were better than any amount of money. To keep them, he had to complete the job.

Soren finished soaping his body, scouring himself and scrubbing away the memories of her soft skin and equally soft words. The shared jobs and romantic meals. The movies and laughter. The future with her, he'd allowed himself to plan. *Dumb bastard!*

He rinsed twice, turning the water to ice cold the second time to blast himself awake. Then, he stepped out of the shower. Back under control.

She was a target, now. Nothing else. Letting her walk was a mistake, one he'd correct. Standards mattered. That was the outcome to focus on right now, not how a cheap little demon half-breed outsmarted him.

As he stepped out of the shower, and lifted a hand to clear the steamed up mirror, letters slowly formed in front of him: "Y O U - L E T - H E R - G E T - A W A Y"

"I know," Soren said under his breath, then a little louder, "I'm getting to it."

"T O O - S L O W," appeared beneath the previous message.

Soren grimaced, annoyed. "Where is she going?"

"D E T R O I T"

"Detroit?" He frowned at the glass. "Why the hell—" He stopped. Adjusted. "Why Detroit?"

"F I N D - T H E - I R I S H M A N"

He grabbed a towel. "Cuinn?" Conn O'Cuinn was a Celtic Soldier demon he'd worked with a few years ago. They were close. Like brothers. The man saved his life! He had no idea why Anastasia was heading that way. He didn't think she even knew Cuinn. He'd kept the past close to his chest. This didn't add up.

To the invisible hand, he merely said, "It's done."

But the last message got him thinking, "D O - N O T - L E T - H E R - D I E"

The words pulled him up short. Before, the instructions were to kill her father and then capture her and wait for further orders. Is she in real danger now?

In his chest, a tiny pang pricked him. What was that? Fear for her? Regret that this Italian idyll was really over? He shook the thought away. *No! Pathetic.* The bitch had tricked him. Left him for dead. Then legged it with his cash.

Soren clenched his teeth, grinding his back molars together until they cracked with a satisfying pain that briefly shot fire through his jaw before the healing began. He forcefully swiped away the words on the mirror with the towel. Time to get moving.

In the bedroom, he roughly finished drying himself and got dressed. Quality was paramount: gold buttons, soft sheen, fine thread of the suit. People responded to quality. They saw craftsmanship and knew he wasn't some street thug. Worth something.

Ignoring the half-open drawers now empty of Anastasia's clothes, Soren carefully packed a holdall of necessaries and left the apartment. His black Lamborghini got him to the airport fast, and by midnight, he was on a plane to Detroit. He'd be waiting for her when she landed.

12

LAZY CIRCLES

THE SMOKE from Tazia's cigarette hung in the air, forming a dirty haze around her body. Jet lag had kicked in several hours ago. She should have crashed, but the nicotine was doing its job keeping her awake. Instead, she sat smoking and watching her target.

From her rooftop perch in downtown Detroit, she observed the street that split the block below. The city plaque called this the Historic District. To her, a convenient perch to keep watch. On her right was the old red brick tenement he'd entered an hour ago. She'd seen him reccy it yesterday, and today she'd been waiting.

She'd sensed his approach for three blocks before he strode into view, not hugging the shade and skeletal remains of the buildings but claiming the median. *Look at him, he owns the place!* The sluggish air smothered his scent until he passed right below her, and she identified him—Soldier.

He carried a rifle in his hand and a shotgun on his back. Its barrel extended by a vicious welded spike. The stench hit her: layers of blood, offal, and brain matter. *You never heard of cleaning your fucking weapon, soldier?*

At this moment, it wasn't the shotgun, but the rifle tip protruding from a third-floor window she had her eye on. Now and then, the setting sun caught the metal with a blinding flash. He kept watch on the store frontage opposite and obviously didn't care who saw him. Faded travel posters of Hawaii still clung to the windows from its former use as a travel agency. Now, someone had painted an English flag above the door.

Shortly after he'd arrived, an old army truck pulled up. Three vampires piled out carrying boxes and chatting loudly.

The first, dressed in a suit, unlocked the solid metal chains that secured the entrance and shouted orders, his shrill voice cutting the silence of the street. The other two, more casual in jeans and tees, carried the boxes inside, sauntering through the doors to take full advantage of the shadow-covered sidewalk.

Tazia shook her last cigarette from the pack, grunted with annoyance, and lit it with the remains of the last. She balled up the wrapper and threw it on top of the spent butts that littered the ground at her feet. The nicotine didn't only keep her alert; it calmed her. Without it, she'd have to resort to other things. She squeezed the pocket of her black leather jacket; sometimes knowing the pills were there was enough.

Far above her, a hawk shrieked, its cry splitting the stillness. It had been flying in lazy circles, but now looked more agitated. It swooped on the air currents and then hovered overhead, wings audibly flapping. Was it watching her? Or him? *Time you moved on, bird*.

Birds told the story of the Risings the world over. Songbirds fled first. Then came the rat-birds, black clouds of pigeons and crows, living on maggots and garbage. Birds of prey followed, feasting on rodents the corpses attracted. When the predators left, the vultures moved in to pick the bones. They never left.

Tazia had run into a Trickster demon in a bar the previous

night. He'd told her vultures had been in Detroit for the last five years. It was the first city to fall.

So why is the hawk still here?

She stood up to stretch out the cramp that gripped her legs. Even before that Trickster last night, she'd heard scraps from demon travellers. They'd told tales of half-dead humans littering the streets, their souls sucked dry, shell-like remnants with not even enough blood left to sustain a vampire.

After that, she'd not wanted to come to Detroit. There was no point. No business to be done. But here she was, chasing down some demon squaddie with a patriotic chip the size of an iceberg on his shoulder, at the behest of her dead father. *Fucksakes!*

She took another drag, savouring the tang of the tobacco on her tongue as she let out the smoke in little controlled puffs to regulate her breathing. Now, Detroit was just one of many demon infested industrial cities around the world. The travellers' tales had become everyone's truth.

The sun had lowered further. A shaft of sunlight cut through the tall buildings to her south, hit her outstretched arm, and blistered her skin. She stifled a cry and snatched the arm back before taking shelter in the shade cast by the casing of a long-silent air conditioning fan. It didn't seem like the sun would ever set.

The blistering heat rose with the demons and their endless scuffles for territory. Organized by cutting the city up by colours or tags. So quiet you could hear a pin drop. It left Tazia with a problem: how do you infiltrate a city as tight as a drum?

She had already done some digging about her target. After a few nights spent in rat-holes, drinking bad whiskey, she'd confirmed Conn O'Cuinn was known as "The Irishman" (demons were never creative). His territory included the old district of Corktown, but overspilled it in every direction.

He had a fierce reputation for protecting the Irish Club he

ran and the men who worked with him. Thanks to Joshua, Tazia already knew the bar was just a front. She'd known Irish activists before. Those memories weren't the fondest.

She'd located the bar, but getting in was proving troublesome. The demon ran it like a private members' club so that he could keep a good handle on the lives and loyalties of his clientele. With no open-door policy, you waited for an introduction. Tazia didn't have time for that.

So, she'd created a few rumours about her presence, letting slip that she had some inventory for sale to the right people, then followed a few markers until, finally, she'd located a demon who may just get careless if she pushed hard enough. In the meantime, Billy searched for any sniff of a gun deal around Detroit. She hoped he would turn up some merchandise soon. Until then, she tracked Cuinn.

A slight breeze dislodged the shroud-like nicotine cloud that had settled over her head and shoulders. Again the hawk shrieked. Something was building. *A warning?*

Tazia crouched back down and waited.

13

BLOOD SUCKERS

THE SUN HAD BEEN low in the sky when Conn O'Cuinn took his place at the broken third-floor window of the derelict tenement building. Its remaining rays highlighted abandoned cars and vandalized parking meters in the road below. Filth lit in false beauty, he thought. Why the feck was he still in this hell-hole and not back in Ireland with its crystal clear waters and green fields?

Instead he had to deal with these dirty little feckers. Vampires. Worse—*English* vampires. Leftover demons who took up residence in dead human shells. They had no allegiance to a higher purpose and no honour. He'd spit if he wasn't lying down.

At least, the sun, would be useful for a change.

He balanced the rifle with his left hand, to reach behind and pull the wet shirt away from his back with his right. As the fabric released in one placed, it was sucked right back in another. *Just grand.*

The day had started as stifling as usual. Demons brought the blistering heat. Lawns, parks, fields—all charred to dust.

But in this feckin' city, the heat was a special torture. It created endless cloudy days. It drenched everything in water sucked from the surrounding rivers and lakes and left behind thick, cloying humidity.

He preferred the occasional clear skies. It forced his enemies to retreat during daylight and he could sleep in. And, God knows, he needed the sleep.

Conn closed his eyes and fought the desire to nap. True rest had escaped him yet again. Instead, incessant dreams of the past. Old decisions circled his nights. It made no sense, he'd dealt with them long ago.

He opened his eyes. Light pooled on a little section of pavement outside the store opposite. Through the sights of his rifle, shiny specks of granite in the sidewalk slabs danced in the rippling heat rising from the ground, transfixing him for a moment. *Focus silly lad.* His target sat on the other side of the large plate glass window.

The red and white flag daubed above the door made the hair on his neck bristle. English vampires in his city. Unacceptable. Today they would receive a lesson in respecting boundaries.

Conn shifted his elbows a fraction and looked up from the gun to readjust his focus. He checked the sky. Although a haze of pollution had followed the sun's descent to the horizon, the evening rays would still serve to dazzle the occupants well enough.

Three of the bastards—drinking beer and playing cards like they owned the place. Boss man with his usual faithful dogs. Blood Suckers always had goons, never had the balls to do their own dirty work. He hated vampires as much as the English.

The hawk called to him. *I know, mo chroí.* Almost time.

For a moment, the wind breezed in through the window, cooling him. It dislodged the longer sections of his brown hair and ruffled the collar of his denim shirt. Sweet relief.

Cigarette smoke came with the breeze. He looked around. Nothing. The hawk circled a building just to his left; she cried out again. She knew. Didn't matter. Someone who smoked on a job was either stupid or didn't care if they were noticed. Either way, he would track them down soon enough.

The sun dropped a fraction further and shone fully into the front windows of the storefront. Like someone aimed a huge flashlight. Finally.

Every muscle in Conn's body contracted. He kept his breath steady. Acting before the blinds were pulled down and his view became obscured, he focused on the three figures inside the building.

Adjusting his position for one last time, Conn trained his sights between the eyes of the boss and started to squeeze the trigger—

What? *No!*

He looked into the bloodstained face of his dead wife. She stood motionless, her eyes trained on him. Sudden sweat broke on his forehead and slid, stinging, into his right eye. He blinked. She was gone. A trick of his mind? A ghost?

Hands shaking, his finger finished depressing the trigger, and a loud crack sounded as the bullet released. He cursed and tracked it. It went wide, exploding a bottle of whiskey standing on the bar behind the target. The vampire stood showered in broken glass and amber liquid, while his goons turned to the window to look. Frozen and blinded by the glare, they had nowhere to run. The window itself remained in place, but web-like cracks extended from a single bullet hole halfway up. *This ends now!*

He dropped the rifle and raced out onto the stairwell. Snaking down to the ground floor, he leapt the last few steps and out the door. As he charged across the road, he reached for the shotgun on his back, brought it over his head, and launched through the weakened window of the storefront. The two dogs stared, rooted in place as Conn appeared in a cascade of broken glass.

Landing lightly, he straightened up and shot at close range, first at one demon and then the other. Both fell to the floor with jagged holes in their chests. He stalked over to the table where the boss had hidden, kicked it aside, gripped his hair, and lifted him off the ground.

The demon looked at him, mouth opening and closing, mutely begging for his life and raking at Conn's hand. No bravery. No purpose. Not even grace in the face of defeat. Just another pathetic Blood Sucker.

Using the shotgun's bayonet like a dagger, Conn thrust it directly between the vampire's eyes. The demon screamed and jerked before hanging limp.

Pulling out the bayonet, now covered in a new coating of blood and brain, Conn dropped the vampire's body and replaced the gun on his back. The two others were writhing and moaning where they'd fallen. The wounds steamed, holy water doing its work. Agonizing and effective. He didn't linger.

At the door, Conn pulled a grenade from his weapons belt. Clutched the lever, and pulled the pin, he rolled it straight to the place where the whiskey-soaked body of the former owner lay.

As he jogged back over to the other building to collect his rifle, an explosion rocked the street. He ducked as glass and bricks flew through the air, but the power wasn't enough for the debris to reach him. Glancing back, the front of the store was destroyed. Vacation posters floated in the air like scorched confetti.

The fire took hold, and the smoke began to obscure the English flag on the front. Through the smoke, she still stood. Accusing.

———

Tazia had stood to watch the action. Before the stink of smoke overwhelmed her, she'd smelled pungent whiskey, vampire blood, and the gunman's perspiration. The last was a puzzle. It reached her as soon as the initial shot went wide. Not typical for a professional sniper and then he fouled the shot? Interesting.

She stubbed out the remaining half-inch of her cigarette on the ground with the metal toe cap of her boot, and then bounded lightly to the low dilapidated parapet to gain a clear view of the street below. Right on the edge, her balance shifted to one foot and the rest of her body overhung the building. She stayed there suspended until she had a clear view of Cuinn as he jogged away down the street.

Tazia maintained her vigil for a moment longer, picking him out through the smoke by the regularity of his stride. Just like a large wolf scanning his surroundings. The ink on her back tightened around her spine. Every inch a predator. Soldier demons had few physical weaknesses, and she knew of only one way to kill them.

Years ago, her father had taken a Soldier prisoner. He'd kept him caged. Tortured him. Goading him to change into his Core form over and over. Studying him. Finally, when he was done, he pierced the Soldier's brain with a thin, flexible metal dagger. He'd shoved it through his eye socket under the steel-like bone plating that shielded his skull.

It's an image that had not faded.

Not the kind of up close and personal I'd imagined with you, Conn O'Cuinn.

Just before the Soldier slipped out of sight, a hawk swooped down and landed on his arm. He turned and whispered to the bird, stroking her head until she nudged his fingers.

He chuckled, the sound reaching Tazia as an echo that bounced down the empty road and then distorted into a good-humoured growl. He reached down to the pouch hanging on his weapons belt to obtain a morsel of food and fed it to the bird. As he turned, the final weak rays of the sun briefly lit his profile. She saw his tender smile before they exited the street.

Tazia smiled broadly at the exchange between the man and bird. Was the interaction his salvation or hers? Perhaps a weakness she could exploit. At the very least, a way to connect. Anyone who could feel affection for a bird must hold more than murder in their hearts, surely.

Unflinching, Tazia dropped over the edge of the roof, free-falling five stories before landing lightly on the pavement below. She left in a different direction from Cuinn. She had one goal, to find a way into the Irish Club.

14

IRISH HOSPITALITY

OLD TRINITY HAD BEEN a Victorian Catholic church. To Conn and his men, she was the 'auld lady,' half-ruin and half-refuge, tucked in the middle of his territory. Red brick with a few tired Gothic touches. The verdigris spire still thrusting Irish green above the rooftops like a battered flag. Most of the stained glass clung on, boarded up against scavengers.

The double-front arched doors were useless, chained and rotting. The real way in was down a side street where the air stank of piss. A steep run of steps dropped to more double doors with a steel grill at face height and iron bars across a run of shallow windows. No sign advertised it, only the old Corktown street post on the corner bent so low it might've been pointing straight down at the entrance. He kept it as a warning for anyone without business here.

Inside stretched a cellar, ceiling ribs arching like bone overhead, fire kicking against the damp. Scarred but solid wood tables and scavenged chairs filled the room. Saints looked down from old church tapestries. Conn reckoned they worried more about the souls than the smoke and whiskey. His people were never shy of a glass. Cheap plastic shamrocks studded any surface that would take them, a gaudy little good luck rebellion. A place to drink, bleed, and crawl away whole—if he let you.

For his lads, there was no better roof.

When Conn returned that evening, it was quiet. A few regulars sat playing cards and chatting near the fire. The air currents helped to stir the stink of booze and bleach, and the iron tang of blood that soaked the floorboards from the cells out back to the bar floor. The stink welcomed him home.

The players looked up and hailed him as he entered. He lifted a hand and casually smiled a greeting.

To the left, Kevin worked the oak bar, tallying bottles. Beer and good whiskey fought for space with the demon fare like blood, and worse. He looked around a human thirty, a shade younger than Conn, but built close enough they could've passed for brothers. Red flickers ran through his hair under the lamps, freckles catching the light. He wore the practical uniform of the Unit: shirt, jeans, boots, and belt.

Kevin looked up, grey eyes asking.

"Done," Conn said, and cut straight behind the bar, through the door to the back rooms.

His small apartment was here along with the cells, a guest room, and a secure strong room guarded by an electronic keypad and a steel door. It was here that he went to deposit his rifle and the remaining grenades, before heading to his rooms, keeping his shotgun with him.

He could still smell the Blood Suckers. Irritated, he ripped off his top, threw it in the tub to soak and changed his jeans. Before putting on a new shirt, he washed his upper body thoroughly with hot water and medical soap. Four centuries alive, and he was proud his body stayed solid.

As he washed, her face came to him again. So long since he'd seen her. These past weeks, she'd been in his head more and more. Like he could touch her. No reason, no change.

The guilt was always there, but no worse than before. So why now?

Clean and smelling strongly of carbolic, he returned to the bar. Cradled his gun on hooks in the wall behind him and started to flick through the pages of a red notebook pulled from his back pocket. Running through figures and stock lists.

Without warning, the front door crashed open, slammed against the doorstop, and bounced back into the face of the intruder. He had his shotgun in his hand before it settled. Kevin matched him with his pistol. Both weapons levelled and waiting.

A man entered, dragging a young woman behind him. "Sit!" The barked order echoed off the walls as he unceremoniously dumped her on a stool.

She crashed onto it and clutched the edge of the bar at the same time. There was a look of open-eyed amusement about her, which seemed out of place judging by Franky's near-apoplectic state.

Franky Lavender (his daft moniker) was one of a kind. The mauve tint of the skin gave him away as a demon despite looking every inch like a soft-bellied, bald-headed granda. As an empathy demon, though, the old bastard only needed to be near a mark and their mind emptied of secrets. Dangerous talent. But genuine kindness, too. He wasn't from back home, a pity, but his loyalty to the Cause was genuine. More than that, he was protective, especially of his boys. Conn was always glad to have him on side.

Right now the air was crackled, simmering. Conn could damn near taste the sharp edge of his temper. At the sight of Franky, he pointed the gun at the ceiling.

"Is this the guy?" Franky said, looking at the girl and jerking his thumb at Conn.

She leaned forward on her stool and gave him an exaggerated once-over. "Nope," she said.

Her eyes reviewed him, assessing from his messy crewcut to his open-necked blue shirt. She settled on his light blue eyes and smiled with what he took as approval.

Conn assessed in turn. Vampire, sure, but more to her scent than that. Human definitely, then a muddle of other layers. *Even a touch of Soldier?* That would be a turn-up.

Franky breathed heavily from his earlier exertions and puffed his way through an explanation. "She turned up at Dan's place… looking for a contact… said she was sent by an Irishman from over this way… knew she was lying her mouth off, but I can't see… her mind's all mussed. Cheeky little minx. Thought you'd better check her out."

The girl stared at her captor, who still had a hand on her arm. "You seem to have formed a rather bad opinion of me, Franky."

Minx was right. She a close eye on both his own gun and Kevin's, which was still aimed in her direction.

"I'm not dangerous, boys. You can put those away."

Intriguing. Despite doing her best to cover them, he smelt her nerves. "Name?" Conn brought his gun down to face her again. Kevin didn't move.

"I'm Anastasia, but you can call me Tazia. Everyone does. Unless you prefer Taz? Not Tazzy, though. Not unless you're pushing your luck." Smiling and looking a little more relaxed, she extended her hand to him in formal greeting. It was ignored. She sighed. "Well, so much for Irish hospitality."

Unsurprisingly, the comment fell flat. Though Conn gave an internal smirk. It was almost funny.

Addressing him, she held up her hands. "Look, okay, I bypassed a few hurdles to get to you. I was given a heads-up by a guy in a bar. He didn't know where you were, but they did point me in Franky's direction. He didn't look the type to talk, so I got creative. So, shoot me—figuratively, of course." She grinned widely at the men.

"You did play me, you little bitch!" Franky's anger piqued again, but this time, it seemed more directed at himself. After all, he had walked her straight there.

Conn raised an eyebrow at Franky, along with a slightly regretful shake of his head. He was fond of the old man, so could easily forgive the odd bad judgement. Besides, the girl didn't look much of a threat. "It's all right, Frank. Not important. What are you wantin' with me, Tazia?"

"Guns. I hear you're in the market?" She was not being coy, nor did she lower her voice.

The plain-speaking worked for him, though looking around the bar at the curious glances of the remaining patrons, he replied, "Depends on what you have, darlin', and also depends if you can use your inside voice."

"Oh!" For the first time, Tazia took her eyes off the guns and looked around.

She was playing it sweet. But Conn had already noted she kept one foot on the floor and a hand on the bar, ready to make a leap out the door. Her right hand was never an instant away from her knife, either. Poised and alert, she was trained.

She dropped her voice. "I'm not exactly the quiet sort. Shotguns mainly. Like that one." She nodded at the gun he was holding. "Without the adaptations. Handguns, rifles, incendiaries." She smirked. "I haven't been here long."

"Sounds like quite an armoury, darlin'." Demon gun-runners, tended to cloak everything in secrecy, even inventing code names for the more usual goods. She was refreshing. And she'd clocked the holy water, smart.

He pegged her around mid-twenties, but with the demon blood, who knew? Probably well over a century. Old enough to know she had openly flouted the rules of engagement. Stupid or bright? He wasn't ready to bite yet. There was too much he didn't know. But so far, he liked what he saw. Especially that smooth skin, wide-smiling mouth, and the way she moved her body.

His assessment didn't stop there either. He'd noted her weapons, smelled the blood on her boots, demon and human. Saw her non-stop assessment of the place: exits, clientele, weapons. Interesting. "You planning on passing through, or staying awhile?" Conn asked her.

"I'll be here for a few weeks. Arrangements are fluid, at the moment." She gave him a slight smile, her level tone giving nothing away.

Conn returned the shotgun to the shelf behind him. Instantly, the atmosphere lightened. Kevin copied his example and put his own gun back in his belt. Franky finally relaxed his grip on her arm.

"Well, how are you keepin' now, Tazia? I'm Cuinn, this is Kevin, and I think you've already met Franky." As he spoke, he couldn't keep a smile from his lips. He leaned forward, arms wide with his knuckles resting on the bar, looking her straight in the eyes.

"That eye thing—blue to green—quite a trick. Sexy," she said, with such an exaggerated wink he almost burst out laughing. Instead, he shot her a grin but said nothing. Flirting was clearly not her thing.

She glanced at Franky, who tutted at her cheekiness and shook his head, then settled on the stool beside her.

Kevin offered his hand next. "How're you doing today, Tazia?"

She shook it. "Very well, thanks. Hey, now that we're all friends, how about a drink?"

In unison, the three men flicked their heads at the hand-painted sign hanging on the wall behind them. It declared, No Vampires. No English.

"I see," she said. "Just out of interest, what's worse?" She directed the question at Conn, the smile still hovering about her lips. It was friendly, not a challenge.

He smirked a little, but still held her gaze. "Well, I guess you can't be helpin' where you were born, darlin'."

"So, if I was English, I'd be let off the hook?"

"No one's off the hook for being English." His manner was lighthearted despite the grate in his voice. He still didn't reach for a bottle.

"Well, I'm not English. Lived there for a while for sure—sound like it when I want to—but I'm Italian by birth. And, you probably already figured I'm not all Blood Sucker. Got a bit of everything in me, I think. Not exactly clean, but a bit of an improvement, huh?"

Conn hesitated, then shrugged before grabbing a bottle and some glasses, one for each of them, and poured. With the whiskey in front of them, he asked, "So what's your story, Tazia?" Time to get a better handle on her.

"Been in the business a while. Mostly in Europe. Worked with Patrick Mulrooney for a spell," she said.

It was too sweet. The way she dropped a name he would know. Rehearsed. He knew Patrick well enough. Dubliner. Human, but well-respected. At least he could check her out.

"Well, Tazia, enjoy your drink while I make a few calls. Don't be leaving now, will you?" She was a long way from being off the hook.

"Not even thinking about it. Looks like that game needs my expertise." She grinned at him and went to join the patrons sitting in the booth closest to the bar playing poker.

With a nod to Kevin, Conn headed into the back.

15

____

SCREAMING INK

CONN MADE several calls from his room out back. As well as Patrick, he also contacted other colleagues in his network. Standard process. He didn't make mistakes with newcomers nosing around his patch.

As Tazia promised, Patrick gave him the most information. Conn reviewed the classified report he sent over with a practiced eye. Twenty years ago, she'd completed a hit on a retired Ulster screw now living pretty in Tuscany. An unexplainable disappearance. Nasty death. They engaged a vampire in Turin who sent a kid. Female. Mixed race— interesting. Job done well. The picture said it all. Conn nodded approvingly.

Other notes: weapons training in North Africa. Looks like an officer "addressed" discipline issued. Conn winced before raising an eyebrow. Why would a demon ever submit to such treatment by a human? List of abilities: weapons, hand to hand, as well as strength, speed, resilience. The usual. Failed at anything needing focus and patience. *Huh!* Spent time in HMP Hastings back in the nineties. Interesting. Half her records had her dead or missing. Typical. Most recent—gunrunning. That ticked his boxes. Some royal vampiric blood, apparently. Same as every other Blood Sucker bragging about their crown roots. Just noise.

From his local contacts, he learned she'd recently arrived in Detroit and wanted to meet him. By her actions, she didn't seem to care who knew she was in the city; either a stupid move or part of another game. Conn wasn't fully satisfied with this last point. Unanswered questions got his men killed. He didn't like that.

When he returned to the bar, the poker game was still going on. He watched the proceedings carefully. Smiling and chattering with Franky like she'd known him half her life.

If this were a setup, it didn't seem like Franky's power would tell him. Yet, the old man looked like he had warmed. Frequent smiles and even a quick encouraging squeeze on the knee when she finally won a hand!

Time for a test.

Conn motioned her to a table, poured her another whiskey, and got straight to the point. "So, you said you had shotguns?"

"How many are you looking for?"

"Never-ending supply, darlin'," he said with a grin and took a sip from his whiskey.

She took a slurp from her own. "Should have something in the next few days. They'll be old but tested."

Since the Risings, this was the way. Once cities started falling by the dozen, the politicians packed themselves into bunkers with the military hotshots, and all the good toys, to wait it out. Leaving the rest of the world to rot. Demons made do with scraps. Old rusting weaponry, even antiques, all shone up. Short supply meant high prices and bloody hard bargaining.

"Sound good?" Tazia asked.

She was bluffing. The fast blink. The extra slurp of whiskey. But for now, he decided to ride it out. He nodded.

"You'll be wanting a sample, I assume?" Her strange phrasing mimicked his own Irish way of talking. He noticed, but said nothing.

"Yep, bring me in a couple to look at when they're ready and then we'll talk money." He was done. Stood up.

"Rather talk money now, Conn, if you don't mind. I like to be up-front. I don't like surprises."

He sat back down. "Call me Cuinn, Tazia. There's only one person here calls me Conn." He gestured toward Franky.

She was testing him. *You get one pass.*

"Fair enough. The guns are two hundred a piece."

He relaxed into his seat. "Ah, Tazia, there's always a deal to be done, darlin', surely?"

"Depends."

"On?"

"The deal." She paused a little before winking at him.

He appraised her. The slight raise of her chin, the wink, more rapid blinking. How had this kid survived? She was off her patch but acting tough. This wasn't about the money; she didn't want to be seen as a push-over.

Conn raised his eyebrows and pushed on his chair so that he was balancing on the two back legs. He looked her up and down again. "All sorts of ways to reach a deal. Some of my suppliers prefer to be paid in other ways. Blood's always popular with the vampire crowd, or I can arrange for anything else you fancy…"

Tazia laughed. "Not interested in kink, Cuinn, and I can find my own food. I told you before, I'm different." She continued, leaning in, but maintaining her smile. "The deal's two hundred a piece—take it or leave it. I can sell elsewhere." This time her gaze was solid.

She finished her whiskey in another gulp and made as though to leave. He put a hand on her arm. "Okay, Tazia, don't rush off now. I'll pay it if they look good. Bring me two samples and we'll go from there." He poured more whiskey into her glass and then raised his own. "*Sláinte!*" Deal over.

She relaxed in her chair, her shoulders sagging a little, and chinked her glass with his. The fierce red shards of energy when she'd entered the bar had now smoothed to orange. Sill on guard, but looking for peace. He guessed her aura was like his eyes. Changeable.

This young woman, he decided, was an easy read and would be no trouble.

Conn studied her. The hair made him laugh; dirty blonde, unruly, sticking out at wild angles where she'd hacked it short with a knife to keep it out of her eyes. He did the same.

Those eyes were what caught him. Brown, but dark enough they edged to black when she locked them on his. Old eyes, heavy. She carried death with her. Her mouth softened the look: lips naturally full, a faint curl she couldn't seem to help. Trick or habit?

She didn't flinch under his attention. Sat proud, neck straight, shoulders squared, arms built by the job—enough to keep a weapon steady. And yeah, her curves were worth a glance, but Conn had seen too many pretty faces to be fooled by them. What pulled him back was the fight in her stance. Those relentless eyes.

And over the blood on her boots, the faintest thread of another scent. Sweet and nutty. Dragging him back to the homeland and the oil his wife had applied to her hair. It awakened a protectiveness in him. But that was his issue. She didn't need it. She was obviously doing fine. Final assessment: she could handle herself.

"If we're going to deal, I need to check something else out, darlin'." This was also standard procedure, but one he despised.

"I thought you'd already done your homework. It looked

like you made a few observations just then, too." Her cheeks dipped red, but she smiled broadly.

"No more I'd say than you've done."

She shrugged and smiled in one movement.

"Soldiers have a few special qualities, Tazia—"

Her smile faded slightly.

"Abilities. We can pick up on more private intentions and desires. Not a tracking thing, more… instinctual. You follow?"

A nod.

He paused again before going on. "Before I deal with anyone, I give them a once-over."

"Will magick screw that little skill of yours? Cos the ink on my back fairly screams at me all the time, so I reckon it'll play havoc with you."

Ahh. That's what's throwing Franky off.

"Yes, I can sense magick, but the rest will still be there. Enough for me to be happy. Or not."

"Looks like I've got no choice." She looked away from him, her arms crossing over her chest. The jagged red energy stabbed at him again.

Conn looked down into his drink, considering. He spoke again with a note of sympathy. "Look, darlin', bring me the guns and if they're good, we'll talk more, okay?"

She regarded him, temper flaring. "And you'll conduct your little experiment then? Do you think I'm screwing with you, Cuinn?"

His sympathy vanished. "Maybe. Plenty try it. But I hope that's not the case with you, *mo chroí*, cos I'd rather you stayed alive."

The conversation was over. For now, he had the upper hand.

16

DEMON BLOOD

"BILLY? WHERE THE FUCK ARE YOU?" There was a picture of sorts, but no sound. Sat on the bed hunched over the tablet, Tazia clicked connect for the fourth time. *Piece of shit.*

Detroit was a dead zone for internet and cell phone service. Sporadic at best. Even Billy's stolen satellite hookups crapped out half the time.

The squat wasn't much: one room, but it had running water and a generator she fed with siphoned gas. That was the only thing worth praising. It was also crawling with lizards and cockroaches, and a few shadow demons scurried around the ground floor. They kept themselves to themselves, quickly merging into the darkness before she could acknowledge their presence with a well-targeted boot to the arse.

After a pause, she heard a voice full of static and an outline of a face. "Billy?"

Another pause and the screen cleared. She was looking at a face-full of metal ornamentation. Joshua grinned. "Hi, Taz!"

"Hey Josh, how did you get in there?" She relaxed her shoulders. It was good to see a friendly face.

"I'm still in the Mac, I saw your call and jumped in. He's

sorta busy at the moment." Joshua manipulated the code to look slightly embarrassed.

"Oh right, I get it. Which one is it today?"

"Who knows? They all look the same, right? The dude's insatiable. What did you need him for? Trouble?"

"Any news on Hux?" Not knowing where he was bugged her. Her fingernails were suffering. A couple now gnawed down to the quick.

"Nothing as far as I know." He cycled a shrug.

"Okay. Inventory, then? I had to promise some to Conn O'Cuinn. Now he wants a sample and I've got nothing. Has Billy's picked up on anything?"

"Is the Soldier as hot as he looked?"

"Not bad, I guess." She remembered the heat of Cuinn's hand on her arm. Hell, she wouldn't say no.

"Awesome. You go girl!" Joshua grinned.

Tazia dragged herself back to reality. "Josh, what about guns?"

"Billy did intercept a call some demon piece-of-shit made just outside of Detroit yesterday. Sounded like a delivery. Hang on, he made a transcript. I'll see if I can find it and show you."

She waited, drumming nails on the tablet until the file pinged through. Couple of scrolls and she got what she needed. "Cheers, Josh." Then she cut the feed.

The gang of demons trading the guns would be violent and unpredictable. Still, easy would be boring.

———

The gun pointed at Tazia's head was exactly the type she was after. That her concern was more with the weapon than her skull didn't bother her. *Yeah, nothing new.* With odds of eighty-twenty—against—she talked fast. "I'd be far more useful to you alive, you know. Got some good connections. Can pass a lot of business your way."

"What makes you think we need any business, honey bunch?" The gravel voice breathed blood and beer; his sweat pure mildew. Tazia moved her head away and gasped.

Roamers. Sneaky bastards. Since the Risings started, gangs of them had been crawling out of every crack. Treating violence like a road trip. They'd hit a town, bleed it dry, take what they wanted, and move on before the smoke cleared. Guns were a side gig.

The demon ran a cold, leathery hand over Tazia's cheek, down onto the throbbing vein in her neck, and across the top of her cleavage. "Maybe you would be good alive, sweetie pie." He chuckled with a sound that hit the same note as a Harley sucking up the miles on an open road.

Why did the mean ones always use endearments related to dessert. There was nothing scary about pie. "What's your name, sweetie?"

"Jarob, darling. You may have heard of me. Got a bit of a reputation with the women around here." *I bet!*

She crouched on the ground behind a spiky bush positioned just above the deserted roadhouse she'd tracked them to, a few miles outside of Detroit. Three hours of watching and waiting had led to a playlist and earbuds. Now, she felt stupid. If Hux could see her, she'd be on the end of a lecture about focus.

She'd counted only three demons before Jarob crept up behind her. How many more? She'd also clocked an old rusted pickup with wooden boxes in the back, covered with a tarpaulin. The guns?

"Do you like money, Jarob?" She made eye contact with him. The barrel of the gun was huge in her face. She ignored it, looked him directly in the eyes, and wildly batted her eyelashes like Jessica Rabbit.

"I like money well enough, sweetie. Why? You gonna pay me not to make you scream?" He laughed again, the sweetly tuned engine now interrupted by a rattling spark plug as the sound caught the wet in his throat.

"I know a guy who'll pay well for that load of guns you just picked up." She gestured toward the truck with her head and watched carefully to see his reaction. If she'd guessed wrong, and they weren't the guns Billy had heard about, she'd see it in his eyes. "He'll pay better than any of the contacts you usually use."

As she spoke, she stood up slowly and turned her body to face him, putting her hands on her hips and thrusting them forward, a little awkward, but he couldn't miss it.

He straightened himself and took a small step back, soaking in her energy as well as the flirty overtones. The shotgun had dropped to her chest. "Who?"

Tazia smiled—her guess was correct. She shook her head slightly. "Oh no, he's my contact. I set up the deal. Then we both walk away from this happy."

Jarob still looked at her like she was a lollipop and he was getting ready to take a big lick, though his interest in the deal seemed to be deflecting his attention from the obvious tightness in his trousers. "Numbers?"

"All you have plus more if you can get them. Ongoing arrangement. Interested?"

"You part of the deal?"

Tazia gave him her best lascivious grin despite her urge to throw up. "When the business is done, we can talk about that, honey."

He grinned back, oddly confident. Did he really think he was such a catch? She took in the leathery, pock-marked skin and the pronounced set of stained, pointed teeth. You really need an ego adjustment, baby-cakes. He was a Bone Cruncher. Pure breed. But she couldn't quite place him.

"Sounds like we could deal—for the right price," he said.

"Well, I can't put a price on anything till I've seen the quality, can I?" Tazia rubbed the dust from her hands.

He took a step back and gestured with a flick of the shotgun for her to begin walking down the hill and over to the truck. For the first time, rotting meat added to the surrounding stink. It caught thick in her throat.

Turning in the direction of the smell, she spied a man's body discarded on the far side of the roadhouse. Two vultures were fighting over a dismembered arm, each pulling from a different end, black wings flapping in the effort to gain ground on the other. *We've all got to eat.*

A couple of gang members lolled on the old wrecked porch attached to the bar, drinking beer. Acrid smoke from their fat cigars burned her eyes. No visible weapons. The other one was sitting on his Harley, also drinking, with his shotgun arranged in a holster slung low on the side of the bike. Energy waves were an easy green. No sense of any inside. So, four in all. At least she'd counted correctly before she got distracted.

Jarob pulled back the tarpaulin and motioned her to open a box in the truck. He kept his gun on her. She picked up a crowbar from the truck bed and popped the top of the first box. Ten shotguns. Well used, the wooden stocks were worn smooth, and a buildup of gun oil smeared the length of the barrels. A few looked newer.

She nodded at him approvingly, then hopped up on the truck bed and tried another box, going for one stuck right at the back—she'd been fooled by dummy merchandise before. It also had ten. Similar condition. She grabbed one, then jumped down again beside him.

"Have you got ammo for this?" Tazia was keeping it very formal to make up for her earlier behaviour. Although a knife was strapped to her leg, she wanted a shotgun to take out

Jarob. With one of these, she'd have just two shots. She'd have to make them count.

Jarob shrugged. "Whatever you need, honey bunch." He took the gun from her and ordered the guy on the bike to load it. The demon looked like he was going to argue until Jarob aimed his weapon toward him to reinforce the point. With a brief glare at his boss, he took two cartridges from the satchel on his bike and handed the loaded gun to Tazia.

When she started to walk away with it, he followed her. There were now three demons without weapons at immediate hand, just one with a gun. Odds increasing. Maybe even fifty-fifty. That was a number she could work with. If only she could remember their damn breed family!

She strode to a piece of open ground, keeping the truck between herself and Jarob, and shot a sweet smile at the demon who'd given her the gun. "Hey, honey, would you set up your can over there for me?" She indicated a piece of land about twenty feet in front of her. That would give her enough time.

As the demon walked, Tazia casually cocked the gun and tapped her foot lightly, grinning as the others gathered round to watch. The ink on her back clenched. *Oh well, here goes.* As he stepped back from the can, she brought up the shotgun and fired.

Her aim was perfect—if shooting this type of demon in the heart was a good idea. It wasn't. The blast knocked him flat, but metal flashed under his skin. He glanced down, then back at her, and roared. *Shit!*

A Bone Cruncher with a chest plate. *(Stomach.)*

She twisted toward the truck, but Jarob was gone. Instead, she aimed at the demon closest to her, just ten feet away. The shot struck square in his fat beer belly. Blood and guts sprayed, just reaching her boots. He dropped to his knees, glaring—then started to rise. *Fucksakes!*

The head, then.

Gun empty. Knife out. She twisted—and Jarob was already on her, automatic aimed at her chest. No love in his eyes now. Just red pinpricks, and his finger tightening.

Nothing between them. She raised her knife and sprang—

A shot rang out, but not from Jarob's gun. It came from behind her; from high on the hill. A rifle shot. And it was a killer.

Jarob dropped to his knees, clutching his gun with whitened knuckles, his finger failing at the last moment. Smoke curled from a wound in his left eye. The other glazed over. He toppled backward. *Of course, the eyes! Sneaky motherfuckers!*

In her peripheral the uninjured demon made his move— jumped off the porch and reached for the holster on his bike. At the same time, victim number one lurched forward.

Tazia ripped Jarob's gun out of his dead hands and fired at them in turn. They both fell to the ground, smoke coursing from the wounds in their heads.

"Bullseye!"

Holding his innards in place, the last one lunged in a side tackle. She flew one way, as he took out her legs, and her gun went other. The impact rolled her back towards the knife. *Lucky!*

She held him off with her left arm, scrabbling for the knife with her right. Fingers found the hilt—dragged it close—and drove it into his left eye as his full weight bore down. He shrieked next to her ear, like a cougar in heat, which would have been funny if it wasn't so bloody loud.

Momentarily deafened, Tazia levered the demon onto his back, straddled him—stinking gunge soaked her inner thighs— and forced the blade down through the bridge of his nose. On into his right eye as he flailed, punching on both sides of her ribcage.

He gurgled. And was still.

She straightened slowly. Ribs busted, but that would heal. Shame about the jeans.

Tazia wiped her face as best she could, pushed off her boots, and stripped off the stinking pants, dumping them in the back of the truck bed.

While she replaced her footwear, she scanned the arid hillside above the roadhouse, all the time grumbling to herself. "Who the hell was that?"… "Didn't need bailing out."

The keys to the truck, still laden with its cargo of guns and ammunition, were stuck in the ignition, and she turned the engine over. It hesitated once, then sprang into life.

As the old vehicle heaved itself over the gravel, a cloud of dust rose in the distance. Someone was leaving at top speed.

17

STRANGERS BEARING CANDY

THE CLUB WAS loud and brash inside, neon lights and industrial metal. Outside, Tazia watched drug dealers and prostitutes patrolling the streets, not the greatest area of town. Just the sort of place young people would gather. A perfect hunting ground.

Detroit emptied fast when the government pulled the plug. The poor never got out. Maybe they loved their city, maybe they just couldn't scrape bus fare; either way, they clung on at the edges. Five years later, 'New Detroit' squats on the bones: tin sheets slapped onto typical suburban houses, alleys turned into markets, hustlers and demons circling the stragglers. Not a place you settled in. That's where she found the club.

Inside, Tazia blended effortlessly with the mainly human clients, though she spotted a few vampires who were doing the same as her. She finally caught the eye of a young girl. Around eighteen, healthy and clean, with a toss of cheeky dark curls.

She made a show of looking her up and down and was shot a confident grin in return. They danced together and quickly made body contact. When Tazia suggested they leave, the girl grabbed her hand and pulled her from the club. She felt a brief flash of sympathy. Never heard of strangers-bearing-candy, kid?

As a rule, Tazia didn't kill her victims, but with the food source so far away, tonight was different.

They walked together for a little, talking quietly in the alleyway at the back of the club until Tazia leaned her gently against a wall and kissed her. Once distracted, she put a hand up to her throat and squeezed. The girl's eyes flew open, and her whole body juddered in panic. Tazia murmured whatever scraps came to mind—half-comfort, half-lie—until the pulse thinned to silence.

She made an inch-long cut in her throat with a feeding knife, then took the girl's weight in her arms and fed. The warm deep droughts tasted like a sweet honey and vodka cocktail. Shame it wasn't tequila.

When she was done, she placed the girl on the ground. Lighting up, she interspersed drags with her excuses to the bricks opposite. None sounded good.

"Taz, who are you talking to?"

Hand straight to her thigh, Tazia dropped her cigarette and looked around for the source of the voice.

"Tazia—here! Turn around. Down here."

She looked back down at the body. Instead of a glazed stare and lolling mouth, the corpse now smiled up at her. It tried to adjust its position against the wall, but remained mainly slumped. It did manage a tiny wave of the hand, though, with a finger ripple.

"Hi, can I bum a smoke? Haven't had one since Billy put me in that metal box." The voice came through the girl's mouth, but the inflection and vocabulary were all Joshua's.

"Josh?" Tazia stared in amazement at the girl. "That you?"

"Yeah, it's me. Cigarette, please. I'd get up, but you didn't leave much blood in here to help me move a heap of bone around. Feels like I'm gonna keel over any second. The nicotine will help."

"Doubt it, just give your head a buzz," she countered, but retrieved the lit cigarette and put it in the body's slack lips.

"Better than nothing." The corpse puffed awkwardly. The cigarette dangled from its mouth the whole time, but when Joshua spoke again, it fell to the ground. "So, who were you talking to? I couldn't see anyone else here."

Tazia looked at the wall. "Myself. I was hungry. Had to kill, but, you know, felt bad. What are you doing here, anyway?" She replaced the cigarette. The lips puckered around it with a little more determination, sucked, and Tazia removed it again.

"Thanks. Oh yeah. Dick… Tech-Head sent me. He needed to reach you fast and couldn't get you on the radar. I've been waiting for you to get near a dead body so I could jump in. Where have you been all day?"

"Needed to see some guys about some guns, remember?"

"Did it go okay?" This time, Joshua managed to get the upper body almost upright on the wall, though the head still lolled to one side and curls fell across the eyes.

"Fine." Tazia remembered the mysterious marksman.

"Good. Well, the reason Billy got his knickers twisted is that he updated his flight checks and found that a 'Richard Hunter' landed a few hours before you got here. There's no listing for a return flight, either, so looks like he's still here. He wanted to let you know. Feeling guilty he'd only checked the flights after you landed, not the earlier ones." He paused. "Can you move her hair? I can't see you. And give me another drag?"

Fingers shaking, Tazia fumbled the curls away from the eyes and held the cigarette for Joshua while she desperately tried to get control of her churning stomach. Hunter was one of Hux's fucking aliases.

Letting the cigarette hang, she slid down the wall next to the girl. How the hell did he know about Detroit?

"You gotta take care. He could be anywhere." The cigarette fell out of the girl's mouth and got caught in her curls.

"He was in a rush to leave, then," Tazia muttered, more to herself than to Joshua.

"Erm, Taz?"

Tazia ignored him. "Why use a name I know?" Richard Hunter was on as many security lists as Soren Huxford. "Sending me a message?"

"Taz!"

The acrid smell of burning hair drifted to her. She flicked the cigarette onto the ground, slapping the girl's hair to put out the tiny fire that had started to catch. Her movements threw Joshua off centre, and the body slumped once more, marks of blackened ash stark against her pale face.

"Keep it together, dude. You can take him. Taz… I can't stay. This body's just not got enough left in it. One last drag?" It slouched back on one side, head still raised a little.

Tazia put the cigarette to the lips one last time. With one puff, the head lolled. The neon sign over the club door burned extra bright for a moment and then faded. Joshua was gone.

Head spinning, she looked around the silent alleyway. She needed to get back to her squat—and the guns. She stared at the girl's dead body one last time. Rearranged it against the wall and wiped a thumb across each eyelid. Then got the hell out.

———

Soren Huxford stepped out of a doorway a little further down the alley. He stared after Anastasia, watching her final steps before she rounded the corner and disappeared. Reckless getting this close. But he'd stayed downwind. He couldn't help himself. Shadowing her all this time without making contact was torture.

He'd followed her to the gun drop that morning, watched her stick those stupid earbuds in her ears. No surprise when that demon closed in.

Getting more and more agitated, he'd watched the proceedings, willing her to remember what would kill a demon of that type. A rare specimen, tricky. When her attempts were duds, he had to step in to keep her alive. Just doing what he was paid to do.

He swabbed at the pool of sweat collecting at the back of his neck. The heat contributed, of course, but being so close to her raised his temperature. It was infuriating his body still remembered her.

Her inattention was typical. So damned distractible. During their years together, she'd left the planning of jobs to him, cos she just couldn't focus. Great fighter, though. The memory drew a smile. She went into every tangle with all guns blazing for the fun of it. Street moves, surprise approaches, always trying something new. She brought the same philosophy to the bedroom. Much more acceptable.

Soren leaned against the wall and drove his forehead into the brick. The skin split, and blood oozed. Before the pain hit, the cut had already knitted back together. Just itching a little. But it pulled the memories short. Stupid to go there at all.

She was no longer his lover. She had betrayed and humiliated him, shown him up to be weak. For a woman who couldn't feel, she did a damn good job at pretending. The contract now was just to track her. But something in him needed her dead!

He smashed his fist against the wall, grinding knuckles into the brick long after the skin had torn and the bones cracked. This time, pain hit and steadied him. But the fantasy still followed: to squeeze her throat the way he'd watched her kill that young girl, see her panic as he took her breath from her.

But first he wanted her confession.

The thump of music faded.

Yes, her confession. To hear her say she'd felt guilt for leaving him under those rocks to die. He didn't care about the money she'd stolen. But just the words. He didn't know why he needed it, but he did. One confession, and then he could kill her without any regrets. Couldn't he?

The music rose again. Soren breathed deeply, flexed his injured fingers, and wiped the blood on his fatigues before starting off into the dark. He already knew where she was going—he'd been watching her for days. He was biding his time, but it was coming.

Soon, baby. Soon.

18

METAL STUDS AND FOREPLAY

AS TAZIA NEARED the steps going down to the Irish Club, the first drunk intercepted her. He homed in, arms outstretched and lips puckered, then lost his footing and slammed into her shoulder. Her metal-studded boot left him airborne for a moment before he bounced off the cracked pavement and came to rest against a long-abandoned Chevy van.

The second drunk came off worse.

This one was a hulk, stepped up from the Club's entrance, fly already wide open. He made a beeline for her, his lolling tongue matched by an equally limp penis he cradled in his hand like a sad little slug. As he stumbled toward her, he tried to stroke it awake, but was way too drunk to make it count.

Tazia carefully put down the gym bag, stood arms crossed, and grinned at him. He grinned back, eyes glazed.

When he reached her, he swiped at her neck with one large sweaty hand. Filthy nails and stiff black hair bristling on the knuckles. She ducked. A swift kick to his knee sent him buckling. Confusion bloomed on his face. He giggled, grabbing at her ankles.

He thinks it's foreplay!

Her kick caught his head and his nose exploded in a spray of deep blue blood. It was enough. He collapsed in the road, dead to the world, snoring through the one intact nostril that now bubbled translucent black monster snot.

Tazia picked up her bag and blew him a kiss.

Cuinn greeted her at the entrance to the Club, his body wedged in the door to keep it open. "That was quite an entrance, darlin'."

She raised her eyebrows at him. "Classy clientele, Cuinn."

"Ahh, they're okay when they're sober. Just too much of the good stuff."

"I'll take your word for it. Do you want to see the merchandise?" She nodded at the gym bag.

After the nightclub, Tazia had spent the night before curled up in the back of the truck selecting the guns she wanted to take to Cuinn. She'd chosen each one carefully, finding its story, and then polishing it to a proud shine. It was her happy place, safe and familiar.

"Sure, let's go inside." Cuinn pushed the door open for her, his arm held high so she had to step underneath. "It's closing time, so it is. Not busy."

Inside, a couple of customers sat at the bar making the dregs in their glasses last, while Kevin washed down the tables, putting the seats up ready for the floor mop. He nodded a greeting to Tazia. Cuinn caught his eye and, with a nod of his own, indicated he was going to the back. The barman immediately slid into pole position behind the bar. The way those two ghosted each other was more than a little creepy.

In the back, six doors came off the central corridor. The hallway turned right, going out of sight. There were the same high arched ceilings as in the bar itself. The smell of damp got worse the further they got from the fire. She guessed the lock-up Joshua had mentioned when he'd spied on Cuinn was around the corner.

Cuinn stopped at the first door on the left and unlocked it, gesturing for her to go inside. He followed her in, switched on the overhead light and closed the door behind him. Hearing the lock click back into place, her heart beat faster.

The apartment was small but functional. A room leading off, possibly to a bedroom and, from the scents of shower gel and mildew, she assumed there was a bathroom back there, too. The main space had living and dining areas plus a small kitchenette with a fridge, stove, and sink. There was also a small desk in the far corner piled high with a computer, papers, and a printer-fax-scanner combo. Very old-school. Billy would like it.

Everything looked well-used, comfortable, and tidy. His smell was everywhere, and she felt her skin pricking, a tickling sensation she found welcoming. *Careful, Taz. He's just a mark like any other.*

She put down her bag on the small pine table in the dining area, unzipped it, and took out the first gun lovingly. Supporting it with her left hand, she stroked the barrel with her right, and then turned toward him, carefully aiming the gun away before handing it to him.

"Well Tazia, if you ever touched a man the way you touch that gun, they'd be mighty happy now, wouldn't they?" He flashed a gently teasing smile of amusement.

"I don't know. Experience says that men don't want to feel the tender side of me." The words were out before she could stop them. As her colour rose, she quickly added, "What do you think, it's a good one, huh?"

"Yes, she's just *fine*," he said.

His emphasis pleased her. The sort of appreciation for someone beautiful. Or, in the way Hux referred to his car. For her, it would be her Bowie.

He carefully examined the gun, turning it in his hands, feeling the weight and the balance. He placed it to his shoulder and looked down the barrel, taking aim, squeezing the trigger slightly. Not loaded, of course, but he was getting a sense of it.

When he was done, Tazia took the gun back and gave him the other, a rifle. Not exactly what he'd asked for, but she thought it the sort he would choose for himself. Older and well-used, perfectly weighted. Someone's pride and joy. The careful polish she'd given the metalwork had revealed italic engraving down one side. Fancy words to a long-dead owner.

"Ah, she's grand." He was still turning the rifle in his hands, admiring and testing it when he spoke.

She gave him a big, shy smile. "I thought you'd like it." She saw a flash of something in his eyes as he looked at her. A connection?

"So, they worth the money?" she asked, breaking eye contact first.

"Yeah, darlin', I'd say so. How many have you got?"

"Sixty in all. This is the best and worst of them."

"Good. I can have the cash for you in the morning, early." He replaced the gun in the bag, along with its companion, and handed them back to her.

"That's fine. You keep those until then—I trust you." It was a gamble, but that connection could strengthen. She smiled and turned toward the door.

"Tazia, hold on, darlin'. Business with me is never just about the guns, now." He put a hand on her shoulder lightly to prevent her from leaving.

She frowned at him. Confused. She'd done what he'd asked: arrived on time, brought him samples of her merchandise—

"The demon needs to check you out…" He smiled as he said it, but didn't lift his hand.

Tazia felt herself blanch. She wrestled with both her pride

and temper. Cuinn's eyes were soft as he watched her struggle. She noticed but it didn't help. She nodded stiffly at him. What choice did she have? She would have to submit to the scrutiny of this inner demon.

Before, he'd called his Core his "instinct." Well, her own instinct hit now—she'd be okay. Surely the tattoos would protect her? And he wouldn't fully change. Not like the one her father imprisoned.

"Fine. Do it then. Whatever," she said. She turned her back to the door and leaned against it. As Cuinn approached her, she didn't take her eyes from his.

He placed his hands on either side of her, trapping her there. "Darlin', it'd be better if you told me anything I need to know now before we start. If I pick it up and you haven't, it could be bad for—"

Footsteps charged down the corridor towards them: "Cuinn, you're needed. Now!" There was no mistaking the urgency in Kevin's tone as he shouted through the door.

Cuinn's face turned stony. His eyes flashed ice blue as he pushed Tazia firmly to one side and unlocked the door to fling it open.

Kevin struggled a little to control the alarmed look he wore. "Frank's picked up on a group of vampires coming down from the north side—he reckons they're headed this way."

Remaining silent, Cuinn marched back to the bar with him. Tazia was forgotten.

She started to follow, but paused when the door to the bar closed in front of her. Turning, she ran quickly to the end of the corridor, where it curved sharply to the right; a solid metal door blocked off the end of the hallway. A keypad glinted one lit eye at her—it was the lock-up.

With a face set to mild concern, she retraced her steps back down the corridor to the bar door with renewed urgency. With a plan ticking over, all she had to do was leave an impression.

19

———————

WAR PARTY

WHEN TAZIA GOT into the bar, the regulars were already heading for the exits. An uneasy energy rode the air. Cuinn took charge with a shout as she came through the door. As he gained order, six more Soldiers came through the front door and gave him their attention.

They were all of a similar height and build, tall and broad-shouldered with sharper buzz-cuts than either Kevin or Cuinn. They looked fresh, obedient, and cloned for battle.

Cuinn handed out guns to the demons he called up. Squad members. But a few of the regulars got one, too. The distribution process was impressive, well-rehearsed. It made her review her own weapons. Tapping her hand on each. Knife? Check. Pistol? Spike? All good.

In short order, the red energy in the room calmed to an alert amber. Shouted instructions became silent hand signals she translated as positioning orders. Two armed demons at the door. Two others across the street. The final two headed to the roof. They were ready.

Cuinn and Kevin also went outside to stand in the shadows of the steps leading down to the Club doorway.

Ignored. Tazia stood beside one of the demons by the door. She picked at her nails with her feeding knife. He looked sideways at her. She gave him her best grin. "Exciting, huh?"

He didn't reply.

"All this fuss for a few itty-bitty vampires."

He controlled his scowl long enough to suggest she might want to move back a bit.

"It's okay, I can look out for myself." She grinned again. If this was organized vampire action as Kevin had indicated, it could be a revenge attack for the destruction of the English HQ she'd watched. If she played this right, luck may have just fallen into her lap.

Deciding she would do better outside the bar than inside, Tazia pushed her way past the guard at the door. He briefly looked like he was going to stop her, but didn't. *Good call.* She dropped into the stairwell beside Cuinn.

"Tazia? Inside. Now."

"Uh-huh," she said, raising an eyebrow at him before jumping the stairs in a quick leap and walking across the street. Cuinn's annoyance washed over her, and she flashed him a quick wink before she looked down the street for the oncoming vampires.

They were a good way off and didn't appear to be hurrying: twenty in all. Most looked fairly mature, not fledglings who barely had a working brain cell. At the back, two demons dragged a woman between them. She was gagged, arms bound behind her.

Tazia raised her head to catch her scent, same as Kevin. A family member? That made a difference. If she saved someone important, more than kudos could be earned. Maybe enough for Cuinn to trust her.

She recognized another scent, too. *Seriously?*

The demon who led the pack looked Hollywood. Lean,

tall, and dressed head to toe in clichéd black leather. But unlike movie vampires, this guy was true evil. She had first hand experience.

She knew him as Antonio Giovanetti, favourite offspring of a vampire family she'd had dealings with in Turin. Close personal dealings. He was the sort to kill for fun not food. Wherever he went, a litter of lapdogs trailed after him, sucking up his scraps.

Tazia scooted back across the road, keeping her body low to the ground. She dropped her voice to barely a whisper. "Cuinn, there's twenty—mature—they mean business. They've got a female with them—one of yours. They won't bargain. Any idea who she is?"

"Jesus, it's Rose!" Kevin made as if to jump the stairs right into the arms of the oncoming vampires. Cuinn grabbed him and shoved him back into the stairwell, growling a low warning to stay down. Kevin complied but his anguish lit a fire up the ink on her spine. Twisting her insides too. *This was new.*

She had to move. "Stand by for my signal. I'll drop the headman—I know the bastard—I can work it. That'll fix the others. I know how their minds work." Without waiting, Tazia took off back across the road.

After a moment, she stepped out and sauntered forward to meet the oncoming demons.

———

Antonio spotted her immediately and raised his arm to halt the procession. He approached her slowly, head tipped to one side. "Anastasia of Savoy? Bella, is that you?"

"Certainly is, Antonio." Tazia stopped walking and let him come to her. They were still too far away from the guns; she needed to coax him on. "What are you doing in Detroit?"

"Seems as good a place as any. Lots of business now the monkeys are gone. I heard about your father, *bella*. I'm sorry for your loss, he was an example to all." Antonio spoke the words dryly.

Tazia shrugged. "I suppose. It's out there already then?"

"You know what it's like. Territory struggles starting."

"In Turin?" This was news. She'd been so intent on her quest that she hadn't stopped to consider the effect her father's death would have on the vampire community in Italy.

"*Si*. Two families vying for the city I heard, mine and another. We will win, I think. But it is not a concern of mine. I am here now." He pushed long blonde hair out of his eyes, as it found the tiniest breath of wind.

"Yeah. Looks like you've got struggles of your own. Why the war party?" She indicated the vampires behind him.

"Oh, just a little issue to resolve. Irish demon owns a bar here. He killed my cousin a couple of days ago. Can't ignore it, even though I hated the bastard." Antonio absently scraped the pad of his thumb with the blade of a thin, silver dagger he played with. Cutting open a scab that stank of iron.

"Does it have to be tonight?"

"Why?"

"Got a bit of business with him. He owes me and can't pay till tomorrow. I'd really like him alive till then."

"He will probably live. He's a Soldier, after all. A warning, no? He killed one of ours, so we kill one of his." He glanced at Rose, who glared red eyes back at him and let out a low growl from deep in her throat.

"You know about Core demons, Tony? They've all got one inside. If she turns, you'll be dead."

"Already thought about it." He lowered his voice, smirking as he leaned over to whisper in Tazia's ear. "We will set her on fire. It will happen quickly. She will not even know. Not pretty anymore like my little Tazia."

Tazia turned her face into his lowered cheek, her eyes catching his and her breath tickling his ear. "Can I do it?"

"You want to kill her, *bella*?" His eyes roved over her face.

"For old time's sake…" She whispered back. "I've got the feeling that if you do this, I won't get my money. May as well get some fun out of it." She continued walking backwards as she spoke until they were level with the steps where the demons' guns would be aimed in his direction.

Antonio stepped forward to follow her. Oblivious to the Club's location, the distraction of her smiling face and swinging hips worked perfectly. The vampires behind him followed, most looking bored.

"Do you remember the old times, Tazia, huh?"

She stopped, letting him catch up with her. "You bet. It's been quite a while."

"We were good together, yes?"

As he reached her, she wrapped her arms around his waist. "We sure were. Do you remember how I taste?"

He didn't have to be asked twice. He pressed himself against her, a strong hand behind her neck, pushing her lips to his. The kiss was deep and savage—and it ended abruptly.

Tazia snatched up the metal spike she kept at her hip and stabbed it into his left side. His eyes flew open.

She twisted it.

The fine teeth on each side of the spike ground the flesh before she yanked it out and lunged at him again, this time between the eyes. The fresh kidney paste clung to the blade and gathered on his forehead as she pounded it home.

When she pulled out the spike a second time, he crumpled at her feet, dead fingers pulling strands of her hair as he fell.

At the first strike, Cuinn and Kevin opened fire, blasting hearts from the first vampire pair, then the next, each shot measured and perfect. The rest of the squad took aim too. Bullets hit home, taking out more. One hit the shoulder of a target who screamed and twisted, his arm hanging by just a few ligaments at his side. He went down for good a moment later.

Screams and moans rose from the vampires who'd been hit first as the mixed holy water and shot started to do its work. The sound increased as more demons were methodically brought down. The ones at the back found their feet and ran in different directions. The Soldiers pursued still shooting.

One vampire came directly for Tazia. She stood, spitting out the taste Antonio had left in her mouth—coffee and stale blood—all the time curiously eyeballing the bullish form running straight toward her. What the hell is he doing?

At the final instant, before making contact, she realized he intended to run her down if she didn't get out of his way. She jumped and twisted in mid-air, bringing her foot cracking into his face. His neck broke instantly, and the body fell to the ground.

Remembering Rose, she replaced her stake at her hip and, trusting the Soldiers were good enough shots to avoid her, she ran through the dying and fleeing vampires until she was at the woman's side. While releasing Rose's hands, Tazia noticed the hostage was pregnant. She was also livid.

Rose pulled the gag from her mouth and, with a stream of profanities Tazia approved of, began systematically breaking the necks of the unfortunate vampires within reach. She sprung from one to the next, all the time growling and hissing her anger. Only stopping when there were no more at hand, and Kevin was standing by her side, pride and relief in his expression.

Cuinn walked up to Tazia and watched their reunion with a wide grin on his face.

"So that's what a Core looks like?" Tazia asked. She didn't want him to know she'd seen one before. Too many questions.

He smiled. "No, that's what a pissed off pregnant woman looks like. Her Core is still well and truly inside."

"You're kidding me?"

"Nope, darlin'. Scary, huh?"

Tazia watched as Kevin tenderly pushed back his wife's hair, now spattered with blood, and kissed her lips.

The rest of Cuinn's team had emerged from their various positions and milled around along with customers. Dying vampires were everywhere, and one of the squad performed clean up, staking those still alive.

The majority of the party moved back inside, and soon the sounds of revelry broke out. Loud music. Glasses chinking together. Kevin took his wife into the Club, murmuring his thanks to Tazia on the way.

"Shouldn't we burn the bodies?" she asked Cuinn.

"The sun will get them tomorrow. Let the vultures have them tonight."

Tazia sensed he still wanted her to remain, and so she waited, slightly unsure of what to expect.

He put a hand gently on her shoulder, and guided her to the wall of the building opposite the bar. He stayed close to her. Too close. "Stand still, Tazia."

She started, thrown off balance. One minute they celebrated. And now? He leaned in, arms caging her as they had before in his room.

"Sorry, darlin'" he said. The air rippled between them, and then he was gone.

Every muscle screamed to her to bolt. But she held and watched it come over him. His eyes changed to a deep amber-red, and silver sparks glittered deep within them. Waves radiated from him too; deep strokes of red quivered and bristled. They dug deep into her energy. With her fists balled, fear pinned her down. This was different than the beast her father had captured. He looked the same, but she felt the predator walking inside her, pursuing her thoughts.

Images spilled. She wrestled to hold them back. The Core

pried them from her. Sifting through them for threats and secrets. She saw them as he did. All of it. Her birth, her father's shadowy presence looming over her. A child's hope and love, ripped up and replaced with despair and brutality. All the atrocities she'd committed at his command. How he'd taught her to steal lives with evil games. And how she still fought him right until the shaman set the ink.

The loss of her soul hit her squarely again. She choked with the pain of it.

Not content to just observe, the Core scoured through her emotions to bring forward feelings that her bound soul had always protected her from. It rooted them out and shoved them back to her, raw and unfiltered. Panic and loss. She knew Cuinn felt it, too. He must!

Yet still, it wasn't finished. It leaned in closer, getting deeper, deeper. Breath hot on her face, electric energy lifting her hair. Dipping its head to her chest and down to her belly, she sensed it inside her, exploring every emotion, every experience. Rising and rasping its cheek against hers. Then—slow, deliberate—its tongue dragged from the cleft where her neck met her shoulder, up to her jawbone.

Tazia's eyes flew open in panic, and she sprang forward uncontrollably, pushing it away. It was enough to jolt Cuinn back into reality. He stepped away from her, back to himself. His face pale, eyes spinning.

"Taz—"

She swung without thinking. Fist cracked hard into his face. He just about maintained his balance, but his lip split and the deep blue of his blood began to flow over his chin.

"What the fuck was that?" she shouted, her voice raw and breaking, her mouth just inches from his face. "I just fought for you. Killed to defend you. Showed loyalty to someone I don't even know. Wha… what did you do to me?"

She pulled up tall in front of him. "Well, you know me now, Cuinn. You know everything, don't you? Was it as good for you? Was it? Do you feel it like I do? Fuck, how can you do that?"

Tazia stalked away.

20

———————————

THE WAITING GAME

SOREN WATCHED the events unfold from the roof of the building opposite the bar. He'd changed his hiding place when he saw Cuinn's two recruits scale the church and take up vantage points higher than his own.

He hadn't seen Cuinn at first, not until the exchange between Anastasia and the Italian vampire had played out and the shooting stopped. Then, as Cuinn stepped out of the stairwell, he'd saw him. He looked the same; the Soldier never changed. It was good to see family.

Soren's thing with Cuinn had started as uneasy admiration. Ten years back, a simple hired gun job. One turned to many, and Corktown became his neighbourhood for a while.

Their different worlds didn't matter. Human and demon, fighting side by side. All that mattered was respect. Then came brotherhood. Then Bali. He'd screwed up. Blood arced across the walls. Cuinn stepped into the smoke, grinning like a madman.

That was the moment. Forget God. He had Cuinn.

Now, outside the Club, Soren watched Cuinn's intimacy with Anastasia and the fist he received in response. There was more going on besides a gun deal. It made no sense: Cuinn hated vampires, and she was too close to one to get a pass.

But for Soren, the biggest piece of the puzzle was not Cuinn's partnership with Anastasia. It was why his employer wanted them both alive—and together?

It was too soon to pay them a visit. He'd wait longer.

———

An hour later, Franky Valentine found Conn alone in a booth of the bar. He felt a man overwhelmed with pain, strangely at odds with the revelries surrounding him.

Franky shuffled sideways into the opposite side of the booth, skillfully negotiating the protrusion of his short tail. He settled and gazed at Conn who had yet to acknowledge him. He raised his voice above the music. "You not celebrating, son?"

No reply. Two short, deep furrows stretched vertically down between Conn's brows, and his eyes glowed deep blue flashing with neon-like green flares as he searched for something. Now and then, his brows raised or his frown deepened.

Franky watched these expressions come and go and noted the large tumbler of whiskey Conn nursed in one hand and the half-empty bottle he pushed around with the other in concentric circles—a motion Franky quickly got bored with.

"Conn?" His voice had a snap this time.

"Franky?" Conn completed the pattern, then glanced up, banging the bottle slightly on the table. "Drink?"

"No, I've had enough. Haven't you?" Franky raised his eyebrows.

"Nah, she's still half full." Conn picked up the bottle and tilted it slightly to demonstrate the level of the remaining liquid.

Franky noticed another empty bottle at the far end of the

table by the wall. It was also a bottle of the good stuff. This was serious.

He'd seen him like this a few times. The same pattern: a bad fight or argument, a few hours of lone drinking, until finally, he would spill his guts.

Franky sighed, leaned back in his seat, and settled in for the long haul.

21

STOP THE DRAMA

BACK IN HER ROOM, Tazia rested her forehead against the cool fridge door. Her first thought was to run back to Billy. She'd even thrown clothes into the duffel on the bed with perfect aim. But she'd stopped as quickly as she'd started.

Was it worth this? The humiliation.

She'd just risked her life for him. And licking her! What was that? Ownership?

"I saved Kevin's wife." She chanted the words, rolling her forehead from side to side, hoping the cooling action of the fridge's surface would calm her mind. Gentle rocking changed to banging.

Chanting became louder, each word accompanied by a thud to the appliance. "I. Saved. Kevin's. Wife." Louder and louder until, "I saved his fucking wife!"

Sliding down onto her back, she wasn't sure she'd ever make sense of Cuinn's behaviour. What she did know was that she'd prevented all hell breaking loose on that street. But more than that… She'd actually felt for them!

With the revelation, her spine turned ice cold.

Outside the Club, Tazia wanted to keep Rose alive. Not for

the job, but to spare Kevin the pain. What did it mean? Were the tattoos loosening their control? *Was this progress?*

She looked at the wall wide-eyed. "I didn't want Kevin to suff—"

"Oh, for goodness' sake, Anastasia, stop the drama!"

Tazia jumped, then instinctively rolled to the other side of the fridge nearest the door. Knife in hand. Exit close. She scanned the room. Alone. Just for a moment, she looked back at the wall. *Really?*

The voice sounded like it came from the corner, where the big, old-fashioned armoire stood. She pushed herself up and crept to the wardrobe, forcing the door open with a crash, knife ready. No one was hidden inside, but as it rebounded shut, she noticed the reflection in the mirror; it wasn't her own. She stoppered the door with her foot, and stared.

A woman around fifty. Long straight hair, the colour of aged red wine. Wide silver-grey streaks laced through it matching the pallor of her thin, sharp-boned face. She glared out from the mirror.

"High Advocate?" Tazia asked. It seemed a good guess.

"Well done, pet." The angel licked her right index finger and ran it over her perfectly manicured eyebrows.

"What do you want?" Buzz gone, Tazia went back to her position by the fridge. This time leaning against it to cool her back.

"That's not the nicest greeting I've ever had, but under the circumstances, I'll let it go. You've had a hard day." A snakish smile curved over her face as she spoke. Her eyes remaining tight and still.

She somehow manipulated the door of the armoire to open just a little more. Everything behind the angel undulated like a heat haze. Tazia blinked. It continued to move. Sometimes shifting into a cave of white sparkling crystal. Strobing light bounced off the walls; glass jars sat on shelves behind her, sparking with lights of their own. Then, back to a blur.

"Where are you?"

"This?" The High Advocate gestured over her shoulder. "This is my refuge."

"And who are you? Is that someone else's body you're wearing?"

"Oh, her? She was alive once, long ago. My favourite of the forms I adopted when I walked on Earth, but her soul is long gone. She's like a comfortable pair of pyjamas." She tittered in her high-pitched way, and a long crack crisscrossed over the surface of the mirror. It split her face in two, cutting across her chin and up over her right ear, displacing the top slightly from the bottom imitating a Picasso.

"Whoops!" she said and stopped laughing. "So, you're thinking of giving up your quest, Anastasia? It seems you've quickly forgotten your responsibility to your father. There he is, rotting in the mire, being eaten away, and you're on the verge of throwing in the towel?"

"Did you see what Cuinn did to me?" Tazia's stomach clenched. She rolled her shoulders. The rhythm of her body still felt wrong after he'd crawled inside her.

"Of course."

"Well—"

"You've endured a lot worse in your long life, Anastasia! Besides, you were safe, pet, I ensured it. The Soldier only saw what I wanted him to. I kept everything... hazy."

"Oh, but..." She stopped. "That's good, I guess." *But so not the fucking point!* She played with her knife, scratching the fine hairs from her arm with its tip.

"You have to be tougher than this, Anastasia. I'm helping you all I can, especially with the Soldier, but I can't be expected to do everything now, can I?"

"Helping? How? You're the cause of all this!"

The angel narrowed her eyes. "Let me give you another incentive, then. I can always point your demon hunter friend in your direction."

"Hux?" Tazia's stomach flipped. "You know he's here?"

The angel smoothed down her hair. "I see everything, girl, and he wants to find you very badly. If you give up on our plan, why would I not help him?" She twisted a lock of hair in her fingers, round and round like a small child, and giggled. "It may surprise you to know, pet, but he's been working for me for quite some time. Even when he was kissing your pretty lips." She tittered once again, and the crack lengthened.

Tazia scowled, but her breath shortened as she absorbed the news. *He set me up!*

"You look tough, but I can hear your heart thumping from here, dear. He really makes you weak at the knees, doesn't he? And for all the wrong reasons!" She laughed again. The crack spread further, and the windows in the room shook a little.

"Oh dear, it looks like I'll be leaving soon. This portal isn't up to much. One final thought for you to consider—" her brittle voice dug deep "—I know things you don't. I can pull the strings of those who have yet to wake. That friend of yours back in London? Sweet boy, but very far from home."

"Billy?" Tazia's heartbeat surged.

"Do as you are told, Anastasia, go along with the Soldier's plans. Be… agreeable. Or more than just you will regret it!" She snapped the last words, all traces of friendliness gone. Tazia's hair ruffled in a sudden gust of cold wind, and the floor under her bottom shook. The crack reached the edge of the mirror with a pop, and the angel's reflection disappeared.

Tazia crawled from the floor to the bed, shoving the duffel bag over. As she lay there on her back, staring at the mildewed ceiling, sweat prickled her scalp. Her breath came in short bursts. Billy's voice in her head, "Breathe, Taz. Breathe."

To gain control, she imagined her mind as a blank sheet of writing paper. List the risks. Plan the mission.

First, her father.

She still felt guilt, yes. But loyalty? Fading. Maybe separation was bringing her clarity. She scratched through her father, but could not quite erase him completely, not yet.

Next, Hux.

The High Advocate would hand her over to him, no question. Her chest tightened again. He wanted her dead, but at least she had a chance with a human. Know thine enemy, right? She sure as hell knew him well. As long as she could keep a few steps ahead, she could come out alive.

But what about Billy? It appalled her to think the angel had some sort of control over him. What the fuck did she mean anyway, that he was "far from home?"

No, Billy was her lifeline. She wouldn't let the Advocate get him. If saving her father would keep Billy safe, then she would do it. She'd do anything. The mission was clear. Hux would be proud.

Now, Cuinn. She rolled onto her front, breathing easier but needing the comfort of her pillow.

The events of today had proved one thing: the only way Cuinn would ever give up his Cause for her was if she tricked him into it and despite the abuse he'd put her through earlier, she'd recognized his reluctance to let the Core take control. Maybe she could still influence him—use his men against him?

She pushed down the newfound connection she'd felt for Kevin earlier. This was not the time for her tattoos to release their grip. The Advocate was right; she had to be tougher than this. Had to play the game.

Her earlier plan reemerged. Billy could easily break into the security system of Cuinn's strong room. Maybe there'd be money meant for his bosses? Cuinn had to have a boss, right— back in Ireland? If she could sow suspicion—take the money—

maybe they'd turn on him or punish him. If the Cause rejected him, that could be enough for him to give it up. Long shot, but it was all she had.

She pulled the pillow from under her head and chucked it across the room. No comfort there. Like the plan, it stank.

When Billy finally appeared on the screen. He was still in motion, swerving into his seat, looking hot and sweaty. He managed a few words between heavy panting. "Hey, babe… was running… you okay?" *Fitness freak.* Like his bedroom workouts weren't enough.

While he waited for a reply, he pulled off his t-shirt, ran it vigorously over his head, and threw it onto the floor. He pushed back the hair on both his temples. The hair on top now perfectly flopping into his eyes. *Typical.*

Tazia waited it out, amused. A wave of calm flowed over her as she watched the performance. He grounded her. "Hey, Billy. You look… hot!"

"Always, baby. Always!" He smirked at her. "Hey, what's going on? Looks serious."

"Things didn't go so well with Cuinn and I just had a visit from the High Advocate, too. She's now a red-haired medieval bitch, by the way."

She explained some of what had happened over the last twenty-four hours. She left out the Core. He didn't need to know that. Then tested out the idea that had been forming in her mind since she'd seen the access panel outside Cuinn's lock-up.

"It's weak, babe. Busting the security system is straightforward. But we need more. I can't see any punishment thrown at Cuinn more than symbolic—you can't kneecap a Soldier demon! He'd probably laugh it off—not bring on a crisis of faith. You don't even know if there's any money in the strong room."

However she spun it, the plan was full of holes.

Tazia collapsed onto her side, her head propped up on her hand so she could still see the tablet. The tension around her eyes and jaw still felt like a vice. "Let's assume there *is* money there. What if one of his own took the cash? Like Kevin. Cuinn adores that guy. If he thought Kevin had turned, it would floor him. Surely? Any punishment dished out would be the cherry on top."

Billy still looked unconvinced.

She pushed on. "Come on, Billy, I'm fucking trying here!"

"Go on then. Convince me!"

"I could get to him then, when he's low. Maybe talk him into leaving the Cause. I can be persuasive…"

"If you're suggesting taking him to bed, babe. I admire your spirit, but sorry. I think the plan's still a bit… limp. You're a kid compared to him—and a vampire! Doesn't he hate your kind?"

"I'm a hundred and fifty-ish! And, I'm not all vamp. He just has to demonstrate a bigger allegiance to me." She trailed off.

"I don't know. It's still wea—"

"Weak. Yes. Got it. Fucksakes!" She rolled her eyes, sat up, and dropped the tablet into her lap. "Look. There was something else today. Between us. I think we both felt it. It was like he knew me."

"An energy connection?"

"Yes. Like nothing I've felt before. Like we were… familiar. Whatever! I can't explain it."

She looked at him expectantly. He was fiddling with a pen he'd picked up from the desk top, twirling it over and over. "Billy?"

Finally, he spoke. "Is all this really worth it, love? I'll admit it's the best we've got, but it's still not likely to work and it sounds dangerous." He looked up, eyes intensified to the deepest brown.

Tazia pondered her answer carefully. She didn't want him to know he was in danger, too. "There's more at stake now. The Advocate told me she has a direct line to Hux and can have him here like—" she snapped her fingers. "This is bigger than saving my father."

Billy leaned back in his seat to grab a long-sleeved shirt from behind him. She saw him shiver as he pulled the cotton fabric over his overheated body. As he buttoned, his mind was clearly ticking over. "To be convincing, you'll need to exploit that… connection, I guess. Through energy runs natural magick—bigger than all of us. Maybe you can use it, but someone will end up hurt."

She nodded, but looked at the space just past his eyes. "I've done worse."

Billy took a breath. "Okay. Tell me what you need."

Desperate to lighten the mood, Tazia grinned at him and imitated Joshua. "You rock, dude!" Really, she needed to throw up.

He ignored the mock flattery. "If it starts to go wrong though, Taz, remember Plan B."

"Plan B?"

"You come home. We'll figure out how to deal with Hux and the angel when you get here."

She nodded without conviction. Plan A had to work. She'd be too dead to try Plan B.

22

WHISKEY

FINALLY, Conn started talking. Franky had sat patiently, matching him glass for glass in the hope each one he drank would save Conn twenty minutes sleeping it off. Words started to flow after an hour. They were a little hesitant at first, just the occasional blast.

Then the floodgates opened.

"Yer see, Franky, whenever the Core walks, it forces itself on them. *It's* doing it, but all they see is me. I can't stop it. I just have to watch—feel what it feels. And sometimes it's just black. I don't even remember." He paused, squeezing his eyes shut for a moment. "And there are risks, too, yer know? Not just for them if they wind the monster up wrong, but for me. If I lose control—I might never get back." He poured another tumbler full of whiskey and knocked it back in one gulp.

For the life of him, Franky didn't know why he wasn't just slurping from the bottle. Why civility when the kid was practically falling off his chair?

Conn continued, his accent thickening. "It happened once. This auld fella, back in Cork. He did a walk, looking for signs a jackeen was a spy for the Crown." He mouthed the final word like it was poison.

He blinked hard, the blue in his eyes swimming out then back again. "He never came back. The traveller wasn't a Loyalist, but he *was* batshit crazy talking about the Fair Folk like he could see 'em! Padraig—" he squinted like he was chasing the memory "—that was the auld fella's name. Came back from the Core, but just as much a madman as the fella he'd walked in. Last I heard, he was hiding out in the mountains, scaring the shite out of anyone who happened to pass by. Still there they say… or maybe he's dead. Hell, maybe both."

Franky tried to follow the train of thought, knowing full well that the mixed-up story about the legendary Irish Soldier was no more than a tale to scare young'uns. In his drunken state, Conn believed every word.

"Surely, just a tale to teach the kids, son?"

Not hearing, Conn wobbled to standing and raised his glass at Franky. "To Padraig! The greatest Soldier to stand o' the Green!"

Franky echoed his sentiment: "*Sláinte!*" At least he was talking!

Abruptly, Conn switched subjects to Tazia, rubbing at his cheek. Although Franky hadn't seen what had passed between them, he could smell Tazia's scent on him only too well.

"Oh, the poor girl has suffered, Franky. I saw it all. Just a wee thing. Wrenched from her dead ma right out the ground. All those demons grabbing at her, fighting over her. Shockin' it was. Sure, she suffered even as she took her first breath."

He plonked himself back in his chair and downed the last of the whiskey. Despite his efforts to place it carefully back on the table, the glass fell the final inch and landed with a bang. The sound echoed and the last drops of amber liquid spattered his hand. For the first time since he sat down that night, he didn't immediately refill it.

Conn sucked up the whiskey drops from his skin one by one between his words. "And… that… Leech… standing over her! Oh, how I wanted to kill that fecker! I couldn't see his face, but it was her da. I felt it. That's never how a father should treat his own daughter, even if he is an evil bastard. The lowest. Made me sick to even watch it."

He sat back in the chair and crossed his arms. "You know what though, Frank? She loved him! I could feel it, clear as anything. How? How could she love someone who treated her like that?"

He finally seemed to want Franky's input.

"Sounds like he was all she knew, Conn. You know how prisoners can end up over time, caring for their captors. You've used that technique yourself in the past, kid."

"Not on children, Franky! Never on children!" Conn tried to stand up again, but the action proved too ambitious and he lurched back in his chair before fully reaching his feet.

"All right, son, stay down. I know you haven't done that. I'm just explaining away how she might still love him." Franky's tone was intended to calm, but something in what he said obviously sounded wrong to Conn.

"No, Frank, she doesn't love him now. He did something to her, stopped the love." He seemed to be struggling to make sense of what he'd seen. "She was tied down—front forward over a rock. Just a kid still… There were men around her, chanting. Drum beats. But I could still hear the screaming, then the whimpering. Jaysus, the pain she was in. One man leaning over her and dripping colours on her back. Ink and blood. I could smell the blood."

He stopped and for a moment. Franky thought this tough, seen-it-all soldier would vomit. He poured them another tumblerful of whiskey each. "Torture?"

"No. Well, not just torture. There was a purpose. Magick, to be sure—control." He looked wide-eyed at Franky. "Her soul! I remember. I could smell a soul on her and then nothing. Those tattoos they gave her—they control her soul!"

They both sat in stunned silence for a moment. Neither knew what it was like to have a soul. It was a thing for humans. Some demons ridiculed it. Others pursued it like gold. But for Franky, he'd felt it too often through his readings not to fear it. A slick oily covering distorting every decision, every thought. Made him sick to the stomach every damn time.

Both men drained their glasses, and Franky sought to change the subject. "What else did you feel?"

Conn looked up from his empty glass. Apparently now sober, he picked up the half-full bottle and crossed to the bar to replace it under the counter. Then he gathered the other empties and stacked them in a crate.

The boy's not done.

When the crate was still half empty, Conn came back and sat down heavily. He took a breath, steadying himself, before looking Franky straight in the eyes. *Okay, kid, out with it!*

"She's scared of something, Frank, but the Core didn't pick up what. Someone is after her. It'll end in fight or die, and she doesn't want to do either. I don't know… She's not a threat, I would have seen it. It's strange, man, but I feel like…" He struggled for words. "Like I'm waking up from a dream she was in. No. More than a dream. She's so familiar to me. Like I know her!"

It was a bombshell. He knew it, kept his eyes on Franky the whole time to see how it landed. Franky wished he could give him answers, comfort him, even, but he had nothing.

"Conn, son, even if you do feel a connection, there's a reason why she's turned up here now. I don't know why you didn't see it, but she needs something from you. I don't know what. But I do know it's too soon to give it to her. You've just met her, lad. You can't trust her, yet."

His words missed.

No acknowledgement. Conn dug at some invisible gunge from a crack in the wood with his fingernail. "Looks like it's bedtime, Frank." He stood confidently and headed to the door.

Franky sighed and pushed himself to his feet. He'd try one more shot before leaving. "Will you just do me one favour, Conn?"

The Irishman looked at him, eyes settling into a full, rich emerald green. "Sure."

"Just don't agree to anything she asks. Not until you've talked it over with the men you trust your life to every single day. Talk to me. Talk to Kevin."

He paused as he levelled with Conn and put his hand on his shoulder. "Son, I don't know if we should be scared of her or roll out the welcome mat, but she wants something. I think she's here to test you. She'll be playing on your emotions, too. Just let us help. Goodnight."

Conn patted the old man's back. "Goodnight, Frank."

As the lock turned behind him. Franky felt Conn's thoughts reach out to him. *Thanks, Pops.* The gratitude felt genuine. He looked back through the barred windows and saw Conn turning off the lights and heading to the back rooms, gently rubbing his cheek.

As he crossed the road, heading home, the stench of vampire bodies hit him. They were already turning bad in the heat, and the vultures were hard at work. *It's coming, kid! The balance is shifting, and there's not a damn thing we can do about it.*

———

Jegudiel looked across the room at the sleeping form of Conn O'Cuinn. He'd fallen, still dressed, face down on the bed.

Though she was simply a dark form in the mirror on the wall, she projected her influence towards the sleeping Irishman.

In her hand, she carried the glass jar in which the essence of Conn's dead wife, snatched from the Red River, was held prisoner. Jegudiel turned the jar over, tumbling the spirit until it became agitated. As it stirred, so did Conn.

The angel was planting a dream.

It was a fresh spring morning back in his Irish village home in Cork, and Conn was training his hawk. Down below, he could see his fellow villagers going about their daily chores, his wife waving to him and his son chasing a small dog that had wandered into the enclosure overnight.

For a moment, the dream reinvigorated him. He breathed deeply, peacefully, but the respite would be temporary.

Jegudiel turned the jar over slowly.

Time had moved forward. Conn charged toward the village but could not get further than the gate. Everywhere he looked, invading vampires set fire to shelters. Choking smoke filled his throat and obscured his vision. Defenceless villagers were dragged into the open and each one skewered with a thin, pliable cutlass through an eye and on into their brain. The smell of the blood of his friends and family filled his senses.

In his room, Conn abruptly turned over onto his back. The sweat trickled down his temples and onto his neck, soaking the pillow under his head. Eyelids flickering rapidly.

Jegudiel smiled at the signs of his discomfort and agitated the jar more vigorously.

Standing in the middle of the carnage was a tall, thin vampire. He looked regal. His beard was pointed, the moustache clipped precisely, and the curl of his dark hair flattened with beeswax. Guards flanked him on each side. Occasionally, he would look sternly in the direction of a loud scream, or he'd wipe away a stray drop of blue blood that reached his clothes or boots, but that was all.

In bed, Conn twisted, trying to find an escape from the vision, but the angel gave him none.

Unseen hands dragged him toward the vampire, the smell of crushed grass under his knees. He was thrown on his back at the vampire's feet and a cutlass held to his eye. He fought to raise his Core, but could not. Blood magick hung thick and metallic on the air.

In his room, Conn let out a whimper. A cornered animal. He jerked his head away from the invisible cutlass.

Jegudiel giggled, the mirror vibrated, and the nail in the wall that supported it came a little loose.

The vampire leaned over Conn and spoke, his voice brittle: "Boy, be sure that I will kill everyone here, then the next village and the next. All who support your campaign will be murdered." He got down on his haunches and looked Conn deep in the eyes, his voice switching to a playful tone: "But I give you a choice, Conn O'Cuinn. Let's test that loyalty you Soldiers prize above all. Turn and walk away, and I will give you till sundown to sound the alarm and save your brigade. Move them on, out of the landowner's grasp. But, if you choose to take my offer, no one here will live. Not your son. Not your wife."

In bed, Conn wrestled with the decision just as he had so long ago. He ground his teeth, and tears mixed with the sweat dripping from his forehead. The angel stirred him further, a second voice nagging in his ear. "What will you do, Conn? Fight and die anyway, or be loyal to the Cause you're sworn to?"

Not waiting for an answer, she looked back into her cave, noting how the sun was rising and casting rainbows through more jars on the shelves. There were other things she should be doing. Yes, time to hurry this along—the girl and the Soldier. Everything had to be just so.

"Let me go." Conn had made his decision, and the

vampire nodded. "I am impressed, boy. You can see the bigger picture. That is loyalty I have rarely seen." His captors released him. Conn memorized every crease and line on the vampire's face, absorbed his scent into his blood and bones. Then walked away, helping no one and looking past every dead or dying body.

Jegudiel watched the memories fly back and forth across Conn's face. She saw the dream bring back to him his worst moments, but still didn't spare him. With one final flourish of the jar, she forced more pain.

His actions had saved hundreds of Soldiers who'd continued on fighting for their bit of Ireland for many years to come. Now, she snatched that pride away and replaced it with the memory that tortured him in his waking life as well as his sleep: the bloody bodies of his wife and child, their lifeless eyes staring into his.

As the images hit, Conn cried out his wife's name, and Jegudiel's laugh rocked the mirror. The nail released its grip, and the mirror crashed to the ground, sending a jagged crack snaking over the surface. Her view of him was gone.

23

DAMN HOT, SOLDIER!

THE NEXT MORNING arrived as hot and fetid as the one before, and despite little sleep, Tazia shifted as soon as a single shaft of light pierced the window coverings. The beam crossed her bed, highlighting specks of dust in the air above her. She wished the plan she and Billy had hashed out was as clear as each of those particles.

She groaned and waved a hand into the dust, disrupting it so it didn't look so damned precise.

She needed to get moving. Soon, Cuinn would arrive to pick up the merchandise. Guns for money: an exchange she'd done a hundred times before. This time there was a lot more than cash at stake. Her heart was already thumping. The whole thing felt out of her control.

For one thing, she had to let go of her anger toward Cuinn. But she couldn't be too accommodating, either. It would make him suspicious. Billy had told her to "act natural." What the fuck did that mean, anyway?

Another groan, this one bordering a growl. Whatever happened during the meeting, she had to find a way back into the Club. Get Cuinn comfortable enough to trust her.

She sat up, dug around for her sneakers. The more she stretched, the further they drifted under the bed. She gave up and dressed, retrieving her already stinking clothes from the floor.

Reconsidering the sneakers, she pulled on her Docs. They sported a nice metal toe cap, and space to slip a thin dagger inside the left one. The boots were the better choice.

Outside, Tazia waited for Cuinn by the doors of the storage garage she'd nabbed when she first arrived in Detroit. After releasing the locks on the doors, she paced up and down the same ten-step strip.

While showering, she'd settled on a strategy: if she had to, she'd use the Core's walk to wheedle an invitation out of him. Surely he'd feel bad about it? The worst would be to look into those ever-changing eyes and see not even a small drop of empathy. If he couldn't give her that, despite the fact he'd seen her scars, then she didn't know what her next move should be. It would probably involve a shit-ton of tequila.

With military punctuality, Cuinn's truck turned the corner at exactly zero eight hundred. Tazia heard the diesel engine long before she saw it and watched as it approached. Despite the rust, the truck handled the cracked pavement easily.

He wasn't alone. Kevin sat in the passenger seat with a shotgun held diagonally across his body. She was annoyed with herself for missing this possibility. Why would he turn up by himself for a gun drop and cash exchange? Far too risky!

Stomach churning, she raised the door of the garage so they could see there was no one hiding inside, just her and a truck bed full of guns. Then leaned against the wall, one knee bent, the knife in her boot a second from her hand. The metal studs on her sole tapped out something by The Ramones against the wall.

As the truck pulled up, Cuinn steered it around and parked perpendicular to the row of garages, blocking the alley. He backed it up just a little. With lowered tailgates, the boxes of guns could be shifted easily enough from one truck bed to the next.

Kevin jumped down from the passenger side, holding his gun stiffly in front of him. As he approached, he gave her a stern and unblinking nod, not the friendly smile she'd received only yesterday. She shot him a quizzical look. He held it admirably, revealing nothing.

Tazia's confusion turned to annoyance. What could have happened since yesterday when she saved his wife? Did Cuinn tell him what his Core had seen? What the hell did he say?

Cuinn stepped off the running board, slow and heavy, making quite a mark in the dust. His greeting was better humoured, a smile, but the dark rings under his eyes gave him away, and delivery was flat. "How're you keepin' there, Tazia? It's a great day for it."

She raised her eyebrows, impatience and anger stabbing. "It's as hot as shit out here, Cuinn, and it stinks just as bad." Despite herself, she glared briefly at Kevin, who was still unresponsive. Her promise to keep herself in check forgotten, she jumped up on the bed of her truck and started to pull the boxes forward. She crow barred the first one open, ready for Cuinn to inspect.

"Okay then," he said. "All business, I see."

For a moment he paused, running a hand over his face and through his hair. It was still wet, and his movement left a scent in the air for her to catch; salt from his sweat tickled her tongue and mixed with the fake fruity tang of shower gel. The heat wasn't good even for pure demons, it seemed. His stubble, though sexy as hell, was sloppy.

Seeing his slow movements and obvious discomfort, Tazia felt a pang of regret at her earlier rudeness and tried to make amends. "Looks like you had a late night. Me too. We should have arranged to do this later once the sun was down." She gave him a small smile of reconciliation.

It seemed to work. He smiled back. "That we should have, darlin'." With a lighter step, he climbed onto the truck bed with her and checked over the contents of the first crate. All was in order.

As Tazia started to open the next one, he stopped her, putting a hand on her arm. "It's all right, I know you'd keep your word."

At his touch, she jerked her arm away, the movement unnecessarily violent. On high alert, Kevin stepped forward and raised his gun in her direction.

"Stand easy, soldier." Cuinn's tone was soft. He continued, "Sorry, Tazia. I didn't mean to spook you. This heat is making everyone jumpy."

Tazia rubbed at the burning sensation left on her arm where Cuinn had touched her. It felt scorched, like the flame of embarrassment in her cheeks. *Don't show it, you idiot!*

She looked him full in the face. "Damn hot, soldier!" The wink she added was probably unnecessary.

He grinned back at her. The tension lifted from them, but not from Kevin, who looked uneasy with the situation playing out in front of him. His efforts to run interference, for whatever reason, were failing, and he suddenly got busy. He abandoned his shotgun, leaning it up against the wheel of Cuinn's truck, and started tugging at the nearest crate. "Let's be getting the merchandise out of here, then, shall we?" He looked pointedly at Cuinn.

"Sure, we can do that..." But Cuinn just continued to hold Tazia's gaze longer. His words faded weakly, and his eyes started rapid-firing between blue and green and every shade in-between.

Kevin responded by pushing the offending crate roughly against Cuinn's ankle. "Some help would be good, man!"

Cuinn dragged himself away from Tazia's eyes and kicked the crate further into the waiting truck, then finally turned his attention to the others. With the three of them shifting the boxes, they were all soon transferred.

When they finished, Kevin retrieved his gun and got back in the passenger seat. Not even a passing glance in Tazia's direction. Cuinn pulled her aside to give her the payment. The two of them went inside the garage, cramming themselves into the space between her truck and the wall.

It was sweltering and airless. Their scents intensified. She briefly regretted her choice of yesterday's clothes, but forgot again as musk thickened the air and the ink stroked her spine.

Money exchanged, Cuinn appeared reluctant to leave. He pushed away the hair that had fallen forward over her eyes. "You do look tired, darlin'," he smiled. "Why not come to the Club later and we can drink to our new partnership? Or are you gonna be holding last night against me?"

Tazia hadn't prevented his familiarity, her heart raced at mention of the invitation she needed. But what about Kevin? Even now, she could see him glaring into the truck's passenger side mirror, watching what was going on in the dimly lit garage. "Looks like not everyone is as pleased with our partnership as you, Cuinn."

"Ahh, don't you be paying attention to him, Tazia. Just come to the Club tonight. We'll drink a little, play some poker, have some *craic*—you'll have him eating out your hand in no time. Him and Franky."

Tazia raised her eyebrows. "So, Franky not a fan, either? Wow, I should stop vampires coming to kill you guys every day!"

"They're good folks, Tazia. They just need some time. They—we—don't trust easily."

He stood back and smiled again. "What do you say? Will you be there, darlin'?"

"Yes, I'll come, but no poker. Franky already knows I don't have the face for it!"

After they'd gone, she took the money back to the squat to find a hiding spot. Money had never been much of a motivation, but now that she had to fend for herself, it could come in useful.

The meeting had gone well considering what she was up against. She'd got what she wanted: a connection with Cuinn and an invitation to the Club. Exactly what she wanted. The plan could work. So why the regrets?

24

____

MENDING FENCES

TAKING a place at the bar that night, Tazia felt nervous. Usually she could bluff confidence she didn't feel—tonight wasn't one of those nights.

Cuinn had poured her a drink and invited her to take a stool. He'd smiled and winked a greeting at her, but had yet to say anything—too busy serving customers: a collection of demons, mostly pure breeds. Only a couple had the familiar Celtic Soldier appearance she was used to seeing here. One had the look of Jarob, the gun-dealer from earlier in the week. *Nasty.* Looked like Cuinn dealt with anyone if they had what he, and the Cause, needed. Except vampires, of course.

It was stifling and overcrowded. Patrons sat in huddles, some in quiet conversation, others partying, or playing cards. Condensation ran down the mirror behind the bar, but the fire still burned.

Tazia chased a bead that formed on her glass, beating it to the bar top by catching it on her fingertip. She sucked it up, wondering how the hell anyone could work in this atmosphere. She regretted her choice of short skirt and bare legs, which kept sticking to themselves and the wooden bar stool.

Cuinn busied himself pouring pints and keeping up a cheerful conversation with each of his patrons. Dark stains soaked through his shirt and under his arms. Now and then he tugged at the neck. He was out of luck, no ventilation in the whole bloody place.

Franky sat in a booth on the far side of the room. A padded bench and long table had changed its use from crypt to meeting place. Thin shelves cut into the stonework now housed his empty beer glasses. It looked like he'd had a few.

He was alone. She decided to take the bull by the horns. If she could win him over even slightly, Cuinn would trust her more.

"May I join you, Franky?" she asked for the sake of politeness, but was already slipping into the booth opposite him. His consent was to raise his glass at her in silence. *Tough room.*

"It seems both you and Kevin have a problem with me and I'm not sure why."

He remained staring into his glass.

Tazia leaned forward across the table. "Didn't I prove to you both yesterday that I can be useful?"

More silence.

"Good God, Franky, give me a break here!" Irritated, Tazia pushed herself away from the table and sat sideways along the bench so that her back rested on the rough brick of the crypt wall. But she'd hardly settled before twisting back. "What exactly am I doing to him that's so bad?" Her voice came out in a low hiss.

For the first time, Franky looked straight into her wide eyes. He leaned forward himself so they were nose to nose. "You. Are. A. Manipulative. Little. Bitch." His voice cracked over the final word.

They both moved back abruptly. Cuinn had said they were "good folks." *Yeah right!*

It wasn't the words that shocked her—she'd been called a lot worse—it was the venom behind them. Had he managed to read her intentions after all?

Warming to his subject, he took a good long gulp of his beer. "I don't know what you've got planned for Cuinn, Anastasia. I saw it in you the first time we met. There's more confusion now," he gestured at the air around her. "But no one turns up in Detroit to do a little gun dealing on a whim and just happens to track down Conn O'Cuinn. There are far easier ways to make a fast buck in this town."

He took another long slug from his beer. Tazia waited for the question.

"I can't see everything going on with you, girl, but I can see you don't give a damn about money. So why are you here? Really?" Franky leaned back and crossed his arms, eyes piercing. His turn to wait.

Tazia's bravado left her. Her shoulders slumped, and eyes dropped to her drink. For a moment, she considered walking out. Surely, if she could get to Billy before the High Advocate did, they'd be able to think of a way to defend him?

She flicked Franky a look. He was peering at her strangely now. Like he could see into her mind. His aggression was replaced by curiosity. Strangely, the tats on her back were quiet.

Moving her eyes back to the table, she spoke, and it was as close from the heart as she could get without spilling her guts. "Franky, I know you're suspicious of me. Really. I get that. You're like Cuinn's dad…"

At that, she paused, thinking about her own father. Would he defend her? No, of course he wouldn't.

She caught Franky's eyes, willing him to understand. "I get that," she repeated, "looking out for someone." Finding the right words was a struggle. "Did you think of that? That the things we do aren't all driven by selfishness." She gave a small, regretful laugh. "Did you ever think, Franky, that I have a duty, too, every bit as strong as Cuinn's? And just like you, I have people to look out for?"

A moment of sympathy flashed through his eyes and was gone. He shook his head slowly, his mouth hardening, but said nothing.

He wouldn't back down. She sighed again and shook her head. "No, of course not. I'm a bitch, after all!"

This is useless. *Plan B, then.*

She stood to leave, but as she started to slide out of the bench, Franky grabbed her arm. "Having people to care about and Causes to fight doesn't make any difference, Tazia—" he yanked her toward him so she was inches away from his mouth "—it just makes you dangerous!" He threw away her arm as if it was something disgusting.

Speechless, Tazia turned away to leave and slammed straight into Cuinn's chest. With his broad frame preventing her exit on one side and the table blocking her on the other, she had nowhere to go. He must have been watching them from the bar and had seen enough to step in. "Sit down, Tazia, please."

Trapped, her hand had settled on her knife.

He gently placed his own hand on hers and leaned into her ear, his lips almost touching. "I thought we were friends, darlin'."

"I don't know what we are." She still felt threatened, but took her hand off the knife and sat heavily down in the booth again. Cuinn slid in beside her, heat rolling off him.

He had brought a bottle with him and four glasses. Before he poured, he called Kevin over and gestured for him to sit down next to Franky.

"There are things to do, Cuinn. Customers to serve, so there are," said Kevin.

"They can wait."

"But—"

"Sit."

Kevin sat, chewing on the inside of his cheek. Not meeting her eyes.

Cuinn passed glasses around. He raised his own to them all. Before drinking, he addressed Franky and Kevin. "I told Tazia we'd drink to a successful job together. That's why she's here. On my invitation."

It was a challenge.

Both Franky and Kevin raised their glasses, though Franky still studied the glass rather than look either Cuinn or Tazia in the eyes.

The three spoke in unison, "*Sláinte!*"

Cuinn smiled and turned to Tazia, raising his glass again. "*Sláinte*, Tazia, to a job well done!" He chinked the glass against hers, which still sat untouched in front of her, then downed the whiskey. Immediately he poured more into each of the empties before anyone had a chance to leave the table.

Tazia took a big breath, picked up her glass, and knocked her drink back in silence. Cuinn kept topping her glass until the tremor in her leg dulled and she stopped gripping the table in front of her. She was still debating whether to make a leap over him and run out the door.

Like he read her mind, he splashed whiskey into her glass again and gently put a hand on her leg to try to still the tremor himself. "Get another bottle there, Kev," he ordered the younger man. "This is gonna take two."

———

Another bottle down. Conn saw shoulders easing at the table for the first time that night.

For him, it was a balancing act to get Tazia feeling more comfortable while not pissing off his men. Christ, but it was a bloody work in progress.

Franky and Kevin kept a very close eye on his interactions with Tazia. When he spoke to her, they watched. When he looked back at them, they dropped their eyes. *Feckin' eejits.*

She, on the other hand, was now leaning back in the booth, her arms resting on the table and playing with her glass by passing it from one hand to the other. Conn saw how often she smiled as she listened to him talk and had stopped eyeing the doorway for a quick getaway.

Slowly, the four of them chatted more easily. Stories started slipping out, even a few half-arsed jokes. Not comfortable, but a truce sure enough.

By the time the third bottle ran dry and the Club had thinned out, Conn leaned forward. "Tazia, are you up for a little recon tomorrow?" He watched her response carefully, saw her brow furrow and her pupils contract. He needed her to see the invitation had no agenda.

She nodded. "Sure, Cuinn. Just need an extra pair of eyes?"

"Yeah, darlin'. I want someone who isn't known, who can get a little closer than I'd be able to."

She nodded at him again. "Sure."

Both Franky and Kevin leaned back from the huddle. The air tightened again.

Closing time had come and gone, and tonight wasn't a night for a lock-in. Bed was calling. "Time for home, gentlemen," he said to Kevin and Franky.

Franky now hunched over his drink, looked dejected. Was it the booze, or his questioning Conn's judgement? He respected the old man, but the criticism was starting to wear thin.

Kevin, on the other hand, acted like he'd been released from jail. He shot up out of his seat. "Time, gents. Out!" He barked at the remaining customers and started clearing glasses and swabbing tables loudly.

Conn sighed. Unification could wait. Now sleep. "I'll walk you out, Tazia."

She looked at him, eyes narrowed, and took a big step away.

He suspected being escorted to the door wasn't behaviour she was used to, unless, of course, she was being kicked through it. Hell, he could see she was suspicious of it. For the *craic*, he opened the door for her too and bowed his head. "Your highness!"

She smirked and nodded her own head before walking through.

"Till tomorrow, darlin'. I'll come to your place at zero eleven hundred, okay?"

She turned back and raised an eyebrow. "You know vampires sleep during the day, right?"

"These guys never seem to sleep."

She jumped up the steps outside and was gone in a second.

He turned to find both Kevin and Franky looking at him, arms crossed and standing side by side. They said nothing, which alarmed him more than if they'd both spoken at once.

"Jaysus, is this an intervention?" *Not in the mood, gentlemen.* "It's all right, I know what I'm doing. Just give her a chance."

"I'm not saying you shouldn't, Conn. I'm all out of reasons to give you to make you question her motives. I just want you to keep your eyes open, son." Franky slapped him on the shoulder before walking out the door Conn still held wide open. "See you tomorrow, boys."

Kevin went back to cleaning up.

"You think the same as Franky?" Despite his tiredness, Conn wanted the other man's opinion and gave him the opening.

Kevin made a couple more circular wipes of the bar top with his rag and paused. He stared at the shining top. "To be honest, Cuinn, I don't know what to make of her. You're seeing something we're not and I'm just wondering what it is, so I am."

He stopped, shrugged, then pointed his hand with the rag still clutched tight toward Conn. "It's not like you to think with yer dick, so I wouldn't insult you to say that's what's going on here. But there's something, all right. It's… intense, is all I can say. Like magick's in play. Just be careful, man. She's not army. She shouldn't know all our goings-on."

Conn locked the front door. Kevin would let himself out when he was done. Imitating Franky's action, he slapped the barman on the shoulder as he walked past and into the back rooms. *Sleep.*

25

ABSOLUTE FOCUS

TAZIA FELT she was reliving her experience from a few days before. This time, though, she was perched on a roof, watching the movements of vampires entering and exiting a warehouse. Instead of spying on an Irish demon she'd yet to meet, he lay just twenty feet away. She now knew the sound of his voice, his scent, the feel of his touch, and how the warmth of his smile allowed her to forget those marks on her back for a while. Funny how quickly things changed.

They had come by foot. Not in Cuinn's territory—a gruff old F-250 truck would have brought too much attention. Gruff was his word; she'd called it *a noisy pile of shite* in her best Dublin accent, earning her a look like she'd insulted his ma and a forty-five minute route march. A *silent* march that Tazia found as irritating as hell. *North Africa had been better!*

Lying on her back, she stretched her arms above her head and alternated between watching the vultures circle over Zug Island—now used as a body dumping ground, she's heard— and staring at the sky. The day was overcast. Not one spot of blue. The sun, just a patch of bright mist, dropped quickly toward the horizon.

In the heavy haze, the vampires on the ground moved back and forth without the aid of cover. They shifted blue plastic barrels from a truck to the warehouse.

She drummed her fingertips beside her and counted down from one hundred to see how long she could stand the heat searing through her t-shirt before moving. She made it to sixty, twenty more than last time. Back on her front, she recommenced the tapping, this time mouthing lines from "Down With The Sickness." The song had stuck in her head all day.

They'd been here for hours, and Tazia wondered for the hundredth time when Cuinn would give her the all-clear to approach the vampires below and get an answer to what was in those plastic barrels. He didn't think much of her joke about chicken noodle soup, or the pulped remains of some poor horse headed to the pet food factory.

Tazia looked across to Cuinn, who lay flat on his stomach, a rifle resting in his left hand and butting up to his raised right shoulder "just in case." He was not ready to fire it and was not even looking through the sights. He hadn't twitched since they'd arrived. Absolute focus, like he was carved from stone.

The muscles at the base of her skull were cramping, so she rotated her head warily, hearing every creak and click before the muscles settled back into place again. *Fuck this!*

Tazia jumped up, and moving away from the edge of the roof overlooking the vampires, she circled backward and then over to Cuinn, noisily coming up on him from behind. She settled beside him, also lying on her front.

He turned his head to look at her. "You're not the greatest at following orders, darlin', are yer?"

Tazia shrugged slightly, acknowledging the truth of his comment. "Can I get down there, yet? We've been here forever."

"Maybe. What's your report?" He turned back to the view.

"Report?" He sounded just like Hux.

She pushed away her hair and scooted a little closer to the edge as if she'd suddenly see something new from this angle.

"Yeah, Tazia. Numbers. Routines. Behaviours. You know the drill. Sure you do." He looked at her again, waiting.

*Christ, this **was** North Africa!*

"Oh. Ten vamps. Misfits. No vibe—nothing tying them together but the job. Six have been in and out, the other four went in soon after we got here. The four that went in were all mature, probably around two hundred. The six outside are younger, three just babies. Five deliveries so far. They're coming at ten to fifty minute intervals and taking around twenty minutes to unload. Last two loads had fifteen barrels—"

His look stopped her mid-flow, and he smiled broadly. "Now there's me thinking you were just enjoying the sunshine and singing heathen songs."

"Did I really sing out loud?"

"Aye!"

"Oh!" She smirked, too. "Did I miss anything, Captain?"

"Lots." He looked back at the view below. "They each have at least one knife, and the two standing guard have sidearms. Four older vamps are now on the fourth floor by the window. And Tazia…"

"Yeah?"

"It's OC."

"Sir. Yes, sir." *Not my army, honey.*

She got the look—the one Hux gave her all the bloody time. "Anything else?" Delivered with a grin this time.

"Last thing, yer man second from left has got a fresh limp and was at the fight the other night with the Italian you killed." He stopped and looked at her. "I didn't think any of those got away, but I missed one. That was sloppy!"

At least he criticized himself too. It showed his professionalism. Up to now, she hadn't allowed his training to be a consideration in her plans. She didn't have a choice, so what was the point? Now it alarmed her.

Tazia regulated her breath before she wound herself up. She'd go up against him soon enough. *Just focus on the job, Taz.* "So, is it time?"

He looked her straight in the eyes. His final check. "Yes. But no risks, Tazia, and no screw-ups, please? Just get in, see if you can find anything out about what's going on and who's involved, then back out. I'll have them in my sights the whole time."

She gave him a small nod.

"And Tazia?"

"Yep?"

"Never use the word *vibe* on a job again!"

She winked at him and was gone before he could list more things not to do.

―――――

Her plan was simple: she'd walk past the warehouse, casually engage in conversation with the vampires, and get a look at what was in the barrels. If she could also find out who their boss was, that would be a bonus.

Her bigger goal, however, was to impress Cuinn and prove her allegiance once and for all.

The last thing Cuinn had said to her was to not take any risks. But she'd have to do this her way. She'd settle for not taking stupid risks as a concession to his order.

Tazia circled the building, approaching the warehouse from the south side of the city. Looking up, she saw the hawk following her path high above her. Cuinn would be doing likewise, watching her. The bird and the soldier were in harmony; it gave her confidence.

She sauntered to a delivery truck that had pulled up outside the warehouse. Two vampires jumped up on the running board at the back to open the doors, just as she called to them. "Hey there!" She smiled. "Do you have a light, boys?" She gestured with the hand in which she held the cigarette to ensure there were no misunderstandings. The knife strapped to her thigh glinted in the sun.

One of the vampires, the older-looking one, dropped down from the back of the truck. A skinny-Jim, but sturdy by his well used arms. His moustache and muscle shirt owed a lot to the eighties. He looked her up and down. "Where did you come from, honey?"

"Round the corner." She gestured behind her. "I was passing through, looking to pay a visit to an old friend."

She got closer to the vampire who had spoken, stopping a few feet from him. The younger guy had a hand on his hip, halfway to the knife that she already knew was stuck into the back waistband of his jeans, and the other holding a bag of candy. He crunched. She focused her attention on the older guy. "You may know him, actually? Tall guy. Italian. Long hair. Name of Antonio."

"You talking about Antonio Giovanetti?" The vampire on the ground had taken a few more steps and was wiggling a lighter from the tight front pocket of his jeans. As she nodded, he walked over and lit the cigarette for her, his suspicion gone.

"He's dead, honey! Sorry." As abruptly as it came, the vampire looked genuinely concerned about delivering the news and hovered next to her while she took a long drag from her cigarette and he lit one of his own. "Some tussle with that Corktown Soldier. Antonio decided he'd teach him a lesson, only they got jumped and most of the vamps were killed from what I hear."

He paused, and she watched as the nicotine started to relax him. He slumped a little, taking his weight more on one foot rather than holding himself so upright. "You a relative of his? You sound sorta foreign."

"Yes, on my father's side." She spoke in what she hoped was a pensive way and dropped her arm to her side limply, slightly shaking her head. "Man, this place. I've only been here for a few days, and it's just… dangerous. I was looking for Antonio to see if he could set me up with some work for a while and thought I'd stay around. But now… maybe I should move on?"

The vampire who'd given her the light appeared to be relaxed now. The younger one opened the back of the truck and put down the ramp so that they could start unloading. It contained more of the blue plastic barrels.

Stubbing out the cigarette, the older vamp headed back to the truck. "Well, sorry to deliver the news, honey, but I'd better get on or I won't have a job either!" He took a few large strides up the ramp.

She didn't want to lose his attention that quickly. "So, you work here?" She looked at him and gestured toward the warehouse. "Do you think they'd have anything for me?"

He stopped and looked at her with a frown. "What can you do?"

"Just about anything, man. I'm strong. Can unload those barrels if you like." Before they could stop her, she jumped up on the back of the truck, flipped a barrel on its side and started to push it down the ramp. She leaped in front of it before it went too far and stopped it at the bottom with her foot before flipping it on its end again.

"How's that?" She gave them a broad smile, the cigarette still clamped between her lips.

He rushed over to her, at least as fast as she was now that he was motivated. "Oh, just fine if you want to kill us, you dumb bitch!"

Tazia furrowed her brow at his change of tone and gave him a wide-eyed, hurt stare.

"There are chemicals in there, girl!" He grabbed the cigarette from her mouth and threw it ten feet away. "One little spark and we all go up!"

"Oh! Sorry!"

The hawk above her was screaming, and even the younger vampire looked up to see where the noise was coming from. Maybe the bird was picking up on Cuinn's discomfort at the vampire's sudden aggression. *Don't you move, Cuinn.*

"Hey, I was just trying to show you I could help. I can take better care now I know. What's all this for, anyway?" She gestured to the barrels.

"Not for us to know, girl." The vampire paused and sighed deeply. "Look, do you want me to put a word into the boss? I think he knew your Antonio. Might be that he can find you some work?"

"That'd be great!" Tazia feigned enthusiasm, taking a couple of steps toward him, a smile on her face. She drew the line at jumping up and down, but she let a little bounce into the movement. What should her next move be? Get inside the warehouse and meet this guy or hang back to get more information?

The vampire started to walk toward the door of the warehouse. "I'll see what he says."

She called after him. "I'll go in with you. Might help if he met me and I can tell him about Antonio."

"Nope, hun, you stay here. I'll be right back." He disappeared into the building.

Decision made for her, Tazia turned her attention to the younger vampire, who was rolling the barrels carefully down the ramp and then rearranging them by the door to the warehouse. "So, this stuff could blow a hell of a hole in something, right?"

The younger vampire stopped and gestured to her to come over to him. He leaned against the last barrel he'd stacked, legs apart and breathing a little heavily from the exertion.

For the first time, she looked at him properly. He was a good-looking guy, about eighteen or nineteen when he was turned. He had blond hair, cut short and pushed back on top, and a short-sleeved tee that showed off some well-shaped muscles and plenty of tattoos. A gym rat.

He looked her up and down carefully, his eyes hovering where they shouldn't. "I know what they're planning to use it for." He smirked at her.

Okay, I'll bite.

"Yeah?" She jumped up and sat on the barrel beside him and swung her legs a little, then twisted around so that her knees were rubbing against the side of his thigh.

He leaned over to her and whispered, "They're gonna blow those fucking Soldier dudes away, baby!"

She traced the tribal ink on his arm with her fingertip. "The Irish dude your friend was talking about?"

He nodded, cocky as hell, moving in for a kiss. His breath smelled of sour apples from the candy he'd scarfed earlier.

Tazia pulled back, keeping him hanging. "When are they gonna do it?"

He shrugged, still angling for her lips. "Soon. We get the last barrels today."

She'd heard enough. Slipping off the barrel, she pushed him away.

He wasn't having it. He shoved her back down, wrist grinding into her collarbone, knife tip pricking her throat. *Wow. How the fuck did that happen?*

She clawed sideways, fingertips brushing her knife handle. *One more centimetre…* "Look, babe, this is a mistake." Her teeth clenched. With his bodyweight pinning her arm, his free hand crept lower. *No fucking way.*

But now her right leg was free…

Too late. The hawk screamed above, and she knew—

Crack! The shot pinged off the edge of the knife, sparks blinding her. *Jesus, Cuinn, too fucking close!*

Before Cuinn missed another shot, Tazia drove her knee up hard between the boy's legs. He arced to one side and landed, crumpled and screaming. As he raised his face to her, the second shot punched him between his eyes with a flat crack, and he was on his back, blood pooling under his head.

Tazia sighed and shook her head trying to get her hearing back in her right ear. Another five seconds was all she'd needed. Cuinn just brought down hell on her!

She found herself stranded in the middle of an all-out gunfight. Vampires streamed out of the warehouse, knives out, and guns firing vaguely at the rooftop opposite. Overhead, Cuinn's rifle cracked, dropping bodies one by one.

A large vampire spotted Tazia and lunged. She vaulted over the nearest barrel, circling fast until she was at his back. He skidded to a stop, arms cartwheeling like a cartoon character braking too late. Tazia kicked him square in the butt, sending him sprawling forward. Her knife already in her hand.

As he rose to his knees, she yanked his head back by his hair and cut into his throat, piercing the flesh with the tip of her knife before pushing down like she was slicing a birthday cake. *Sweet.*

Footsteps pounded behind her. Jaws wide, the vamp pounced from six feet away. As he flew, she lifted her leg, her sole meeting him square in his middle. She flipped him over her and he crashed to the dust behind. Struggling to get to his feet, he let out a stream of expletives.

Laughing now, Tazia stomped to where he floundered. The knife repeated its pattern, silencing his curses to a gurgle. "Save your breath, stupid!" Blood spurted into her open mouth mid quip. She swallowed before she could spit. *Yep. One to tell Billy later.*

The gunfire thinned. Tazia looked around. Cuinn's neat corpses lay scattered across the lot. *Show off!* Her two were all gruesome, with necks open and leaking blood.

She did the math. All accounted for apart from the shadows that moved behind the warehouse windows. Money men? Bosses? Her eyes flicked to the blue barrels stacked by the open doors and estimated the distance from her to them. All that firepower for the Club.

By the crunch of gravel behind her, Cuinn was on the move. A glance behind and she saw him running around the corner toward her, shotgun ready.

She couldn't wait.

Kicking over the closest barrel, she drove her knife down into it and twisted until liquid sprayed and then seeped from it. The chemical smell burned her eyes. She booted it forward, the drum rolling, spilling its shining trail toward the stacked cache.

Lighter out. Thumb strike. The blue flame jittered, then settled.

"Don't—" Cuinn shouted. Too late.

She flicked it. The fire took instantly, racing along the trail. She was already running.

Cuinn stopped too, eyes wide. She winked as she flew past him. Then he spun and sprinted after her.

The first detonation ripped through the air and threw them both off their feet. The shockwave slammed them into the doorway of the building they'd been scouting from. Teeth rattled in her skull. She curled, arms tight, tasting grit and chemicals.

The second blast hit harder. Roaring into the sky. Masonry ripped free. Concrete chunks flung like screeching rockets around them. The building above started to crack, raining debris. Then the flames—white-hot—attacked the dark sky.

Cuinn didn't wait. He yanked her up, and they sprinted blind through the flame-shot black. The heat from the fire slapped at her spine. They slowed only when the bridge loomed ahead and had its cover. Irish territory. Safe—for now.

At the old public boat ramp, the noise of the explosions had receded. Cuinn sat heavily on the river wall, and Tazia, still gasping for breath, slid to the ground beside his legs. The hawk flew down and settled on Cuinn's shoulder. It nuzzled his ear. A slight smell of burning feathers came from the bird, but it was no worse for wear.

Behind them, the warehouse and its neighbour had split open, belching smoke and scarlet streaks into the setting sun.

26

BACKLASH

CUINN AND TAZIA stumbled into the Club to find Kevin waiting alone. One look at their bloodstained clothing and hollow eyes, and he poured doubles, pushing the glasses into their hands. They both collapsed onto the bar stools and downed the drinks.

Every step from the blast site had tested Tazia. She still hadn't told Cuinn what had happened outside the warehouse. She lacked both the words and the energy. That blast was fucking amazing—and terrifying.

It was unclear whether he was angry. Apart from checking she wasn't seriously injured, he hadn't spoken. His shoulders slumped, as if like her, he suddenly felt the weight of every year he carried.

"That explosion, was it you?" Kevin asked, topping up both glasses with a heavier hand this time.

Cuinn nodded. "The recon took more of an active turn."

Kevin rolled his eyes. It looked like amazement, not attitude. But hell, what did she know? This guy didn't exactly have a hard on for her.

"You're okay?" Kevin looked like he wasn't sure whether to stay or go.

"We're fine. I'll debrief you tomorrow, Kev. Get along home to that wife of yours."

Kevin nodded and walked toward the door, slapping Cuinn on the back. He spoke low as he walked past but she picked it up just the same. "Just tell me, man, do I have to be worried? Backlash?"

"Are you serious, lad? There's no one left to worry about!"

Tazia watched the whole exchange, trying to figure out if it meant trouble for her, then went back to staring into her glass. A little dragon, the stamp of the glassmaker, peered back through the whiskey. It seemed to wink at her. Maybe she was just too wired to see straight.

Cuinn heaved himself off his stool to lock the door behind Kevin, then lifted the bottle of whiskey from the counter. With his hand on her shoulder, he guided her to the easy chairs in front of the fire. The flames were low and cast just a slight amber glow in the darkness.

After sitting, Tazia couldn't get a read on herself. Her mind was full of images, but her body felt silent and still. Numb. Even the ink was quiet.

The blast's ferocity had rocked her. Hot ashes scorched her skin. Deafening explosions, blinding flashes—all of it. Like they'd escaped the jaws of a monstrous beast. Was it still chewing on the parts of herself she'd left behind?

While her human side was in shock, her demon side was delighted at the carnage she'd been responsible for. For a few more minutes, she let them both play. Then, with her hand trembling, she gulped from her glass to blank the human out. The demon needed to be in control again.

She lifted her eyes to study Cuinn's face and bearing.

He seemed calm, staring into the fireplace, and swirling his whiskey in a haphazard manner around the glass, the rim only just stopping the spill.

"What can you see?" she asked.

He looked from the fire to her. "What?"

"In the fire?"

"To be honest, darlin', just flames right now." He grinned. "And screaming vampires."

It wasn't the response she was expecting. Tazia had been waiting for him to chastise her. After all, he had said, no risks. His smile loosened her tongue.

"There was a reason, you know, why it all went to shit." She wanted him to know that she wasn't this screwball fuck-up who couldn't stick to a plan.

"I'm sure there was Tazia, darlin'." Although he continued to smile, he seemed serious. Even leaned forward a little more in his seat as if to convince her that he was being straight. "It all seemed under control until that little eejit decided he had eyes for yer. I wasn't expecting him to pull the knife, though!"

"Me neither." She scooted her chair towards Cuinn as though a closer proximity would make her words more convincing. "The chemicals in the barrels were to make explosives. They were coming after the Unit. Revenge."

She sat back. "I guess I just reacted. So much for training, huh?" All that discipline from military types over the years, come to nothing.

"Sounds like it needed to be done. And I guess we don't have to worry about retribution for a while. No vampires left."

He raised his glass to her.

Was his calm genuine? It seemed to be. In the short time she'd known him, Tazia had come to believe Cuinn didn't play games.

"Apart from me." She said flatly.

He didn't give her exactly what she wanted, but what he

did say interested her greatly. "I said before, darlin', you can't help being what you are—"

"That's not what you said. You said you can't help where you were born…"

He shrugged and stared back at the fire before continuing, "None of us can help what we are, or where we come from. Sometimes even what we've done in the name of things we thought were important. We just have to live with it."

The statement seemed to say a lot less about her situation and more about his own. Curious. The fire flared momentarily as it grabbed a new piece of kindling.

Was this it? A weakness? Was he questioning his Cause? She wrestled with her quickening heart—he mustn't get wind of it. The tattoos had woken and gripped tight.

But Cuinn didn't seem to be listening to her excited heartbeat. "I messed up today, Tazia. Missed that first shot." He shook his head. "I could have killed you."

"Were you trying to?" Semi-serious, she couldn't help herself.

"No, darlin'. No way!" He put down his glass and swivelled in his seat to face her. "It was my job to cover you, and I failed."

Tazia watched his eyes oscillating between every shade of blue and back again. She'd learned that blue was the colour of his eyes when he was focusing—or mad. She missed the green. "You don't seem the type to botch shots, Cuinn."

He half smiled and shook his head. "Recently I am. I don't know what's going on with me. Honest, darlin', all I know is my mind's full of the past, and just when I need to focus or relax, it comes rushing back at me." He turned to the fire. "You asked me what I saw in the flames?"

She nodded.

"My wife, that's what. Her dead eyes."

She sucked in a breath.

Cuinn let his head fall into his right hand for a moment; speaking the words aloud seemed to have drained him. "I see her everywhere—in the flames, in my dreams. Fuck, even on the roof just now, standing in the way of my shot."

Tazia listened intently. Flames crackled in the background.

"I can't sleep, Tazia. Night after night, just replaying the past. Going over old decisions, choices I made. Things I thought I'd got over years ago."

Is this that angel bitch?

The exhaustion, the bad judgement, the missed shots. It all made sense. He was being set up to fail, to question himself. So she, Tazia, could swoop in and take advantage of that vulnerability. *And I thought my father was an evil fucker!*

She had to take advantage, of course. Make this the moment to convince him to give up the Cause. Tell him she could make the visions go away. But instead she let the human talk. It was easy. "It happens to me, too." She shrugged as he turned to look at her. "Memories. Things I've done. Promises I shouldn't have made. Christ, the deals to prove myself. Kills I shouldn't have made."

Her head was full. Hux was there. And, of course, Billy. But so were snapshots from her past. Images that still haunted.

Tazia squashed the human. She must turn this to her favour. *Save Billy.*

She pulled herself upright, poured another drink. "I guess, Cuinn, we're always going to have the past coming for us. You don't live as long as us without consequences. But, that said, we can't dwell on it, even if it damns us!" She raised her glass to him. "*Sláinte!*"

Cuinn tapped his glass against hers with a dull clink. "Well said, Tazia. *Sláinte!*"

He put the glass back down and took hers as well. Then, he

reached out, laying his hand gently on the side of her cheek, his eyes slowly transforming to sea-green, and kissed her.

Afterward, Tazia remembered his lips roughened from the fire, the chemical ashes still clinging to his hair, and the taste of whiskey on his tongue. But mostly, she remembered his green eyes.

27

BAND-AIDS

TAZIA WOKE SHORTLY AFTER DAWN, lying in Cuinn's bed. The pillow was still damp from her shower a few hours before. She'd scrubbed off the layers of vampire blood, dust, and ashes from the building collapse and crawled into his bed, exhausted.

Sitting up, she ran her hands over her hair, flattening the strands sticking out at odd angles. It would need wetting again most likely.

She took inventory of her injuries: a few aches and pains, one bad bruise on the side of her face, and a long cut across her knee from jagged glass blown out of some window. Cuinn had patched it up for her, then covered it with gauze. It was not bad having someone to play doctor with.

The hour before bed was still vivid in her mind. The first kiss and the ones that followed. The mutual desire to take it further in front of the dying embers of the fire. Even during sex she'd wondered, was it her demon or human side responding to him? Right now, it didn't seem to matter.

When they were done, they'd showered and assessed injuries, exchanging kisses for Band-Aids and sutures. Despite his armoured chest and steel-like bones, Cuinn had actually come off the worst of the two of them.

Tazia had done her best to stem the bleeding of a deep cut to his right arm. It looked like it was almost down to the bone. As she stitched him, she recalled the piece of molten metal he'd yanked from his flesh as they'd run away. Purple bruising covered his right side from shoulder to ankle. He had no recollection of how that had happened.

As she put her feet on the floor, testing her knee, Cuinn came in with her clothes, freshly washed and dried.

"Your non-blood-covered clothes, darlin'." He smiled and kissed her hard enough to make her fall back on her elbows with a laugh. He butterfly-kissed her stomach, tracing a line of equally light kisses up onto her rib cage and to the side of her neck. It made her shiver.

When he got to her ear, he whispered, "I have deliveries coming any minute, but will you stay for a while longer?"

She sighed, battling with herself. "I've got to go. I've got a call to make, London. It's important."

Cuinn's face dropped. "Who is this guy?"

"Billy?" She gave him a big smile. "He's family. I can't let him down. The text last night said it was urgent."

Cuinn put his hand on her stomach like he would object further. Instead, he kissed her again, and pulled her up from the bed.

Immediately, he clutched his side and winced. Her hand went to her own knee.

"Good God, we're falling apart, so we are!" he said. Cuinn straightened a little more carefully, just as the knock on the front door announced the deliveries he was expecting. "Tonight?"

She smiled. "Try stopping me!"

Cuinn left the room, and she dressed carefully, trying to pull her jeans over her knee so as not to interfere with the dressing. She stopped mid-pull. The mention of Billy recalled how that conversation had ended.

Maybe Cuinn was too exhausted, or too comfortable, but he let slip his own "family" were visiting on Friday—the bosses!

He'd joked that it'd be bad timing if the Council showed up to find the place—and their cash—blown to bits.

The damage was done. As he napped in the early hours, she'd stolen out of bed and photographed the digital lock on the strong room door. Sent it to Billy to work on while she carefully got back into bed beside Cuinn. She just hoped she'd have time to act before anyone checked the security recording.

Today was Thursday. She had just a few hours to finish the plan to steal whatever funds were in that back room. Tonight, she had to screw over a lover. *Again!*

The ink ate into her back—half panic, half excitement. She shoved it down. Demon or human didn't matter now. Only focus. She dragged on her jeans, skinning her knee and ripping off the stitches in the process. Sometimes pain was inevitable.

———

Kevin breezed past Cuinn with a "Mornin'!" ready to help with the delivery. A good night with Rose had lightened his spirits.

He was stacking beer barrels in a small side room adjacent to the bar itself when he saw Tazia emerge from the back hallway and walk toward the door. *What the fuck?*

When he saw her climb the steps outside and get a kiss from Cuinn before disappearing, his good mood dissolved.

Kevin finished the barrels, then shelved the whiskey, steaming silently as he banged the boxes down in precise rows. What the hell was Cuinn thinking? Despite everything he and Franky had said, he was still letting this demon girl into his life.

This just wasn't right.

Another thing—Cuinn wasn't sleeping. Most mornings Kevin found him already up, or still dozing in a chair by the fire. It had only got worse since Tazia turned up in Detroit.

He had to try again to make his brother see sense.

Cuinn brought in the last of the boxes of alcohol and started putting bottles away behind the bar. He walked stiffly and a few times clutched at his ribs. Nonetheless, he whistled an old Irish folk tune. *Cheerful!*

"You still sore?" Kevin asked casually.

"Aye, but healing quickly. Nothing a little time won't sort out, man."

Despite the words, Kevin could see he found the stretch to reach the higher shelves a bit more difficult than usual.

He stepped in to help. "So, I saw Tazia leaving."

"That's right." Cuinn's body seemed to stiffen further.

On dangerous ground, Kevin was committed. "Saw you kiss her, too."

Cuinn said nothing.

"So that's it now? You two together?" Kevin had never questioned Cuinn's relationships with women. They came and went occasionally. Like with most of the lads. No big deal.

"I'm thinking you don't approve there, Kev." Cuinn stopped placing the bottles, turned to face him, still speaking good-naturedly, but his eyes were ice blue. "Give me a reason right now not to tell you to mind yer own feckin' business."

It was a red rag to a bull: "I'll give you a fucking reason, Cuinn. You know nothin' about her. Since she turned up here, things have been fucking crazy, man! Why aren't you sleeping? Why are you coming back here so beaten up? That never happens. And you're even talking army business in front of her! It's not right." He was up in Cuinn's face, and though his arms were still by his sides, his fists clenched.

Cuinn didn't back off, nor did he move forward. He spoke calmly. "You're my friend, my brother, and my Second, Kevin.

You get this one last pass. But be sure, man, if you ever talk to me about Tazia again, and it's not to offer her a drink or to shine her feckin' shoes, you won't make it out of here in one piece."

He turned back to the shelves and continued stacking the bottles as though the exchange had not taken place.

"I don't know what's happened to you, but you're not the same man, so you're not. I'll see you later." As he left, Kevin slammed the Club door so hard the sound reverberated down the road.

28

———————————

IN HIS HEART

THE ABANDONED APARTMENT Soren Huxford occupied looked like a crime scene. A dust-sheet twisted under him on the bed, glass from a smashed lamp scattered across the floor. Flakes of dried blood peppered the rough white cotton. The rhythmic, metallic click-clack of his balisong, opening and closing, kept his heart steady.

Black smears clung to a glass shard beside him, the last trace of early hour slashes across his forearm.

Glassy-eyed, he stared at the door. Waiting for what? Someone to come through it? Her? She'd never come now.

He closed the knife, set it down, and let out a long breath. "Get a grip!"

At the sound of his voice, two lizards froze on the sun-warmed stone parapet just outside his open window, tongues stilled, eyes locking onto his.

He caught up the blond lengths of his hair in one hand and pulled them roughly to one side. *That's her too!* The movement she'd made a hundred times with her own hair. He'd told her to cut it properly, but she'd laugh, tip her head, hair spilling to show the smooth skin of her neck, before hacking at it with the Bowie. So little respect for herself. But so sweet.

"Fucking bitch!" The lizards streaked out of view, looking for cracks to vanish in.

No, I don't mean that.

The rebuke was automatic. Even as a soldier, he didn't join in the barracks talk. He'd not been brought up that way. He'd curse, sure. But insults were earned. She didn't deserve that. Respect and consideration were drilled into him. Even on a contract, it was quick, clean.

If the angel told him to kill her now, could he?

Anger threatened again, his chest ready to burst, but nothing left within reach to smash. *Box it up, soldier!* With clenched teeth, he swung himself around to sit on the side of his bed—

He still had his boots on!

His mother would not approve. Her hair had been long and blonde like his. *It smelled of lemons.*

Focus, Huxford.

His eyes drifted to his dark green combat trousers. They too were dirty and now covered in tiny little holes. Ashes. They'd settled on him as he ran around the devastation at the warehouse, looking for signs of life.

He'd screwed up earlier and lost track of Anastasia. When he heard the explosion, he was already out searching and went running, stomach clenching; she had to be in the middle of it. When he saw the mess of burned clothing and smouldering flesh slowly disintegrating to ash, he'd changed his mission to identification, not rescue.

He pushed aside half-melted barrels, picked through the wreckage, scanning blackened bodies one by one. When he couldn't find her, he dropped to the ground, maybe kneeling in her remains for all he knew, vomiting until only dry retches came.

Caught by the setting sun, the glint of metal two feet from him, stopped him short. Partly covered in soft, blackened muck: Anastasia's cigarette lighter. His blood turned to ice. But still, no body.

Now, sitting on the bed, he looked again at his trousers, at the red stains on his knees and the smears of black sludge on his boots. The sight disgusted him. He tore off his boots and thick army socks, ripped off his trousers and the rest of his clothes, and stood naked in the middle of the room. Better. He could breathe.

Despite the sour water, he scrubbed hard in the shower. A do-over, to scrape off what he'd seen. He rinsed. Clean. Calmer.

She was alive, of course. He'd heard a hawk's cry by the docks and, running toward it, saw her and Cuinn slip out of sight. There she was, limping but safe. *Thank God!*

Soren turned off the shower, wrapped a towel around his middle, and returned to the bed. The breeze from the window chilled his wet skin, steadying his breath, and untying the muscles across his chest.

He'd followed them back to Cuinn's place. Watched Kevin leave, then waited for Anastasia. Like always, he would trail her back to her building, settle in the doorway opposite, and watch til her light went out.

She never knew. Hell, she wouldn't care!

She wandered their apartment naked all the time, smiling, daring him closer. She'd laugh when he lifted her to the bed; and kiss him when he promised her the world. He'd still give it. Despite her games.

But now you're with him…

Outside the Irish Club, Soren had seen Cuinn lock the door. From his vantage point on the roof, he stood confused. Had she left and he'd missed it? He watched the low glow of the fire through the barred windows—the steady rhythm of the shadows moving in front of it.

He'd struggled to make sense of it. When it dawned on him, rage gripped tight, twisting. Cutting. Not with his brother!

Furious, Soren didn't know who to target first. Images flowed. Cuinn's skull split by his dagger. Anastasia's throat in his hands. Maybe both.

He'd stormed back to his squat, smashing at whatever he passed: walls, windows, trashcans, and arrived home with cracked fingers, split skin, and fragments of glass peppering his body. All healed by the time he crossed the threshold. *Too soon.*

Wanting the pain, he'd ripped at himself with the shard of glass, until it seeped from him and he fell into a daze.

But now, again, his anger turned inward. The disgust. The desperation. It lessened when the blood flowed.

He picked up his knife. Using the tip, he carved into his left forearm. Carefully forming each line, each curve. The cuts opened, seeped blood, sealed—and he began again. Over and over.

"Mooning over your demon lover won't get you anywhere, Soren Huxford!"

The sharp voice raised goosebumps on his skin. But he didn't jump. He'd known Jegudiel wouldn't leave him alone for long, and he recognized that lecturing tone.

His handiwork was precise. The first "A" was beginning to heal over. The other letters still stood deep red against his skin: "N - A - S - T - A - S - I - A." Abruptly, he rubbed at his arm, blood highlighting the gooseflesh for a moment until he rubbed again and stained his skin a uniform scarlet.

"I'm talking to you!"

"There was a setback. I'm working on it. The girl is safe." His report was terse. Still giving his full attention to the name on his arm.

"Soren!"

He snapped toward the voice. The features of a woman's face stared at him from the window pane across from the bed. Her nostrils flared, and her head jerked as she glared at him. "You are becoming insolent, boy, and I won't have it!"

Soren put down his knife and headed to the window. His wry smile forming in the pane's reflection and merging with the angel's image. "You call me a boy?" He faced her, standing his full six foot three, his broad frame blocking the light.

Hands in fists, his smile tightened. "I've hunted and slaughtered more men, women, and demons for you, Jegudiel, than any *boy* could have done." He spat the word at her.

"If there was any child left in me when we met, you've wiped that from me." He turned away from her, struggling to control himself. "And you dare scold me like I'm a child now, when I finally see Anastasia means something?"

He twisted back. "You did this to me! You said *get close*. I did. You told me to *keep her safe*. She is. So safe she's in my brother's arms. Now, what do I do? Forget her, and go back to being a *boy*?"

The urge to take a swing overwhelmed him, and he smashed his fist through the centre of the angel's face. The bottom pane of the old-fashioned sash window shattered, and the image disappeared.

For the second time that night, blood gushed from Soren's cut knuckles. He stared, watching it ooze and drip to the floor. When the pain failed to reach his brain with any real intensity, he roared.

"My, my, Soren, that's a nasty temper!" The angel reappeared in the wall mirror that hung on the far side of the room. Her voice softened. "I know she's been hard work, pet. I feel the same way."

He didn't approach her mirror. From where he stood, he

could see his own face reflected with hers. He looked gaunt: deep frown lines, sharp cheekbones. Symptoms of what? The heat? Lack of sleep? Love?

"But I still need you, Soren." Her tone was wheedling. "We're not quite done yet."

"What's your plan for her?" Tension clenched his gut again, but he wanted the end game.

Jegudiel raised an eyebrow. Assessing him.

"I need to know or I walk." This was the line. Even if it meant he'd lose the wards that circled his skin.

She nodded. "Yes. You're right. It's time. The half-breed will help me take my revenge. Once her soul is hers again, I will own her. That's what I shaped her for."

Chills ran through his body. "And the Irishman?"

"Destiny, pet. Conn O'Cuinn will make a sacrifice to free her soul from its bounds and, in so doing, her father from Hell." Her voice became a whisper. "Oh, my boy, it's been so long in coming. All those demons I had you kill, sweeping the path clear. The reward is almost here!"

Soren's mind ticked over. "And if Cuinn doesn't make this… sacrifice?"

"Oh don't worry. Fate always has a backup plan." She giggled.

"And Anastasia? What happens to her once she's yours?"

"When she thinks she is free? That's when it begins. With me by her side, she'll turn creation upside down!"

Her eyes deadened. "But let me be clear, boy. Finish your contract. Keep Anastasia safe, no matter who she fucks, and hand her to me when I ask. If you don't, I will take more from you than your pretty skin charms, pet—I will take your life." And then she was gone.

He almost laughed. Death would be a mercy, but not if it left Anastasia in the angel's hands. Not if it meant Cuinn would sacrifice, what… his life? Something else? This wasn't contract or duty anymore.

Soren loved exactly two people, and Jegudiel would never touch either of them.

———

He needed out of that room. Back out on the road, Soren ended up in front of the Irish bar again, perched on the roof opposite, watching the entrance become slowly illuminated by the sun.

His mind was not on a stakeout.

The conversation with the Advocate had rocked him. He knew what it was to be Jegudiel's pawn: he'd lost all freedom since he'd agreed to help her years ago, and he didn't want that for Anastasia.

But now he knew Jegudiel's plan was bigger than him. Bigger than Anastasia. To *turn creation upside down*? She could do it. And Anastasia was the lynchpin. It started with this sacrifice.

To stop whatever Anastasia was planning for Cuinn, he'd likely have to blow her cover. Then, get her to safety. Irish revenge was never easy, she wouldn't survive it.

His relationship with Cuinn was unbreakable. More than the Unit; the Soldier had given him a family. Showed him self-respect came first. It came to a head in Bali, but if not then, someplace else. Soren owed him everything.

The crash of the door startled him. Kevin stormed down the street away from the Club.

That was it!

Soren grabbed his rifle and followed the Soldier. He maintained his place above, jumping from roof to roof, navigating the change in levels skillfully, all the time keeping his eye on the demon. Kevin turned east.

At the end of the row of houses, Soren snaked down the fire escape, then walked into the middle of the street. "Kevin!" He held his rifle far to his side, away from his body, and held his other arm up high to show he was not a threat.

Kevin turned, pistol already pointed, but stopped. "Hux? Jaysus, man, is that really you?"

"Yep. How are you, Micky-K?" Soren used the affectionate nickname he had for Kevin—the only one who could get away with it. The two men approached each other and back-slapped their greeting, moving to the side of the street to catch up on how long it had been since they'd last seen each other.

"Does Cuinn know you're here?"

"Not yet. Keeping a low profile. On a job." Soren settled himself on a low wall that ran in front of an old kitchen appliance repair store.

"Tracked the target back to the Club last night. She was with Cuinn." Soren watched the Soldier carefully. It was time to find out how much of an impression Anastasia was making in Detroit.

Kevin's body stiffened; his enjoyment at seeing an old army mate appeared to dampen. "You mean Tazia? She's your mark?"

"You know her?"

"She's trouble, isn't she?" Kevin was looking for validation so hard, it was easy for Soren to play on it.

Soren nodded. "Yep. I've tracked her from Turin. And watched her cozy up with Cuinn." He paused. "She's dangerous, Kev."

"I knew it!" Kevin's whole body seemed to exhale. "I've been trying to tell him, but he's just too fucking stubborn to listen."

"Are they… together?" Soren couldn't stop himself from asking.

"Looks like!"

Soren covered the tension in his body with a shrug. "He'll listen to me. I can tell him stories, man. He'll look at her in a different light when I'm done."

"And what's your deal with her?" Kevin asked.

"Unfinished business." He paused. "So, you want my help?"

29

A VERY WEAK PLAN

"IT'S STILL A VERY weak plan, Taz." Billy's face stared at her from the screen of the tablet she'd propped against the backboard of her bed. She'd only gotten back from Cuinn's half an hour ago—and, to her surprise, the connection had gone through immediately.

She sat cross-legged, ignoring Billy, and instead watched as a little blood oozed from the wound on her knee. Now and again she wiped the mess with her fingers and sucked them absently.

"Just stop! That's gross!"

"Sorry." She wasn't.

"All this happens tomorrow? The money is there ri—" He broke off, turning from the screen, and pushed away from the desk a little. She heard the sound of water running.

"There's one in the cupboard in the bathroom, bruv," Billy said to someone she couldn't see. There was a muffled "thanks" in a man's voice, the sound of a door closing and the water receding.

He pulled himself back to the desk and continued as

though the interruption hadn't occurred. "The money's in the Club right now?"

"Hang on, who was that?"

"Who?"

"The guy?"

"What guy?" he said, looking her straight in the eyes.

"Stop messing, Billy. The guy in the shower."

Billy looked like he was deciding whether to tell her. Then he grinned and leaned forward. "That's Thomas."

"He's a boyfriend?"

Billy shrugged a little noncommittally. "Sure."

"You call the guy you just slept with 'bruv'?" She said.

"What do you want me to call him?"

"Honey. Darling. Sweetie. Baby. Stud! Pick one!"

Billy laughed.

"What's he like?"

"I decided to vary my usual menu just slightly. He's still blond, but not Barbie-doll, and…" He moved forward even further and spoke with a whisper and wide eyes, "he actually talks sense most of the time!"

"Wow! Refreshing! The two of you *talk!* You going to keep him?" she asked.

"What, stick a collar round his neck like a fluffy puppy? Perhaps I should add a little bell so I can hear when he's coming?" Billy deadpanned, then winked. "I like him, all right? Leave it at that."

She smiled. "Perhaps there's hope for one of us after all. So, do you have everything you need to break the lock?"

Billy became all business again, too. "Yes, I can break the security system. Those pictures you got me this morning showed the serial numbers. The cameras will be down, too. I've already primed a trigger for the safe. From my side, we're okay." He paused. "Just text me when you're ready to go in. It'll take a couple of minutes for the spell to take effect. Text me the amount and I'll put money in that Kevin-guy's account. I've already set up a back door to the bank—it'll look like he made a cash deposit."

In silence, she fiddled with a Bic lighter she'd found lying around the room, just flicking it on and off.

"What is it, Taz?"

She threw the lighter aside. "I have a bad feeling. Not just about the job itself—we've been in tighter spots than this and still managed to make it work, but about what I'm doing to Cuinn." She looked at him, eyebrows furrowing. "It's wrong, Billy."

"Your lack of soul doesn't stop you feeling the guilt, then?" he said, a little surprised.

"I still have it, and all my feelings, I just mostly don't understand them or can ignore them easy enough."

"Maybe you're starting to like him, too..."

She looked away from the camera, catching her breath. "It's more than that. Yes, I like him, but we're going to destroy everything that's close to him—his whole identity will be gone. And say he did give up the Cause for me, then what? I walk away, do the next thing on the High Bitch's list, and he's left with nothing. Soul or no soul, anyone can see that's wrong!"

"So, don't do it." It sounded simple. "If you do this, and you feel as bad as you think you will, it might destroy you. You'll end up with a pissed-off Soldier demon after you—as well as Hux. Christ, girl, you might as well just disappear off the face of the planet now."

They sat and looked at each other, the connection flickering every now and again, breathing together.

Shit, I need to lie to him.

Tazia broke the silence. "Last night, I dreamed of my father. He was burning in the Red River. Demons tearing at him, climbing over his body to escape. His face turned to me— desperate."

"It was just a dream." Billy said.

"But it's not, is it? He's really there." Then, in a small voice, she said, "I thought I could do it, Billy. I thought I could forget him. Move on. Leave Cuinn alone. But I can't leave him there. I just have to do this one last thing." *And I have to keep you safe, too!*

Through the audio she heard the rain battering the window panes of Billy's flat in London. *Beautiful.* The trees were still green there, too. For now, anyway.

Billy broke the silence. "Well, let's do this! Tonight." He came up really close to the screen, his deep brown eyes with their long lashes gazing at her intently. "We've got your back, Taz. Me and Josh. Don't forget that, love." A kiss into the camera, and then he was gone.

Tazia turned off the tablet. She went to the window, wishing for rain there, too. At only nine in the morning, the heat already shimmered off the cracked pavement, and lizards basked.

Her eyes snapped to a movement in the doorway of the thrift store opposite. The security gate had been forced open, and inside, a figure sheltered. A man.

For a moment, she swore he'd looked right at her. He moved. The sun flashed on something metallic, blinding her. She blinked to clear her bleached vision. Another look. More cautious this time. No one there, but she knew better.

Hux had found her.

———

That evening, Tazia got to the Club at the busiest time. A packed house meant cover—two minutes to slip into the back, grab the cash, and be back on her stool before anyone missed her. She took a place at the bar and winked at Cuinn who was serving. He looked stressed. Where was Kevin?

Franky was in his usual booth talking to a couple of demons she didn't recognize. He didn't acknowledge her presence. The truce had failed to stick. Tazia shoved her glass back and forth. They'd never trust her.

In a lull of customers, Cuinn came over, bent close and gave her a quick kiss on the top of her head. Then he refilled her glass.

"It's pretty busy for you to be on your own," Tazia said. She gesticulated to another group of demons who were just coming in the door. "Wow, they just keep coming!"

"Yeah, darlin'. The Unit's been out training. They're looking to play now." Cuinn continued to clean the bar down while he had the opportunity and then started to lay out glasses of beer for the guys who had just come in.

"Where's Kevin? You seem short-staffed." Cuinn's eyes flared blue before settling back to green. There was an issue with Kevin.

"He'll be back later."

A new group of demons surged to the bar, talking loudly and shouting out greetings to Cuinn. He hailed them by lifting a drink of his own and then pushed glasses of beer toward them, refilling as soon as the empties hit the bar.

Tazia raised her voice to be heard over the noise. "Hey, Cuinn!"

He looked up.

"Can I pop out back? I think the memory stick for my tablet fell from my pocket last night." She shrugged. "At least I can't find it. Can I check?"

Busy, he waved her through with a smile and a nod. She quickly texted Billy, relieved that the cell signal had held, then hopped off the stool, heart pounding. Her fingers shook as she shoved the cell back in her jacket pocket.

In the hallway, she opened the door to Cuinn's room, leaving it ajar, then continued to the lock-up. The cameras were dead, their lights already out, and a surge of blue light passed down the cables and sparked its way toward the security system on the door to the strong room. The keypad flashed, and the door clicked open. Tazia immediately pushed it and went inside. She watched as the lights on the safe on the far wall also flashed and that door released too. *Thank you, Billy!*

She unfolded the lightweight bag she'd stuffed under her jacket, swept the cash inside, counting as she went, then messaged the total to Billy. The bag was only half full. After closing the safe and locking up doors, she slipped into Cuinn's room, ruffled the bedclothes, and nudged the chair out of its normal position. It would look searched. Then back to the bar. Two minutes flat.

Retaking her stool, Cuinn barely glanced up. She reached for a whiskey bottle from behind the bar for a refill, clinking the neck against the glass noisily as her hand shook. She gulped, feeling the burn calm her.

It had been easy. With Kevin gone and Franky sulking, the whole operation had been trouble-free. Perhaps their hostility worked in her favour. She took another swig. Guilt temporarily overcome by smugness.

Half an hour later, Cuinn came over to her, this time giving her a proper kiss. The tip of his tongue tasted her lips, then he smelled her drink. "You found the good stuff then, darlin'."

She winked at him and pulled out a memory stick from her pocket. "Found this too!"

"Good. Does it contain all yer secrets?"

"Well, there may be a few pictures on here I wouldn't just let anyone see…" She smirked.

He smiled and leaned across the bar, whispering. "Maybe I'll get a private viewing later?"

"Maybe." She paused. "Hey, you're busy right now, why don't I come back?"

"Sure, it's mad in here. These guys will all be gone or passed out by midnight."

Tazia winked goodbye at him and headed out, pushing through the crowd.

She opened the front door and stopped dead, the warmth in her stomach replaced with ice.

Soren Huxford blocked the stairs up to the street. Behind him—Kevin.

30

GAME'S UP

TAZIA'S INSTINCTS FAILED HER. Instead of sprinting past Hux or jumping the iron railings, she froze. Her mind wouldn't tell her where to run. At that moment, it wasn't even telling her to breathe. The duffel bag felt too heavy to hold and slipped through her numb fingers to the ground.

She waited.

Even when Hux stepped down to her level, he still towered over her. He said nothing, just handed the bag to Kevin. His blue eyes never leaving her.

The last time she'd seen him, he glared at her from across a crowded airport concourse, threatening her with death. Now, here he was.

Too numb even to brace herself, her mind stupidly rattled through options. Knife across her throat. Bullet between her eyes. How would he kill her?

Instead, he slowly leaned forward and kissed her. Not friendly. Not passionate. A claim.

Her body shook as adrenaline surged back, lips buzzing with heat as he backed away. The stairwell's foul urine-stink hit her nose, forcing tears to her eyes and jolting her from her trance.

She grabbed the knife strapped to her leg and thrust forward, aiming for whatever bit of him it could reach. Of course, he had been expecting it. He knew her moves by heart. She should have done something different. Something he wouldn't have seen coming.

But it was too late.

The tip of the knife passed through his combat trousers, barely piercing the skin of his hip before he stopped its passage by grabbing her wrist. Blood oozed slightly and then stopped, leaving a tiny patch of red. Useless.

He replaced his neutral expression with a scowl, and a low growl sounded from his throat. He forced her hand upward at the wrist and slammed it back against the doorframe of the Club door.

Still weak from the cave climb in Turin, her right hand shattered on impact. The knife dropped. She swallowed the scream just before he seized her throat with his other hand, pushing her head against the door with a savage thump that rattled the metal handle and hinges. He held her there, suspended, with only the very tips of her toes touching the ground.

Hux bent to her ear and whispered, "Game's up, Anastasia."

The pain in her hand pulsed, and the busted bones ground together when she tried to flex her fingers. Blood oozed from the split skin on the back of her head and trickled warm into her hair. When Hux moved back to look at her again, a ghost of his image merged in and out of her vision. She couldn't tell which was real.

She stared him down as best she could, opening and closing her mouth a little, as she tried to speak. He relaxed his grip on her throat.

"Took long enough, Hux. Game's still…" she gasped against his hand "… in play, lover."

He gave her a half smile and slowly shook his head. Admiration or disbelief. She hoped for the first. Even in this position, she wouldn't give up.

"Are we going to move this inside?" Kevin glanced over his shoulder and shuffled from foot to foot.

"Yeah, we're going inside, Micky-K. Anastasia is going to be on her very best behaviour, aren't you, lover?" *Perfect.* "You'll smile and sit quietly while Cuinn and I catch up. And then when we're ready, you'll tell him everything. The whole dirty scheme. Every. Single. Lie." He banged her head against the door to emphasize each word, causing the skin to split further and the blood to gush, hot and clammy, down her back.

Nausea rose, but it was his words rather than the scent of the blood that made her want to hurl for real. This wasn't about Cuinn. Not the money. Not even her soul. This was about Turin. Using him. Pretending. Screwing him over. Everything he'd want revenge for.

"You… know… Cuinn?" Her voice shook and then broke as his hand continued to squeeze her throat.

"Didn't your Techno-Git tell you that?" Hux's smile narrowed further. "He's getting sloppy. Yes, we fought together. All of us—me, Cuinn, and Kevin here."

He raised his voice and added an almost hearty inflection. "In fact, I haven't seen the old Unit for a while. Should be fun for us all to catch up, shouldn't it, Kev?"

"Not sure 'fun' is the word I'd pick, so it isn't!" Kevin took a step down. "Let's get inside!"

Something inside her gave up. She could have kicked, twisted and taken a broken arm to go with the hand. Something. But no. She just didn't want to fight anymore.

Hux let go of Tazia's throat and pulled her to him by her broken hand, bones grinding together once more. He turned her, twisting her arm down and behind her back, at the same time pulling her into his body, with the other arm grasping her across her front. Her left arm pinned to her side, useless.

She bit down hard on the inside of her cheek to prevent crying out, deflecting one point of pain to another. The taste of the blood comforted her.

She could smell him. The expensive cologne she knew from borrowed sweaters she'd snuggled into during the cold Turin winters. The smell of his skin and sweat. His close contact blistered through the back of her thin jacket and left her feeling as though she would ignite. *Of course, that's how he'll kill me—fire!*

He whispered again, "Don't do anything I wouldn't like, Anastasia. There will be guns pointing at you the whole time. For now, we're invested in keeping you alive." Then he added, "But it doesn't have to stay that way."

Hux gently eased his grip on her, allowing her to carry her own weight again, and let go of her hand. Throbbing escalated, and she gingerly cradled it with her other. He already had the nose of a gun in her back, urging her through the door. She led them inside.

31

———————

COMING CLEAN

HUX SHOVED Tazia back onto the stool, hand screaming as she reached out to steady herself. Cuinn returned, still wiping his hands from changing a barrel. "Did you forget something—"

"Cuinn!"

"Hux?" Cuinn lifted the hatch in the wooden bar, a broad grin on his face, and strode over to Hux, who was already standing with his arms out and smiling almost as wide. "What the feck are you doing here, man?" Before Hux could reply, he added, "It must be, what? Two years?"

"Three, I reckon," Hux said. "Great to see you again, Cuinn!"

The men ignored her while they exchanged backslaps and handshakes. Annoyance lit a fire in her. *Fucking bromance!*

Tazia felt a forceful push at her side. She turned. Franky had pulled up a barstool beside hers and now sat with the nose of a revolver prodding straight into her side. *Of course.*

"Just relax, Tazia." He spoke low into her ear, and then turned to join in the celebration of Hux returning to the fold, a big grin on his face.

Positioned by the door, Kevin had yet to take his eyes off her. Even if she got by Franky—and by some miracle, Hux— she'd be unlikely to get past him. She had no chance in a straight-up fist-fight with a Soldier.

Her right hand throbbed, and blood leaked warm into her collar. Hux had efficiently weighted the fight against her.

She sucked in air, but her chest locked tight. She tried again, through her nose this time. Finally, a little oxygen reached her lungs.

Franky pushed his glass of whiskey toward her. "Give it up, kid. There's nowhere to run."

She swigged the whole thing before croaking "more" at him and downed the refill, too. Maybe she did have a card to play: Franky. He wasn't bad, tough as nails sure enough, but he mostly seemed snarky than mean, protective. She reckoned he wasn't looking forward to this showdown with Cuinn any more than she was.

"Franky, I was telling you the truth the other night. Nothing I've done has been for me. I know it won't look that way, but I truly don't want to hurt Cuinn."

He glanced at her. Silent. Maybe pleading family would work.

"Listen! I just... I've got to save my father!" She tried to grip his arm, but pain shot through her hand. She winced and replaced it under the counter.

She was sure she had read a touch of sympathy in his eyes. She pushed on. "I've done nothing that can't be undone. Cuinn will be none the wiser. I'll just leave. He'll never see me again. I promise, Franky."

"Something, or should I say, someone, tells me your promises aren't really worth much, Tazia!"

"You mean Hux?"

Franky nodded.

Tazia leaned closer to him. "You mean the guy who did

this, just cos I hurt his ego?" She showed him her bleeding and broken hand. She felt the pressure of the gun in her side slightly lessen and tried to press home the advantage.

"Okay, yeah, I treated him badly, but no worse than he did to me. We used each other. But this—here now—this is different. This isn't about me getting away with something. It's about saving people. But I won't do it, I'll find another way. Please, let me go and I won't come back—ever."

She'd never begged before. Pride or stupidity stopped her. But now she did. She hadn't lost sight of who this was about— Billy.

Franky regarded her for a long moment. Did he see her sincerity?

"Like I said, give it up, kid." He pressed the gun hard again.

She'd lost him. Her shoulders sagged. Sweat, mixed with the blood from the wound on her head, rolled down the side of her face, dripping onto the bar top.

The Club started to empty and with the departing demons, the temperature dropped a degree or two. It revived her. Another space opened up next to her, and Hux sat in it. Tazia was flanked on both sides.

When Cuinn came back behind the bar and started filling glasses again, Tazia moved her hand to her lap so he couldn't see the state it was in, but the scent from her head already filled the air and he stopped. "What happened to you, darlin'?"

She had no plan. But knew if there was any chance of escaping, it would need to be soon, before the others had a chance to tell him anything. She'd have to bring the fight to her.

On pure instinct, she reached around with her left hand and grabbed at the old fashioned revolver Franky had planted in her side. She twisted it out of his hand and, with all her might, swung it back and cracked it directly onto Hux's skull.

The blow knocked Hux sideways off his stool. As always, he was ready. He put out a hand to steady himself and sprang up before she'd had a chance to do more than slide from her seat.

He touched the side of his head and looked at his hand. Blood stained his fingers. He gave Tazia a thin smile, then grabbed the back of her head and crashed her forehead down onto the bar, pinning it there. Her vision spun, and the revolver slid from her fingers. She felt another weapon against the back of her neck, the metal icy on her skin.

The club instantly fell silent.

"What the fuck?"

Tazia heard Cuinn's voice through the thuds of pain ricocheting through her head. Her ears rang loudly. Darkness beckoned. Then… drifting.

The point of a knife pricking her throat brought her hurtling back to reality and voices. Everyone talking at once.

Hux: "Cuinn, don't touch the gun, man. This isn't how it looks. We just need to talk to you. But I will shoot her if I have to, and I know damn well Franky wants to use that knife."

Then Kevin, his voice shaking slightly: "Yeah, Cuinn, for fuck's sake, just listen, will yer?"

"What is this, Hux?" Cuinn's voice sounded razor sharp before it drifted away from her.

Franky's voice was gentle, coaxing: "It's about family, son. And making you see sense!"

Another few seconds ticked by. The silence engulfed her. Pitch-black welcomed her.

Cuinn's voice fractured the peace: "Any of you fuckers who haven't got a weapon pointed at me, or Tazia, get out now!"

Awake again, Tazia heard feet charging toward the door even before his words had faded. It seemed no one wanted in on this fight. She couldn't say she blamed them.

"Okay, Cuinn, I'm gonna lower my gun. I didn't want to do this, man, but you need to listen to Hux, please." Kevin's voice carried a desperate tone that would be playing on Cuinn's loyalties.

Tears of pain rolled down Tazia's face and mixed with the blood flowing unchecked from her forehead onto the bar. As she breathed it in, it stung her nostrils.

"I'll listen," Cuinn said. "When you let her up."

Hux took the pressure off Tazia's head. She slowly straightened and cracked her eyes open. The reflection of the lights in the mirror behind the bar stunned her, pulsing in and out. Pain from her head wound sprang at her again and ripped its way behind her eyes. Vomit moments away.

Taking a breath, she tried again, focusing on Cuinn. Double-vision settling. His ice-blue eyes stared into hers, a pulse of green willing her to make sense of it all for him.

Kevin spoke first, running his words. "I ran into Hux this morning, Cuinn. He was here to hunt a target. Her." He nodded at Tazia. "I knew there was something, but yer wouldn't listen. Then he told me and we caught her red-handed. Just listen to him will yer, man?"

Hux jumped in: "Cuinn, Anastasia is—was—an... acquaintance of mine back in Turin—"

Tazia turned her head to glare at Hux, focusing all her rage into the look, forcing her usual calm brown eyes to turn black and spark amber. Demon front and centre. He hesitated, but kept the gun aimed at her.

"We had a job together. Worked on the set-up for two years. Then she changed the rules—left me for dead and took off with the proceeds. Been hunting her ever since."

"You're missing out some key parts to that story, lover." Tazia's anger had overcome her desire for self-preservation. "Like, that you weren't working with me at all. Against me, actually—and that whatever I pretended was matched, action for action, by you." She gave a little laugh. "We're not so different, Hux!"

Cuinn shook his head. "So far all I'm hearing, Hux, is that you got screwed over and your ego's sore. There'd better be more than this."

"Oh, there's more!" Hux jerked his gun at Kevin, who threw the bag containing the money onto the bar. "Open it!"

Cuinn looked from Tazia to Hux and stepped forward to unzip the bag. Once he saw the money, he took a step back again. He agitated his hair in confusion. "What's this?"

"Go check the safe, man." Kevin said. "Go on. You'll find the money's gone. It's all here."

"We took the bag from her. She was headed out the door with it. She was setting you up too, Cuinn. Just like me!" There was no triumph in Hux's voice.

Cuinn frowned, jaw flexing, looking from Kevin to Tazia.

Tazia's anger seeped away. She could only whisper, "Cuinn, it *is* yours. I did take it. But I wasn't stealing it for me, I—"

"No! You were using it to set me up!" Kevin slammed the side of his fist on the bar so hard it rattled and Tazia flinched. "There's a payment in my account, for the same amount as the money in this bag! That's how we knew what she was up to. We were just coming here to talk, Cuinn, just to talk. Then the bank text came through and we knew—she was setting me up. Taking the money and making it look like I did it!"

Tazia looked at Cuinn. She couldn't read him. If only she could get him to listen. "There's a reason… I had to… I—"

"Cuinn!" Hux began. "I don't know what this story is she's going to spin you. But she filled my head with crap like this. It keeps you vulnerable. It's what makes her dangerous." He paused. "Let me take her. You've got the cash back and I can get what's owed to me!"

Tazia didn't recognize the tone Hux was using. It was

weird. Had a desperate edge to it. There was something else going on.

"If you let him take me, he'll kill me." She looked at Cuinn. "If you let me explain, you'll realize it's not as simple as they're making out."

Usually calm and in control, Hux forgot his gun, letting it point to the floor, and bounced impatiently on the balls of his feet.

Cuinn turned to him. "Is this it? Or is there more?"

"Isn't this enough? The girl was screwing you out of army funds and setting up your Second to take the fall. She's said so herself." Hux raised his voice and used his gun to gesticulate.

Tazia glanced at him; his behaviour was confusing her. She sensed Cuinn also felt it.

He took an audible breath and as he let it out, his eyes started to level to a mid-blue. It gave her some hope.

But Hux had seen it, too. "No, man, you can't let her get away with this! Give her to me!"

It was delivered as a desperate order. They all turned to look at him.

Hux waved the gun at Cuinn again. "All right, there's fucking more! I was trying to spare you, but… but… Anastasia isn't just another demon girl." He let his gun point to the ground once more. "Her father was the Abbot of Savoy. The leader of the fucking vampire army that took out your family! He's dead now, but she isn't, and she's here to screw with you, just like he did."

He spoke in an urgent whisper. "Your wife and kid's murderer, man. She's his daughter. She's gonna free him from Hell and let him kill more victims. And she needs *you* to make it happen."

Tazia was horrified. Wide-eyed, she pushed Franky away and took a step toward Hux. "How do you know that?" For a moment, she saw nothing but sympathy in his eyes.

32

INNER DEMON

CONN'S GAZE locked on Tazia; his body trembled. To his eyes, she was no longer the abused girl within whose mind he'd walked. Now she was not weak, not vulnerable. Instead, she looked like her father.

He could see it in the way she held her head proudly upright, and in the defiance of her dark eyes. They pierced into him, demanding obedience. Just like her father's. A growl vibrated deep in his throat.

Her voice echoed his, too—the vampire who'd forced him to choose between his family and his Cause. The cut of her words, that edge of power. It was the same tone the vampire used in demanding the sacrifice of his wife and son.

Now it made sense. This girl he thought he knew. He didn't. He'd just recognized his enemy.

It was his final thought before his outer form began to crumble.

Still staring at Tazia, his jaw clamped down, his teeth ground together. He dug his fingers into the bar in one final attempt to regain control. His vision shifted, and he was looking at her through deep red fire. He growled again, louder this time. A warning. The others took a step back.

But she remained still, watching him, talking to him. Her lips formed soundless shapes as the blood pumped so fast in his ears it deafened him. He heard nothing of her words, nor of Franky's, who was pulling her back.

As he felt himself slip away, his awareness faded to nothing, and the determined pulse of vengeance grew in its place. It flowed through each part of him. Charging his veins. Transforming the flesh under his skin.

In the pounding of his heart and the crackle of the surrounding air, he felt the beat of something ancient and powerful. And he welcomed it.

Conn stood aside and surrendered to his Core.

———

The world moved in slow motion to the inner demon; swirls of scent gave way to colour and vibration that guided it toward its goal.

It dropped to its haunches, talons forcing their way through the tips of its outstretched fingers. Vicious teeth pushing up through its jaws.

The agony drove it. A howl tore free. Pure rage and an insatiable desire to reach its prey. It wanted to rip her apart, taste her flesh, and paint the walls with her blood. Its thirst would not be pacified until she lay in bits at its feet.

The Core sprang.

———

Kevin stood silently watching from the Club entrance.

He heard Franky's desperate shouts at Cuinn to get control, but knew it was useless. He didn't intervene; there was nothing to be done. He watched Franky pull Tazia behind him to try to get her out of the demon's path, and it made him smile. The old man protected the very same girl he'd been so disgusted with not moments before. Franky would always be one of the good guys.

As Franky pulled her into a booth, unable to find any other escape, Cuinn dropped to his haunches, now fully Core and ready to attack.

The monster shook its head and howled again, as the final agony of the change faded, and it could focus more clearly on its prey. There was no way back now. Kevin knew the demon wouldn't stop until Tazia's flesh hung from its mouth, her screams fading into the night air.

Even as Hux began his own futile charge, his thin dagger gleaming in his hand ready to intercept the demon's flight, Kevin knew it was over. It was done. Nothing would stop the monster now.

He shifted his position slightly, lowered his gun, and waited for the screams to start.

———

From her position within the mirror behind the bar, the High Advocate had watched these events unfold, and prepared herself, waiting for the optimum moment to act.

As the demon launched, with fully formed claws on outstretched hands, and Soren attempted his own flying tackle to bring it down to the ground, there was a flash of pure white light. The church shook from the cellar beneath to the top of the half-collapsed cupola: Jegudiel was in solid form.

She looked at the five figures she'd frozen in time. For this single moment, all the angels in Heaven and on Earth could feel her presence and would soon be on their way to hunt her down.

She touched Soren first. He disappeared with an almighty bang, which sent him speeding through space away from Detroit. Her boy had betrayed her; she would deal with him later.

Then she laid a hand on Anastasia's arm. The girl came to her senses, took one look at the demon frozen in a mid-air jump, claws reaching toward her, and hurtled through the Club door and out into the night.

The Core demon was next. The angel stroked its head like she was petting the beast. Her touch sent ripples of energy outward across the city, up into the sky, and down under the earth. Pure angel versus pure demon.

The jolt wrenched Conn back into his outer form and submerged the inner demon again into his subconscious. He fell to the ground screaming in agony, searing welts of fire spreading over his body.

Jegudiel smiled grimly, then vanished.

Time ticked forward once more.

33

THIS ISN'T OVER, LOVER!

SOREN REGAINED CONSCIOUSNESS face down on the bed in his North London Regency flat. He struggled to turn over; every muscle felt bruised, and every bone creaked. He would have come off better if he'd been kicked out of a car doing a hundred on the motorway. He had no recollection of the time, the day, or even what month it was.

He made it onto his back and, while he waited for the throbbing in his legs to subside, he gazed up at the high ceiling. The moon shone through the window, but by the way the light hit the plaster ceiling rose and cast weak shadows to the picture rail, it was creeping towards morning. Together with the heavy rain dripping in steady rhythm from the leaking gutter outside his window, it felt familiar. But not comfortable. Never again.

He had to get moving. The mission—his mission—wasn't over.

He sat up, stretched out his arms. Livid bruises patterned his skin like he'd been daubed with violet-grey paint. The colour of an oncoming storm.

Unsteady, he stood; pain radiating upward into his chest and neck. He eased off the holster and gun still slung around his chest. Then pulled free the hunting blade tucked in his belt. It was Anastasia's knife from Detroit.

Had Cuinn's inner demon got her or had the High Advocate saved her, too? Of course, she wouldn't let her prize die.

He needed to get back on task. But first—

He drew the serrated blade across his forearm. The cut wasn't deep, just enough to create a ragged incision and ooze blood. The wound did not knit. It remained open and bleeding. Stinging. A sweet moment of relief. Jegudiel had made good on her promise.

But if the magick had gone, how would he protect Anastasia? Human strength—and a rifle. Not enough.

The wards were a reward for the taking the contract in Italy. To kill the Abbot and bring his daughter to the Advocate. For a moment, the pain of his guilt overshadowed his injuries. He pushed the final thought away; he'd deal with it later. *Focus, Huxford!*

Steadier now. There was something he had to try, one person who could help.

He flicked through the contacts in his mobile phone until he found the name he needed and checked the address. If Anastasia was alive, he could still save her. *This isn't over, lover.*

———

In a repeat of what had happened two weeks ago, Billy awoke to hammering at the door. It was close to dawn.

Tazia? Ignoring the protests of Thomas, who had managed to get an invitation for a third night, he dragged on some underwear to make it to the door in a semi-respectable state.

The hammering started again. He flung the door wide, a grin of welcome already plastered on his face, ready to greet his best friend. Instead, he found himself looking at the large frame of Soren Huxford.

Billy's smile faded.

They exchanged a look.

Stony eyes told Billy everything.

He attempted to slam the door shut. Hux jammed his foot in the threshold, then punched it open with the side of his fist so that it ricocheted into Billy's face. He jumped back to avoid a direct hit and stepped straight onto the side of a four-inch stiletto heel belonging to a red shoe abandoned in the hallway; it dug hard into his bare foot.

"Fucksakes!" He grimaced from the pain and glared angrily at Hux.

Hux looked confused. "She teach you that?"

"What?"

Hux clenched and released his fists over and over, and Billy prepared himself to take a punch even though he didn't understand why.

"Did she teach you to say that… word?"

"Seriously, mate, I don't know what you're on, bu—"

"Doesn't matter. Is she here?" Without waiting, Hux walked into the flat, through the living room and to the bedroom.

Regaining his balance, Billy limped his way to the bedroom a few seconds too late to save the naked Thomas from the indignity of being rolled off the mattress and onto the floor.

Hux threw a pair of trousers at him. "Out!"

Billy stood in silence and watched as Thomas hopped backward out of the bedroom while pulling on his pants. He was tall and muscular, not of the Swede's proportions, but still comparable. He could take care of himself, but was choosing not to.

He glanced at Billy. "Boyfriend?"

"No!"

"You want me to stay?"

Billy looked from Thomas to Hux, who stood in the bedroom glowering at them both. "No, it's okay. I'll call you." He gave him a weak smile.

"Make sure you do." Thomas brushed a kiss on his lips and left.

Penthouse inspected, Hux lingered in the kitchen. His frown was less dark now, more confused, but he still clenched and released his fists like he was using a couple of Gripmasters.

"Happy?" Billy grabbed a t-shirt and a pair of jeans from the sofa where his evening with Thomas had started.

"Have you heard from her?"

"Like I'm going to tell you!" Billy dragged on the jeans but didn't bother with the shirt after all. He couldn't decide what the best path of resistance would be: basic spell work, perhaps, or just run out the front door. But despite the clenched fists, there was something about Hux that didn't feel "assassin" to him right now.

"She's alive then?" Hux said, his tone dialling up to hopeful.

Billy heard the relief; it was strange. "What's going on, Hux? I get a panicked phone call from Taz telling me to get her on a flight. Said you'd given her the beating from hell. Then nothing. Now you turn up here—looking like shit, by the way—and actually look relieved she's not dead? Last I heard, mate, that's the way you wanted her!"

"Not anymore." Hux left the words hanging while he came over to the living room and settled on one of Billy's black leather couches. It looked far too small for him and squeaked under his weight. "Where's she going?"

To buy some time, Billy gave an exaggerated sigh, wondering which way he should play the next part of the conversation. He couldn't let Hux know where Tazia was.

Hux exhaled too. It looked more like an attempt to

maintain control than a delaying tactic. He struggled with his explanation. "Look, I know you and Anastasia had a plan… to get Conn O'Cuinn to make a sacrifice for her. I had to stop it. Make it look… convincing. Get her away from him. She was in danger. Jegudiel told me…" He paused. "Look, I just couldn't let her do it!"

"Hang on." Billy took a step forward, curious now. "You know about the plan with Conn O'Cuinn? And you stopped it to *save* Taz?"

Hux nodded. "She was in danger."

"You said that. But that plan was the only thing that could save her! She has to get her soul back—and who the hell is Jegudiel?"

"An angel. She's the one behind everything."

"Red-haired bitch?"

Hux grunted his assent. He took a levelling breath. "If Cuinn makes the sacrifice, the angel will control her soul. End of times!" He slumped back on the sofa.

There was a long moment of silence as the two men mentally digested what the other had just said.

"Figured you were into women." Hux's statement was simple, if oddly timed; it didn't sound like a challenge.

Billy looked at him. "Wow, random much! I'm into whoever I bloody well like."

"He looks like me."

"Who?"

"Your boyfriend…"

Caught on the back foot, Billy could just manage, "Erm…"

"Whatever." Hux ran his hand over his chin. His usual light stubble looked like it had not been checked for days and was getting beard-like. A scent of sweat and stale whiskey rose from him, and there were blood stains on his shirt. Billy wondered whose blood it was.

"Look, man, Anastasia's in danger. I can help her—if you

can help me. Jegudiel's after me now, too. She won't stop till she has her and I'm dead. Probably got Cuinn on her tail, too. Can I use your shower?"

"Wow, again with the random. Sure, why not? Just move in!" Billy wondered why Tazia had never told him just how distracted Hux could be. It seemed out of character from the 'Ice King' nickname she'd given him. But "end of times." Really?

Hux paused as he headed for the bathroom. "I know you won't believe me, and she won't—not after last night—but I want her alive. I think, I… No, I know, I…" He gave up. "Can you get my protection back?"

"Your what?" Billy's eyes widened.

"For my skin. Jegudiel gave me wards to protect me. Magick. They deflected attacks, healed me. She took them away as punishment. I'll need them back… to protect Anastasia."

Billy noted the dark circles under Hux's eyes, the bruises on his arms, and his over-thin face. He felt a pang of sympathy for him.

"A spell always leaves its mark. You have a shower and I'll try and come up with something." Billy wanted some space to think through the turn of events.

Hux didn't move, looking lost in thought again.

"Hux, go have your bloody shower, bruv, or do you need me to get in there with you?" Billy made the joke to drag Hux out of his daze, but he didn't laugh, just turned and continued to the bathroom.

"Not even a slight smile?" Billy sat down at his computer.

34

____

PANIC

AFTER THE EVENTS in the Club, Tazia fled to Turin. It was instinct. Going to London hadn't been an option. Billy was already in danger. Where else could she run? Hux knew all her boltholes. Turin was home. At least, it used to be. She still had the Savoy name. Maybe someone would stand up for her? Someone had to owe the family, right?

But back here in Turin, she doubted it.

The vampire she'd killed in Detroit, Antonio, had said there were tussles for power already going on. A few calls down, and her hopes for family loyalty were blown. Laughed at. Cursed at. No one was ready to fight with her. Even to hide her. Everyone was too busy muscling into her father's territory or saving their own skins.

Not knowing her next move, she kept busy, unpacked and then repacked in case she needed a fast exit. Weapons too: a handgun, a replacement knife for her boot, and another for her thigh—a hunting knife. It didn't feel right; the balance between blade and handle was wrong, but it would do. One day she'd recover her Bowie from the cave floor. If she lived through the day.

She'd showered, too, and changed her clothes, all the time avoiding the mirrors and keeping the curtains closed in case Jegudiel decided to pay a visit. Also alert for signs of the arrival of an angry Hux or Cuinn, she'd checked windows and doors on a five-minute cycle.

For the first time since her arrival, Tazia was still.

She sat on her overstuffed purple chair staring into the middle distance, noting the gradual rise in her heartbeat and the perspiration beading on her brow. She left it unchecked until it trickled down each temple, and then she smacked at it with her palms and smeared it into her hair. Her nerves were on edge, her cheeks burned, and the back of her throat started to close as panic rose.

This time, she let it take her.

Tazia's mind raced; images and memories flew. Sometimes she was outside herself, observing events in playback. At other times she was in the middle of it, feeling every hurt and emotion all over again. Eyes peered at her. The anger in Hux's clear blue ones morphed to a sympathy she still didn't understand. Cuinn's emerald eyes changed to ice blue to blood red, flashing from lover to predator.

When she saw the image of the Core jumping at her again, she fell to her knees, reaching out blindly to the wall in front. Its face twisted in rage. Razor teeth bared. A spinning vision of blurred eyes and clawed limbs.

And then nothing but running.

She'd run so fast through back alleys and around abandoned vehicles, jumping over garbage bins and demon corpses rotting in the heat. Through flocks of vultures, black wings flapping in her face. Never stopping in case he was behind her. Fire burned in her chest and throat until her legs failed and she sprawled face down on the hot, broken pavement.

The hot, dusty roads of Detroit faded along with the loud

buzzing in her head. Sweat bathed her from head to foot and her breath came in sharp gasps, but that, too, was levelling out. She looked around. Here were her pictures and shelving units, her books, and the little plastic figure of Solaire of Astora, looking strong and determined.

And on the wall opposite, the wallpaper Hux hated so much. He said the purple swirls made him think of an album cover by some psychedelic Swedish seventies band she'd never heard of.

"He had a point," Tazia remarked to the wall once her breath was finally her own again. "You are fucking horrible."

Thankfully, only silence.

"He'll be coming soon—Hux. To finish the job. Nothing stops him—ever. And Cuinn. He'll be here, too. Perhaps they'll come together. Do you think so?" She laughed, though the prospect terrified her.

More silence.

Calm now, she re-bandaged her broken hand, wrapping it tightly to support the bones as they healed. During the attack, she'd pummelled it against the wall, and the bones had shifted out of place. What use was a one-handed half-demon girl against fully fledged vampires, demons, and assassins? *No fucking use.*

Her cell phone beeped: voicemail. The third since she'd exited the plane. The first two were from Cuinn. Up to now, she'd ignored them. But it was time.

The first message was brief, abrupt, and frightening. It had been sent quickly after she'd been thrown from the Club. His voice was steely, telling her he was coming for her, and this time she would not survive.

Tazia shrugged.

The second message had been sent hours later, just as she'd been boarding the final leg of her flight to Turin.

This message was longer, calmer. His voice was still

controlled, but with a slight edge of emotion. They needed to talk. He wanted to hear her explanation. He was in control. He was coming to Turin. He'd land at sixteen thirty.

She looked at the time. It was already four. *Shit!*

Tazia breathed evenly. Maybe there was still a chance she could complete her mission. Her demon—of course—influencing her. Completing the cruel task she'd started. How could she think of it? Yet she hesitated. Perhaps…

The final message was from Billy. Its entirety was composed of, "Taz—call me. Muchos urgent, babe. Do not do anything till we've spoken. Love ya, girl."

Her phone was almost out of charge, so she fast dialled on the landline.

He picked up on the first ring. "Babe?"

"Yep."

"You at the apartment?"

"Yep."

"Taz? Talk to me. Are. You. Okay?" Billy spoke slowly as though to a child.

Tazia did a mental check on herself. "Yes. Disorientated. I've had messages from Cuinn. He's coming to Turin. He wants to meet me—"

"Taz, listen carefully. Do not meet him. It's dangerous. Bad idea, babe. Hux is here. He knows everything. He's coming to help."

"To help! Are you serious? He just tried to kill me!"

"I know. He explained that to me. You've got to trust him now, okay?"

The silence hung.

"Tazia?" The seriousness in Billy's voice got her attention. He only ever called her Taz.

"He hurt me, Billy. Practically fed me to Cuinn. It's because of him I'm here." *Shit, I sound like a whiny kid.* But how could Billy suggest this?

"Taz, he had to do that. Had to try to get you away from Cuinn. You must not meet with him. He must not make the sacrifice for you. Please, babe, do you understand?" Something in his voice calmed her, but too stubborn, she said nothing.

"Look, Hux is getting out the shower, I'll get him to explain it to you, he can tell you everythi—"

The phone call cut out abruptly.

"Billy? Billy? Fucksakes!"

Tazia called Billy's number again, but the phone wouldn't connect. There was just silence. That wasn't right. It was as though the line had been cut—

She froze and tipped her head toward the front door, listening.

Her instincts clicked in a fraction too late. She launched herself across the bed to grab her gun just as the front door shot off its hinges, flew across the hallway, and shattered the wall mirror with a deafening crash. Pieces of jagged glass sprayed across the floor.

Two large suit-wearing figures entered, guns out and shouting at her in Italian to stay still. Demons. Old school. Someone's muscle.

Her fingertips grasped the bottom of the gun holster, but it was too late. One demon grabbed her arms and twisted them behind her, locking her into a pair of solid metal handcuffs. The violence of his assault caused the bones in her injured hand to become displaced yet again, but her cry of pain was muffled as the second guy placed a foul-tasting gag in her mouth.

As she was manhandled over the broken door and onto the street, Tazia's last thought was: why the hell is Hux taking a shower at Billy's flat?

———

"Is that Anastasia?" Hux had emerged from the bathroom redressed in his dirty combat pants and tee shirt, holding his hand out for the phone. Billy wondered vaguely what the point of the shower had been.

"It was. We got cut off and I can't get hold of her again." Billy sat heavily on one of the eight designer dining chairs he never used. The expensively curved wood didn't give under his weight. He blinked.

On his mobile, Hux called the apartment. Billy could hear a female Italian voice telling him the number was out of service. Hux tried Tazia's mobile next. No answer.

The worry lines on Hux's face deepened as he pushed the tails of wet blond hair behind his ears.

To Billy, this change in him was intriguing. His attitude towards Tazia had always been so off-hand. Could he actually care for her? The creased brow, the back-and-forth pacing. He was worried.

"I told her not to meet with Cuinn before we were cut off. Apparently, he's on his way to Turin, though. He's landing soon." Billy felt the need to calm the man who, only an hour ago, had been his best friend's worst enemy.

"I need to get there. If she meets with him, it'll be too late." Hux appeared to calm down; making the decision to go to her seemed to settle him. "Can you get me on a flight? Magick?"

"Flight's no problem—one leaves in two hours from Gatwick and you're on it. The charms will be harder, but doable." Billy walked back behind the desk and grabbed a small hand-held scanner. "Come here," he ordered.

From Tazia's stories, Billy knew Hux hated orders. He gave one anyway. The man frowned but walked to the spot Billy indicated with the scanner.

"Take your shirt off."

The glare he got back made him smirk. "I need to read the sigils on your skin. The angel switched them off, but the ghost of the spell will be there. Back cos it's a larger area. Once I've got the sample, I can digitize and start to unravel it. It's the first step to rebuild it. At least, we'll try, yeah?"

Hux nodded and removed his t-shirt. Broad, well-muscled back, still-damp blond hair settling against the nape of his neck. Definitely an eyeful.

Billy dragged the scanner slowly across Hux's skin, hand lingering against the muscle before moving on. Several times he stretched the already taut skin with the flat of his hand, deep skin tone against Hux's lighter colouring.

He reluctantly completed the task and hooked up the scanner to the computer to start the download. "I've left my mark. If I get anything that looks to be useful, I'll send the resulting spell to your phone so leave it on, okay?"

"Sure. Your mark?"

"Yeah. A magickal signature to retain a link. Don't worry, it will fade too. I'm not making you my bitch or anything." He grinned, waiting. *Nothing?*

Dressed, Hux nodded and started to the door. He turned and spoke to the floor, voice catching. "I will save her, Billy. I have to."

35

FAKERY

ONCE OUTSIDE THE APARTMENT BUILDING, the two demons manhandled Tazia into the back seat of a luxury Audi. She ended up on her front, pressed head first into the fleshy leg of the man sitting beside her, soaking up the scent of fabric softener and lavender soap. *Lavender? Oh, fuck!*

Awkward in the cuffs, she wrestled herself upright to see who sat beside her. As she'd guessed, it was the Soul-Sucker cafe-owner she'd stabbed and stolen money from on the day her father was killed: Bello.

Viscous residue leaked from his face and neck, clotting above the neck of his shirt collar and tie. Red ripples of energy cascaded from him. Thank God, she couldn't see the souls still writhing under his skin this time.

Dabbing a silk purple handkerchief to his forehead, he barked orders at the lackeys who'd fetched her from the apartment. They drove out of town toward the place where her father had been shot. Bello stuffed the damp silk into his jacket pocket and acknowledged her presence. *"Mia bella Sahara Dune,* what a pleasure to see you again."

Tazia grunted, all she could manage with the gag in her

mouth. The little saliva she managed to make burned a chemical trail of solvent and fake lemon-scented upholstery shampoo down her throat. She did her best to scuttle further along the back seat away from him.

"Tell me, Signorina Dune, did your hunter friend find you?" Words slid sideways out of Bello's mouth. "He appeared to be disappointed when he heard you treated me poorly the last time we met." His blue eyes flared red.

Tazia remembered the blue blood spurting from his neck after she'd pushed her broken wine glass into him—and the fact he'd short-changed her reward money. She grunted again, and wished she'd cut his windpipe.

"I thought not," he continued. "Or you would be dead by now. I did hear you had some issues in Detroit, so maybe you, how do you say, 'got lucky'?"

He paused.

"That luck is not likely to continue, *mia bella* Sahara."

Before Bello could goad her further, the vehicle veered off the road and turned into the driveway of a stupidly lavish villa. Porticos, columns, and a triangular roof topped by gold-painted spheres and cherubs. Cement blocks imitated limestone. Despite the fakery, there was money here.

Vampires wearing sun-protecting hats and overcoats guarded the entryway, and a line of security cameras caught every angle.

The place reeked of vampire ostentation—and paranoia.

The car drove between two rectangular reflection pools, and stopped at the huge wooden front door inset with gold in the shape of a Satanic-looking goat that appeared to be leering at her.

One of the goons opened the back door of the car.

Taking the opportunity, Tazia swivelled, and kicked out at him before he was able to drag her out. The effort was wasted. He dodged her foot, grabbed her by the shirt, and dragged her clear of the back seat, throwing her to the gravel. She skidded on her knees before landing face down. Grit and dust flew up to her face in a choking cloud, the disgusting gag briefly becoming her friend.

Bello leaned forward in his seat so he could peer out of the car door. He raised his voice just high enough for her to hear. "Enjoy your stay, Miss Dune."

As the car drove away, two vampires gripped her under the arms and pulled her forward to the front door. Each step thumped pain through her knees.

Tazia reviewed her situation dryly. She wished the last twenty-four hours would just fuck off.

36

ITALIAN SUITS

CONN O'CUINN WASN'T USED to commercial airlines. Normally, he'd buy his way across borders or use transport from sympathizers. This time he'd had no choice. Slipping cash to half the bloody security staff was bad enough. But having the experience of every other passenger in coach was worse—cramped seat, crying babies, and God-awful food.

By the time he landed on the tarmac in Turin, he'd flip-flopped between simmering anger and homicidal rage too many times to count. The flight attendant on the last leg refused him a fifth whiskey after he growled: "Hurry the feck up or leave the feckin' bottle!" She chose to do neither.

He woke from a brief nap just an hour outside of Italy with a banging headache, but it didn't drown out the screaming from the rest of his body. The welts from Jegudiel's touch still burned. They cracked open on his face and arms when he moved and wept blue blood that caused his fellow passengers to gasp in alarm. *Pussies.*

Only an occasional red flash in his eyes remained of the Core demon.

When the plane landed in Turin, Conn pushed himself

through the crowds to get to the black sedan waiting for him on the airport concourse. Provided by "friends" it came complete with a vampire-ready shotgun, pistol with chest holster, and a large hunting knife to tuck into his belt.

The *pièce de résistance* was a laser-sighted rifle, bringing a non-demon-related sparkle to his eyes and a gentle whisper to his lips, "I'll damn well find something to use you on, *mo stór*."

He drove immediately to Tazia's apartment, trying her cell phone at the same time. The number was out of service.

A lengthy travel day had given him too much time to think. In the bar, she had radiated red energy, genuine distress. But secrets too, batting between her and Hux. He'd give her a chance, but her story had to be feckin' good.

Hux's energy still screamed as deep blue as it always had. It was the only colour he heard more than saw. For sure, there was something wrong with that boy. He'd done his best; loved him as a brother, taught him to be a true soldier. At times, Conn had sworn there was more demon in him than in the rest of the Unit altogether.

When Hux dropped the bombshell about Tazia's father, all hell broke loose. Mostly a blur and still not explained. That connection he felt with Tazia? Was it just twisted recognition of a past enemy? Or something more? Too many questions.

Now, he stood outside Tazia's apartment looking at a hole where her door should have been. The battered remains lay on the ground in a coating of mirror shards.

Moving cautiously, shotgun ready, he stepped inside. No one. An abandoned handgun and holster on the bed and the knives lying beside them. Her phone was on the floor, dead and stamped on. The only sign of Tazia were drops of blood on the bed. Not enough to suggest murder. The smell of two additional bodies hung strong in the air: mixed-breeds.

He'd only just missed them.

Hux's scent was everywhere, but wasn't recent. It led Conn

to a closet full of Italian suits, to the towels in the bathroom where shelves were lined with expensive toiletries, but most of all to the bed. The energy pulsed hot, unmistakably intimate.

At least he'd been telling the truth about that. So, what had happened between them to break that relationship? Despite Tazia's protests, Conn didn't buy that Hux had used her just as much as she'd used him. He might be an angry son of a bitch, but human. If being coldly calculating was a competition, the vampire would win every time.

Conn had no interest in Tazia's past sexual encounters apart from how they might put the pieces together. She had been taken against her will; that was clear. So, who had Tazia now?

He wiped a hand over his face, breaking a crusty seal from the welt on his forehead. Not a flinch. Her scent was still strong. Maybe he could track her? It was all he had.

———

Conn followed Tazia's scent until it broke at the edge of town. He circled back, peering down alleyways, into the buildings and piazzas around the city. Nothing.

Stopping at the side of the road where the scent had first disappeared, he batted at the steering wheel with his fingers. Calculating his next move. Through the lowered window, he caught the scent again, from a large black Audi heading back into the city. *Yes!*

Conn U-turned. He tailed the vehicle until it came to a stop at the back entrance of a bar off a central plaza.

He stepped out and approached the driver's side. Before the occupants could move, he rapped on the tinted window. The driver lowered it. Conn slammed a fist across his jaw. The demon was out before he hit the seat and a shotgun levelled at his frozen companion. With his other hand, Conn pointed a

Beretta at the chest of the occupant sitting in the back seat. *Big bastard.* He adjusted it to point at his head.

"Where is she?" he asked.

Signor Bello looked at him carefully. "You are speaking of the vampire half-breed, of course?"

"Of course."

"She is delivered safely to the arms of those who will treat her with much… gratitude." Bello laughed heartily, jowls quivering with mirth.

Conn cocked the gun. "Where is she?"

Bello's laughter died. A scowl gathered on his forehead. His eyes flicked between Conn's face and the gun. He shrugged. "*Allora,* my brave demon, who am I to stop you from your quest to save the girl? She is at the Villa Fortunata, on the mountain road. If she is still alive. Her host wanted her company very badly."

Before he'd finished speaking, Conn had already walked away.

37

FIGHTING SPIRIT

ONE THING TAZIA hated more than head games was waiting. Now she had both. She'd been chained to a chair in the reception room on the upper floor of the villa for what seemed like forever. *Fucking perfect!*

The chair was solid steel, bolted to the floor with plates and screws. Blood spatter on the wooden planks told her this set-up had tested many demons. No wriggling loose and rancid gag still stuffed in her mouth. Playing tie-up had never been her style—that was more Billy's thing.

A quick scan on entry gave her little to work with: a door behind her; the double doors she'd been dragged through to her left; windows dead ahead. They'd parked her in the centre of the room. No furniture to use as a weapon, either. Just reams of little chubby angels gazing down at her from the high plaster ceiling. These guys really loved their cherubs.

A run-of-the-mill vampire would have got to the torturing part by now. Or else moved straight to killing.

As the clock ticked on, it gave her too much thinking time. Why the hell hadn't Bello finished the job himself? Who had he handed her to? She had no energy left to guess. Her anxiety switched to boredom. Every ache, a fresh annoyance.

As she began counting cherubs for the twentieth time—footsteps!

A man entered from behind her. He stopped at her side, arms folded. A well-kept fifty, tall, dark suit and black shirt. Slick hair. No tie, she noted. *Not good enough for that, huh?*

And she recognized him.

Of course. Word of Antonio's death would've flown across the demon network the second it happened in Detroit. She'd be named as the killer. And he would have heard about her return as soon as the plane touched down. A spy at the airport. Maybe one of Bello's men. Hell, maybe a fucking Instagram post.

Signor Giovanetti. The father of Antonio. Enemy of her father. And now, it seemed, hers.

He strolled to the wall of windows facing her. The late afternoon sun lit a path into the room, forcing him to stop short of it to avoid burning. His steps, deliberate and steady, echoed through the empty space, while his gaze wondered to the mountains beyond.

After a long silence, he turned back. His Italian accent was light. "I remember you, Anastasia, I remember you well. You and Antonio caused quite a stir a few years ago, didn't you?"

With the gag preventing speech, she just stared.

"Back then, I turned down your father's request to marry the two of you. I didn't want your soiled blood mixing with my family." He turned casually back to the window. "Perhaps if I hadn't, you wouldn't have killed him. And for who? An Irish Soldier, wasn't it? A peasant for hire. No nobility at all."

Conn O'Cuinn. A peasant mercenary? Remarkable misread. The man bled for his Cause.

"I am aware Antonio could be…" he paused, searching for the right word, "difficult. But did he deserve to die, Anastasia?"

He looked back at her again. "Not really. And nor do you. But you will."

As Tazia absorbed the news, she was calm. She lifted her chin, eyes locked on him. For the first time, she wanted to carry the Savoy name with pride.

She grunted, tilting her head toward the window, eyes wide.

He rolled his eyes, unconvinced.

She grunted again with more urgency, nodding frantically.

He stepped over and undid the gag. "What?"

Her first attempt was useless, just a croak. She swallowed, then: "You're not killing me because of Antonio, Giovanetti."

His brows rose. "No?"

"You want me gone so I don't get my hands on my father's territory. The land you've craved for years. He was always more respected, his line more pure, showing you and yours up for the squalid pretenders you are!" She delivered the taunt with a challenge in her eyes and her father's old fashioned words. She wanted Giovanetti to see it: she was her father's daughter.

In a blur, he backhanded her across her right cheek. The sharp edge of his cygnet ring carved a deep gouge from ear to mouth.

She raised her head again as the blood streamed warm on her chest. "And by the way, your son was a sadistic pig who deserved everything he got!"

Whether he guessed she was goading him didn't matter. She wanted him riled. Needed him to know she'd go down fighting, chained or not. Maybe her father would catch a glimpse from the Red River and finally smile at his daughter's fighting spirit.

He drew back to strike again—

A gunshot ripped across the courtyard.

Giovanetti froze, then darted to the windows as another

shot cracked, pressing himself flat against the wall between the centre windows.

From her position, she had little view, but she thought she'd seen a flash just a fraction before the second shot. And a third. Outside, vampires screamed orders and boots thundered on the paving.

Giovanetti dragged a pistol from under his jacket, and holding it tight to his chest, hissed. "Who is it? Who is defending you? Who is killing my men?"

She gave him a slow shrug. She didn't have an answer and was damn sure whoever was shooting was not doing it to protect her. Probably just to save her for themselves. Hux? Cuinn? Maybe Bello had come to play after all?

Whoever it was, she wanted to thank them. Maybe now she'd get a fighting chance.

38

STORMING

TAZIA COUNTED SHOTS. Quick and consistent, whoever was shooting had some hardware. Cuinn? Hux? Maybe both! Either way, she'd take it.

"Let me go, Giovanetti! They're not my friend! I can help you!"

He shook his head, either in disbelief or just not listening.

Another shot rang out. It shattered the window beside him. A floor-to-ceiling beam of sunlight erupted into the room.

Sunlight slashed across her left side and onto her face; the glare blinded her. Her exposed skin heated up, and she yanked herself back out of its reach.

Tazia figured the shot was so the shooter could see inside the room, maybe even to locate her. And yeah, now they had a full view of her. *Shit.* "Giovanetti!" she hissed. "Let me go!"

This time, she saw his hesitation.

"He's either gonna take the shot and kill me or come get me. Either way, you'll lose. They want me dead, too. Don't you want to do it yourself?"

Had she gone too far? Maybe Giovanetti would simply shoot her? But she didn't think so. He seemed to want more.

Revenge for him was a slow, painful business. He wouldn't want to be cheated out of it.

The vampire decided. He circled behind Tazia, careful to avoid windows and the beam of sunshine to the left of her chair. Gun jammed to her head with his left hand, he unlocked the cuffs with his right, and dragged her into the shade—

Get ready.

Rifle quiet, now a shotgun blasted its way through the house and up the front stairs. Keeping her in front of him, he backed up to the door, and reached for the handle—

Let's go!

Tazia slammed her right arm up, forcing Giovanetti's gun arm away from her. Something cracked. Hers. She grunted, but pain did not hit. He screamed, and his gun flew across the room. He abruptly dropped his hold on her. His arm hanging loosely. Dislocated.

Cuinn stormed through the double doors, shotgun ready.

Already committed, Tazia hauled the still screaming vampire with her good arm, spun, and flung him at the shattered window like a one-armed hammer toss.

In motion, the vampire's skin smoked in the glare from the hot sun. Eyes wide, he reached for her to save him, yanking on her fractured arm. Tazia screamed, turned the pain to fury, and kicked him free. He blasted through the window, caught fire midair, and was ash before he hit the ground.

Cuinn lunged, yanking her clear of the streaming sunlight. They crashed to the floor together.

39

____

ANGELS AND CATS

SINCE LANDING IN TURIN, Soren had traced Cuinn's path. He'd also made the same discoveries. The blood on the bed at the apartment made him freeze. He steadied. *Treat it like a job, soldier.*

Soren's flight was no easier than Cuinn's. Unlike Cuinn, it wasn't due to cramped seating and noisy babies—Billy had secured business class for him—but an exhausted sleep broken by dreams of Jegudiel.

She sat on the head of the statue of Venus, the centrepiece of an ornamental fountain, water drenching her purple dress. Her curved lips and flicking tongue, taunted him. In her hands, she turned a clear glass jar. She stared directly into Soren's eyes like she was perched on his lap, and snapped, "See you in Turin, pet. I can't wait!"

He'd woken with a shout and a kick that jerked the surrounding passengers awake. An over made-up stewardess had come rushing over. She eye-raked his muscles, giggled, and urged him to have a drink.

When the plane landed, he'd retrieved his car, visited the apartment, and driven to his storage locker to load up with weapons. There, he ran his fingers over the classic Bowie he'd retrieved from the cave floor that day he'd almost died. Anastasia's initials carved into the polished wood handle. *Should I?*

With the car loaded up, he pushed the ignition and—

"Soren, pet. It's time for a little chat." Jegudiel spoke from the driver's mirror. She looked serene.

"Not this time." Soren reversed out of the parking space at speed, skidding on the turn before moving into forward gear and screaming out of the car park in a haze of dust and gravel.

The High Advocate transformed. Her eyes glowed pure white, with no irises or pupils, and her hair appeared to burst into flames. Her voice scraped like a blade on metal. "You think I'm done with you, Soren? You think you can ignore me now? I may have already taken your toys away, but I can still do you damage!"

The side windows shattered, glass fragments flying everywhere.

Soren pulled to a stop at the side of the road, ears ringing. He glared around the car. The angel had gone.

Brushing away the tiny pieces of glass that had fractured from the safety coatings embedded in the windscreen, he reviewed the damage. Windscreen mostly intact. Electrics worked. Side mirrors unscathed. Still drivable.

He was about to exit the car park again when his phone rang. Billy.

"Hey, Hux."

"Yeah?"

"I re-engineered that spell and think I've got it. Have you found Taz, yet?" He sounded anxious.

"Still looking. The spell will work?"

"No guarantees, but I tested it on a cat. He didn't seem to feel a thing…"

Soren didn't ask. Usually an animal lover, at that moment, he felt no sympathy for the unfortunate feline. "Good. How?"

"I've sent a file in a text. Once you get it, open it. That should be all you need to do. It'll find the mark I left and shazam! I hope there's no fallout."

The phone beeped to announce the incoming text message.

"It's here." Soren paused and then added awkwardly. "Thanks, Billy."

"Just find her. And Hux?"

"Yeah?"

"I was joking about the cat, bruv." Billy rang off.

Not sure whether that was good or bad, Soren tapped on the file. *Here goes.*

Digits and letters scrolled, floated off the screen into the air. A low buzzing filled the space, like electricity building before a lightning strike. A slight vibration slid warm across the bare skin of his arms, neck, and face, hairs standing up. His skin flushed a deeper pink and then subsided. *Huh. That it?*

Soren flicked open his knife and drew a shallow line across the underside of his forearm. There was little pain. The cut knitted and sealed itself. He gave a tight nod, then cut deeper. Again, the wound vanished. He grunted. Billy had done well.

Pressing the ignition, he eased out onto the road. The car cut out and rolled forward before coming to a stop. He tried again. Nothing. He slammed his hands on the steering wheel and swore.

Shrill laughter filled the car. Glowering, Soren wished with all his might Jegudiel would be solid this time so he could grab her neck just as tightly as he clutched the steering wheel.

She wasn't. The angel's reflection flashed sporadically in the shiny silver border around the car's centre console. Her appearance was back to normal. As she laughed, her body shook. "You think having your charms back will protect you from me, Soren Huxford?"

Maybe it was time to play his hunch. One that had been developing for some time. One he'd never been able to prove—but he had nothing left.

"No, but you're not so safe either. You took a chance getting solid in Detroit. Other angels knowing your whereabouts." All fugitives feared getting caught, didn't they? Would it be the same for her?

The bluff seemed to pay off. Jegudiel's expression changed: cold, hard eyes replaced smiling ones. "Careful, boy."

He pushed further. "A deal. You let me find Anastasia. Then I'm yours."

"And if I agree?"

"I won't go to the nearest church and pray to the angels to come get you." Would it work? He'd never had a reason to pray before.

The angel was silent. "How about I do better than that, pet? What if I tell you where she is? It won't matter; you're too late to save her from Conn O'Cuinn's sacrifice, anyway. She's already with him and about to spin the perfect line. Either that or he'll kill her of course. So, go and save her if you can."

Soren couldn't read her. Couldn't tell if she was lying. "Where?"

Jegudiel told him Anastasia's location. "I'll be cheering you on, pet!" She smirked and disappeared.

The engine hummed and he put his foot down. If he was too late, could he do what was needed?

40

——

KISS

TAZIA AND CUINN stayed where they'd landed, a heap on the floor by the broken window Giovanetti had just smashed through. Outside, the moans of dying demons drifted in; fires crackled over vampire corpses. The only other sound was their ragged breathing.

She eased back, her leg smouldering where the sun had caught it. Too drained to move far, she leaned against the coolness of the wall. He didn't look like he wanted to fight.

"So, Tazia darlin', not the welcome I was expecting to get from Turin. I thought it was supposed to be the most romantic city in the world, so I did." Cuinn shifted to lean against the wall beside her.

"Nah." Tazia shook her head. "That's Paris. We're known as 'Satan's City'."

Cuinn looked surprised, then nodded. "Makes sense."

They stared intently at each other for a long moment. He seemed relaxed, even friendly.

"You said on the phone you wanted to talk?" She said. "I guess this is as good a place as any."

"Aye, darlin'. I reckon there was a lot more going on than Hux told me, right?"

"He seemed to know a lot," Tazia acknowledged. "I don't know how. I haven't seen him since Detroit. Billy has. Said he was helping me back there."

The laugh she tried, ended in a wince. She was wrecked: burns, cuts, bruises, a broken arm, and a hand still hurting from Hux's violence. Despite it all, she wanted to come clean. The plan was shot now. Not even a ripple from her tattoos at the thought of it.

Her heart thumped loudly, but she didn't care if he heard. "I'll tell you everything. It'll be up to you then. Okay?"

He nodded.

"My father was the Abbot of Savoy. But I didn't know your history with him."

Cuinn seemed to accept her simple explanation and nodded again.

"You picked up a lot in my head. How he caged my soul as a kid. What you didn't see was why it all happened."

"True. So, tell me, darlin'."

"He struck a bargain. He would serve Satan when he died. Be his right hand, I guess. It's all he ever wanted. In exchange. Me. Made through magick. Half demon. Half human—with a soul. Special." She laughed. "But, he couldn't handle being so close to it, so he dealt with it."

"The tattoos?"

"Yes."

Cuinn's mouth hardened. "Evil fucker."

Tazia shrugged. "He tolerated me well enough when it was gone."

"When it was time for him to die—to be with the Old Goat. He had nothing to offer me. We had money before the Demon War, power, even. But most was gone. He knew

Giovanetti would make a play. Take what was left. Kill me. He said for the bargain to stick, I had to survive."

She stopped. A flood of guilt. *Was this honesty or excuses?*

"Go on." Cuinn squeezed her lower leg, the only part of her within his reach.

"We brought in Hux. He had a reputation for getting the job done. I had to spin him a line. Tell him Turin demons would pay well for my father's death. He'd keep the cash. And yes, I lived with him to sweeten the deal."

Her voice dropped a little. "I did use him. He didn't know my father's death was prearranged. The bullet was his, but the rest—the rock fall—Fate or Satan, I guess. Hux would die. I'd collect."

Cuinn looked out the window. She could tell he was struggling to remain neutral. She'd behaved just like the other Leeches he so despised.

"If I'd been strong enough to take the shot. Then we wouldn't have needed him." It was no excuse. "I did care for Hux though. More than I realized. Now he hates me."

"He doesn't hate you, Tazia." Cuinn's gaze returned, steady. "He's mixed up, sure. Has darkness in him that he needs saving from. But it's not hate, sure it's not."

That surprised her. His insight into Hux.

He nudged her. "Go on with your story, darlin'."

She swallowed. "Everything went to plan. Hux killed him, but survived the rock fall. I—" she lowered her eyes "—left him there to die. I got the money from the demon we'd done the deal with and ran."

"Soul Sucker?" Cuinn interrupted.

"Yes."

A nod. "And?"

"And that's when the plan got screwed. I met a woman, an angel—"

Cuinn's eyes opened wider. But she couldn't stop to ask.

"—bad though. She told me it was all her plan. My birth, my father, all of it. Only he wasn't chosen anymore. He'd been left to rot in the Red River unless I agreed to help. I couldn't let him stay there." She looked to see that he understood.

He nodded once. "Go on."

She breathed a little easier. "To free him, I had to have my soul back. All of it. Not just the little sparks my father left me with when he bound it."

Cuinn looked intrigued. "And?"

"Billy and I figured out how to break the ink. Someone had to make a sacrifice for me, but it was very specific. It needed to be the loss of something or someone they really believed in and given willingly."

He nodded again.

"We raised my father using magick… and a necromancer. It's complicated, but he told us about you."

Cuinn looked at her sharply, obviously confused, but said nothing.

"My father said that he had once witnessed you making an ultimate sacrifice—for your loyalty to Ireland…"

Instantly, Cuinn's eyes changed to ice blue with small flecks of red flashing dangerously.

Tazia noticed, but rushed on. "He said if you gave up your Cause for me it would be the sacrifice Jegudiel was looking for."

"The angel was called Jegudiel?"

"Yes."

"Are you sure?"

"Yes."

The red flashes in Cuinn's eyes flared again, then subsided. "Go on."

"For what it's worth, both Billy and I never thought the plan would work. Not really. But it was all we had."

Cuinn stared at her, his expression unreadable.

"The angel said she would help. We didn't know how, but I think the dreams you were having—the hallucinations—were to make you weak. I think that was her."

She stopped, exhausted. "Everything else you know. The plan failed. According to Billy and the angel, Hux has been working with her from way back—that's what I meant about us screwing each other over. I don't think he knew you were involved. And, I didn't know he knew you. He obviously cares a lot about you."

"People get close when they risk their lives together. He's a good man and a grand soldier. Is there anything else?"

"No. The plan failed. My father will stay in the river. I don't know where Hux is. Billy said he was on his way here." Pushing back her hair, she scooted over until she was right in front of him.

"I know you'll find it difficult to believe a Blood-Sucker like me, but I am sorry. This whole time, Billy and me, we've been trying to find another way. To leave you alone. Halfway through I decided to leave my father to burn—to leave Detroit —but then she said she'd hurt Billy, too. I couldn't allow that. He's innocent."

Cuinn pushed away the hair from her eyes. His eyes were green again. "I believe you, darlin'. I wish you'd told me instead of trying that half-arsed scheme, though. You could have saved us a lot of pain. I could have helped somehow."

"But why would you help me?"

"Because I care about you." He smiled. "I could never have given up my country and her fight for freedom for you, Tazia. It's ingrained. But we would have found a way! We still can. Not to save your da. I can't do that, darlin', it's asking too much, but to free you from that witch. To save your Billy. There are ways to defeat angels!"

"Will you really help?" She took a breath.

"Aye."

Her chest eased. Lighter than it had been for weeks. She leaned forward and brushed her lips to his. Would he respond? He kissed her back.

"Thank you, Conn," she murmured.

41

SACRIFICE

OUTSIDE THE ROOM, Soren slid to a halt. A sliver of light from the doorway. Muffled sounds. He leaned closer. Frantic. Had he missed it?

Cuinn's voice promising to help.

Anastasia's whispered thanks.

Their kiss.

It's done.

Or was it? *Did* he promise? Echoes in the hall, echoes in his head. Footsteps and whispers swallowed by the dark. Grinding the words over and over until they were just noise.

So fucking tired.

Did he make the sacrifice or not?

Assess, soldier.

It's Cuinn. A good man. He would do it. For her.

Of course he said yes.

Jegudiel's face filled the hall mirror by the door. Cajoling: "See, you're too late, pet. You heard him make the promise to her. He'll give up the Cause. It's just a matter of time now before he makes the sacrifice—unless you stop it." The angel's voice sharpened with urgency. "Quickly, boy! Quick! Only one way to save her!"

He'd promised. The decision made.

Commit.

Soren stepped through the doorway, the dagger weightless in his hand. His thumb worrying at a sharp splinter in the polished wood handle. Back and forth. Back and forth. An anchor against the roaring in his head.

The two lovers looked up. Cuinn started to smile, to greet him.

No. Don't let him speak.

Feelings can't stop me.

She swore she'd turn creation upside down. Tazia will be hers.

The promise is the threat. Only one way to break it.

Do it.

He locked onto Cuinn. Launched. Hit him like a thunderclap, driving him onto his back.

Quick, before the Core gets free. The eye. The weak point.

Soren set the tip against Cuinn's right eye and worked it inward, threading it beneath the bone.

Don't stop. Don't think. Keep going.

Cuinn didn't resist. No fury, no fight. Only a look, brief and calm. As if he expected it. Like he'd already forgiven it.

The blade curled under the steel-like bone of his skull.

Is he speaking? A whisper?

Don't listen. Don't stop.

The blade gave as it reached his brain, then sank deeper.

Cuinn's left eye stilled. And dulled.

Gone.

Soren held the handle, his weight on the body until it was completely limp. Blood, brain, and eye matter smeared on his hand.

Far away, Anastasia screamed. Her fist beating on his back, begging for Cuinn's life. Too late. Done. His brother was gone.

He eased the blade free, his whole body shaking. Gently, he loosened Cuinn's hands where they had grasped his wrists. So gently. He let Anastasia pull him off. He just sat there. She crawled past him. To Cuinn.

"Why?" Anastasia asked, eyes wide.

Soren expected her to come flying at him. To beat him. Even end him. But here she was. One arm around Cuinn, rocking him. Her other arm hanging loose and odd. *She's injured.*

"Tell me why."

"He couldn't make that sacrifice. She'll have you then—the angel. Control you! It'll be the end of all of us." He dropped his voice. "I had to choose—him or you. He was my brother, I—"

"But he didn't, Hux! He didn't make the sacrifice. He told me he couldn't. He told me we'd find another way. Together! He was going to help me."

Soren froze. Surely he'd misheard. "What?"

"He didn't do it!"

"But I heard—"

"HE DIDN'T DO IT!"

"But she said—"

High, girlish laughter echoed around the empty room, bouncing back off the plaster-covered walls. With a deafening bang, Jegudiel took physical form. The sky split with sudden lightning.

The angel stood beside Cuinn's lifeless body with Anastasia still holding onto him and counted down. "Three. Two. One."

On *one*, Anastasia screamed, high, desperate. Like she was being seared with a hot blue flame. Split in two. She pushed Cuinn's body away from her and clawed at her back, trying to reach the source of the agony.

Soren pulled her to him and held her tight. Could hardly

keep hold as she twisted and turned. He barked at Jegudiel. "What's happening?"

"The spell, Soren Huxford. It is broken. Her tattoos are being ripped from her drop by agonizing drop. When they are all gone, she will have her soul again and I will have her. You did a good job, pet! Perfect, in fact."

"No. You're wrong. You lied," he said. "Cuinn didn't make the sacrifice. Killing him—useless. So, why is the spell breaking?"

"My sweet, dear boy, Soren. Why, that was you, of course. You just murdered the man you admired most in the world. A man you thought of as your brother. A man you loved and respected more than any other. Your life will be forever scarred. And you did it all to save Anastasia. You made a perfect sacrifice for her. It's just too sweet! And now I will have her, too." She laughed again. Another flash lit the room. She looked to the sky. "Whoops! Looks like I need to rush."

Appalled, Soren gripped Anastasia more tightly. *I did it. Me. I made the sacrifice. Jesus, no.*

He'd brought about the thing he'd tried so hard to stop.

The Advocate's words in Detroit: *Fate always has a backup plan.*

I was the backup.

Still crouched against him, Anastasia's eyes darkened. She hissed at the angel. "You will not have me. Not ever."

"Pet, you think you have a choice? No, no. You're just one more stone to shift, one more stop before Heaven's Watch itself will crumble." Jegudiel smiled as lightning struck nearer this time. "See, it's already on alert! Seeking us out. But before I go, Anastasia, know that your father is free. He's out of that nasty river. I made good on my promise. Don't forget that."

"Go… away!" Anastasia tried to sit up straight.

"I *will* go. But see you very soon, pet. That's another

promise. By the way, give my love to William. Not even that sweet friend of yours will be able to hide you from me."

Whispers filled the room. A flare of bright white. Soren squeezed his eyes shut against the glare. When he opened them, there was only silence and fading evening sunlight. Jegudiel was gone.

From outside, a distant hawk screamed. For a heartbeat, Soren swore he saw it wheel above the mountain ridge, wings sharp in the setting sun. Then gone.

42

EPILOGUE

"YOU CAN'T MOVE that way around the board, Billy, I keep telling you. I may be crazy, but I still remember Snakes & Ladders, it's a child's game." Tazia shook her head, freeing the strands of hair that she'd only just placed behind her ears, and gave Billy a smile.

"Not crazy, love!" He squeezed her leg and forced a laugh.

"Then why am I here?" She asked it each morning. Waiting for an answer that made sense.

"You've been through a lot. You needed some downtime, that's all." His laugh faded. "Don't you remember me telling you this earlier?"

The memories slipped in and out like a constant dream. A fantasy of angels, demons, and a man with green eyes. "Tell me again."

"Hux and I thought a stay in hospital would help. Safer than home."

Tazia felt like her memories had been pulled one by one from her head, mixed up and replaced in the wrong order. She stepped through it. "Cuinn's dead, isn't he?"

"Yes, love."

"Hux killed him. He brought me to you."

"Yes, a couple of months ago. In the night, remember? I've told you this." He sighed. "Hux called me. Told me he'd killed Cuinn—and why. That your soul had been freed. It had hit you like a brick wall, love. He said you were in a bad way and needed me."

"What about that angel?"

"No more sightings since Spain last week. She appeared to a group of people. Same MO: English woman, fiftyish, purple dress. Hux went there, but it was too late, he'd missed her. He's in Madrid now—that's just fallen. More cities every day. We think it must be connected to Jegudiel. Demons are on the rise everywhere." Billy pressed the heels of his hands to his eyes. When he released them, the whites were blood-shot.

Tazia abandoned the game to reach across the bed to hug him. "You look ill. Thin. Are you still having the dreams?"

"Yeah. Never remembered my dreams before—not ever— and suddenly, every night is intense. Weird stuff. People poking at me, always trying to wake me up. And a blinding light, all night. I need some rest, girl."

He slowly stood. "I'm heading off. But I'll be back tomorrow. Same time." He gave her a big smile and kissed the top of her head. "I love you, Taz. Don't forget it!"

"I never do." She forced a smile back.

Don't leave.

Tazia went to the window to watch him cross the lawn outside. She cheerfully waved in response to his many glances back up at her. With one last thumbs-up, he reached the carpark and got into his hatchback.

As he drove out of sight a magpie settled in the tree beside her window. It squawked as it did each day, then peered at her through beady eyes.

Ignoring it, she turned and looked up at the wall to a picture of a young child on a swing in a beautiful garden.

Despite the intended joy of the scene, the child looked sullen and bored.

Tazia locked eyes with the child. "You thought stripping the ink would stop them. It won't. They'll find you. They won't stop fighting. And neither will I. You'll never have me."

The child's mouth curved into a snake-like smile.

AUTHOR'S (AND TAZIA'S) NOTE

The *Dark Urban Rising* trilogy was my first published work in 2017, then slightly updated in 2019. I had several novels hidden in desk drawers (or more realistically, stashed on old laptops,) but had never felt my stories were ready for an audience until *Fighting Spirit* was born.

In 2025 I decided to review and improve the trilogy. My writing skills had improved and I felt that finally I could represent the stories in the way I first envisaged. The rewrites were an act of indulgence, but I'm glad I took the time. I hope you are too.

— S M Henley, January 2026

Here is the original Author's Note from 2017:

I dedicated this book to myself. Not because I'm a selfish person by nature, but because despite being a lot of fun to write, it has also been very hard work to get it to this point. Granted, there's been no actual blood spilt but most definitely a lot of sweat and tears.

Blood? Nobody died in the making of this book. Apart from that guy, and that guy, and that guy with the—

No spoilers! This might be one of those weird readers who checks out the Author's Note first. Anyway, I said there was no blood. You never listen.

As I was saying, first published books are fraught with difficulties, doubts, tearing out of hair, and possibly, even the odd pitchfork stabbing.

Hush! NO SPOILERS!

Don't get clever.

Are you going to talk about me now?

Just getting to it. This book started life in 2009 (it's 2016 at time of writing). Back in those days I had only written fan fiction; work I was too shy to share. But a funny thing happened as I wrote in one of those wonderful worlds, I stopped writing about a certain vampire slayer, and started to write about a tough British Army drop-out named Suzanne who kicked arse just as soundly as Miss Summers—though without the superpowers.

She was cool. And had an AK47.

Who Suzanne or Buffy?

Suzanne—Buffy didn't need one. And she had better hair. And she was hotter.

Your hair's fine.

Damn right!!

Later Suzanne morphed into Alex. The human became a vampire from a royal line, rejected by her father and forced to make a life for herself away from his court. She also kicked a lot of butt—in between doing her nails and hunting for a secret blood supply.

I liked her too—apart from the nail thing. No patience for that stupid-arse crapola.

Stupid-arse crapola? Who taught you that?

No one. I am my own woman… Billy. Of course.

Finally, Tazia emerged—

A veritable butterfly am I.

—a little bit of both of them rolled up into one, but I didn't want any black and white situations for her. She needed to be more than just a little bit bad as well as more than just a little bit good. What's a story without conflict?

For fucksakes! Was that a serious question?

Probably not. So, are you pleased with the way you turned out?

Sorta. I'd really like a Jeep. Can I have a Jeep? Suzanne had a Jeep.

Maybe.

Please. I'll beg if you like—I have chains, I'll let you use them…

Stop that Missy. I made a note. Watch this space for next time.

So I get another story?

You get to feature… The next one's Billy's, but of course you're a big part of that story.

Turn the page (or touch the screen) to read the beginning of Book 2 of the *Dark Urban Rising* trilogy, *Hero Worship*… I hope you enjoy it, but I can't promise that madam behaves herself.

In darkishness,

S M Henley (and Tazia)

PS But before you do—to learn more about the whole trilogy and to get very special freebies, go signup at http://darkishfic tion.com/stay-in-touch/ There's a free-gift you can get immediately you will not want to miss.

Did you include all that stuff I did in the past, the stuff that Hux doesn't even know?

Yes.
Fucking sicko.
Goodbye, Tazia.
Kisses.

EXCERPT FROM HERO WORSHIP
1. THE IMPOSSIBLE GIRL

The steady slap of polished wood against bare skin should've been doing the trick. It wasn't. Bloody hell, he was even boring himself. Billy picked up the pace—*thwack, thwack, thwack*—more for curiosity than pleasure.

Momentarily, the flesh tensed before settling again into softness. Knees and hands remained rigidly planted on the bed, and a toss of long blonde hair indicated he should continue.

Under the action of the paddle, a vivid red splotch had bloomed, the same colour as the high-heeled shoes that protruded over the end of the bed. Billy peered more closely. The mark looked familiar, like something off a map. France? *Nah*—not square enough. Spain—*nope*. Another slap, and a triangular extension burst onto the skin. *Africa!* Christ, he was paddling geography lessons onto her arse. It made him sort of proud.

The last slap also finally earned him a slight *"ahh!"* from the woman straddled on his slickly wrapped bed. The black silk sheets were a recent purchase made from boredom and a brief desire to be Hugh Hefner. Too slippery. One unfortunate bunny had already shot across the bed and landed in a twisted heap on the floor.

He wouldn't keep them; not the sheets or the blonde.

Regardless of the cartographic potential, she seemed preoccupied. Her sighs all sounded the same, like she was phoning it in. *Brilliant.* He was so dull even his lovers ran on autopilot. That stung more than he wanted to admit.

The last few months had really put a crimp in his performance and, truth be told, left a cramp in his thigh muscles.

Thwack!

With one last energetic slap, which took the bottom quite by surprise, he said, "Time to bugger off, love." The look she shot him back? Pure bloody gratitude. *Shit! She is bored.*

Without waiting for the woman to get up from the bed, Billy pulled on his designer underwear and the shirt he'd removed earlier, and made his way into the living area of his East London Docklands penthouse, a pristine tea warehouse conversion of exposed brick and cast iron.

The stiff black leather sofa still dominated the room, its only saving grace the flat arms, perfect for balancing bottles of European lager on footy nights. Flanked by its two matching armchairs, the arrangement pleased his need for order, at least. Opposite, the wall was covered in parallel rows of his photography: stilettos and steampunk-inspired thigh-highs. Truth was, he barely got a kick out of them anymore.

Only one photograph got his attention: a study of well-used workman's boots back-lit and placed attractively; one leaning its heel against a satin-covered box, and the other resting at a sideways angle against its companion. Placed at eye-level, dead centre.

He clocked the picture now, on his way to the kitchen, and gave a lazy salute.

After retrieving a beer from the fridge, Billy pried off the metal bottle top with an opener styled as Dracula's open mouth. It released with a pop, and he took a quick swig, then studied the gadget. The vampire grimaced at him, its flat central teeth providing just enough space to grip a top tightly while the two sharp canine fangs added no function.

He smiled, thinking back to the day he'd received the opener as a gift and the accompanying lecture. *Vampires only use their fangs for the 'grrr' factor, Billy!* She'd said, dead serious. Then, without missing a beat, up went her hands like claws and she gave him her best, *grrr!* He hadn't resisted, not for a second, and gone full camp vamp, stalking across the flat like a Hammer Horror extra: *Dahling, I want to drink your blood!* They'd both collapsed in tears of laughter.

That was the day his best friend, a tough and often impossible half-demon girl, had chosen to give him a lesson about the supernatural world. When he'd dropped her at a South London psychiatric unit four months ago, those conversations had stopped.

The sound of high heels clipping sharply over his polished wood floor brought him up short. He winced and, without looking up, said, "Shoes!"

"I know!"

He felt her eye-roll.

The footsteps paused by the front door, and the offending heels clattered to the floor.

Looking up, he noted the mid-length, brown, wrap-around dress tied at the waist, not a hint of cleavage. A strangely sedate outfit for the woman's chosen lifestyle. She pulled on low wedge-heeled canvas sandals, kissed the air vaguely in his direction, and was gone.

Billy's shoulders sagged in relief. Even his heartbeat steadied.

He pulled the kitchen drawer open to return the bottle opener, but hovered instead, his fingers running over the sharp little teeth. Dracula's wide, staring eyes looked back at him. The memory of Tazia's laughter ringing out, had brought his empty flat alive. With a sigh he dropped the opener to the drawer with a clatter.

Crossing to his desk, Billy switched the window on his PC to his calendar. Boring meeting after boring meeting. But today a big red TAZ. The only one this week. Scrolling back, the last twelve weeks had been littered with them: daily visits. A haze of shared pots of flavoured yoghurt (*guess the berry, Taz!*), mindless board games (*Snakes & Ladders or Clue?*), and tales of his latest plaything to make her smile.

Four bloody months, and she was still curled up in the corners of her room, shut down. Like someone had switched her off. He was supposed to get her through it, but he was bollocsing that up too.

He switched to his email. A new one from Thomas, just a question mark in the subject line. *Nope.* Billy dragged it to the *Trash* folder. *Fuck it!* Love could wait.

The alarm from the Mac cut through his contemplation.

Video call. His stomach fluttered. Maybe news about that red-haired bitch? His fingers hovered. Did he want to know?

———

Hero Worship is available from all good ebook sellers and in paperback. Go to https://books2read.com/heroworship to link to your favourite.

THE SPOIL HEAP

The Spoil Heap is not a newsletter. It's an introduction to the things you missed. A round-up of what I've already dragged to the surface of **The Midden**, along with a look at what's still buried.

It's there for those with the sense to ask. Just give me an email worth using.

—Digger

https://darkishfiction.com/sign-up

New subscribers receive *Bleeding Ebony* by return. Consider it a first round, on me.

ACKNOWLEDGEMENTS

My gratitude goes to:

My editors, Megan Harris for being gentle with a newbie, and Mary Matthews for her commitment to pickiness; to Kieran Clynes for impeccable beta reading and for living with the characters this long; to www.derangeddoctordesign.com for a kickarse cover; and, finally, to Rick Gualtieri for his words of blurb.

And, finally, thank you to my readers. Your continued support means the world!

ABOUT THE AUTHOR

S M Henley was brought up in an English seaside town singing to Echo and the Bunnymen and worshipping Siouxsie Sioux. She now lives in rural Alberta, Canada, with more pets than people, where everyone is friendly, winters are long, cheese is bright orange, and the occasional moose wanders through her yard.

Her writing spans Urban Fantasy through Horror. The UF is darker than average. It dips a toe into Dystopia and splashes blood freely. The Horror is a little darker and is written under the pen name, Ellis Marsh. Still paranormally themed, characters run from flawed to freaky, blood is optional.

ABOUT DIGGER

Digger introduced himself after the first trilogy was written. He now tends bar and watches the signs.

He knows more than the Author, but not too much more. He writes **The Midden** and curates **The Spoil Heap**.

Learn about the author and Digger on the website: https:// darkishfiction.com

ALSO BY S M HENLEY

Available now in digital and paperback versions, the complete *Dark Urban Rising* trilogy:

Book 1 - Fighting Spirit

Book 2 - Hero Worship

Book 3 - Raw Deal

The Dark Urban Rising Box Set (the Complete Trilogy) (ebook only)

And the prequel novella (ebook): *Bleeding Ebony*. The story of Tazia's time at Her Majesty's Pleasure in 1995. Only available with newsletter sign up.

———

And from the continuation series set in the *Dark Urban Rising* world just after the Tipping Point, *Skye Quest*:

Skye Wolf (a prequel novella) (ebook only)

Book 1 - Dead Playboy (coming soon in ebook and paperback)

———

For synopses and purchasing information and to keep track of new releases, visit: https://darkishfiction.com

www.ingramcontent.com/pod-product-compliance
Lightning Source LLC
Chambersburg PA
CBHW061612190726
48288CB00007B/2284